The Reality Show Series:

Book II

I0610434

THE WHOLE PACKAGE

By Kate L. Hart

Impact books with a message

Contents

CHAPTER ONE

I don't know how long I slept; I must have heard the doorbell. I woke further when I heard Andrea's startled voice say:

"Adam! What are you doing here?"

"I came to get Carrie," Adam said.

"She's asleep," Andrea snapped.

I shook the tired from my eyes and stood up. I walked into the living room to hear Adam saying:

"I drove all the way from Connecticut to get her. Can you just –"

"Wait, what are you doing in Connecticut?" I asked, walking around the corner into the front room. Adam ducked around Andrea. He put a hand on each of my arms.

"Hey, are you okay?" he asked. He studied my face intensely.

"Sure," I said. I forced a smile for him.

"I am in Connecticut because I promised to take care of your mom if anything happened while you were on the show. Remember?"

I only half remembered Adam make the promise, and then it was more as a way to keep me from wiggling out of going on *The Whole Package* in the first place. He must have read something on my face.

"I'm so sorry, I didn't realize…" he said. "I'm sorry I got you into that mess." Adam still studied my face.

"No, it was all for fun. I took it too seriously. So, you've been in Connecticut this whole week?"

"Of course," he answered, continuing to look at me in a way that made me self-conscious of the rat's nest my hair

1

had.become. I'd never seen Adam in jeans and a tee shirt before. His arms bulged out of the sleeves. His face looked rough with dark whiskers as if he hadn't bothered to shave that morning. He looked like a walking cologne advertisement.

"I can't believe you took time off work to stay with Mom," I said again.

"Well –"

"No, no," Andrea said, "Karl gave him contacts to make down there. He's on the company's dime. Staying at the Marriot because –"

"Because it would have been weird for me to stay at your house with Addie alone there," Adam cut in.

"Oh," I said. Addie would never invite him to stay. "That's so sweet of you."

"I got you into this mess. I just... I wanted to make sure everything was taken care of," he said.

"Thanks," I said. I didn't know why Andrea rolled her eyes behind Adam.

"If you grab your stuff, I can drive you to the hospital," Adam said smiling at me. He always dipped his dark widow's peak in my direction when he focused his puppy dog brown eyes on me.

"Yeah, of course. I'll be right back," I said. I slumped back into the guest bedroom combing my fingers through my hair. Andrea followed me. I grabbed for all my stuff that spread surprisingly far in only one night.

"Be careful with Adam," she whispered urgently, "I'm pretty sure he has a crush on you."

"I kind of thought he might. But then he sent me on a show where I had to proposition another man for a million dollars, so probably not," I whispered back.

2

"He came into work two days ago to sign some paperwork for this new account he won't shut up about. Seriously you'd think he wouldn't gloat over every –"

"I get that the two of you compete over everything, but can't you figure out a way to get along? We all have to work together, somehow."

"No, this isn't about work. Adam kept telling me, and anyone else who'd listen, you were just acting. You were only pretending to like Ethan because that's the only way to win the million dollars. He insisted you were just after the money," Andrea whispered.

"I wasn't..." I whispered, hating myself for it.

"I believe you, but Adam doesn't. He honestly thinks you were playing for the money."

"Then why does he think I left?" I asked.

"I don't know, but he thinks you're in love with him. He's implied as much over the last year," Andrea said.

"Andrea, seriously? Who does that?"

"Conceited men," she said. "Trust me."

"Andrea, you don't like him. I get it."

"This isn't about me, it's about you," she insisted.

"I don't really get what you're so worried about. I recruit for him. It would be a conflict of interest for him to –"

"Exactly. He gives you accounts; the two of you need each other to make money."

"He knows we can only be business associates," I whispered at Andrea.

"That doesn't mean he isn't into you," Andrea said. "It just means he has to be careful how he acts on it."

I stopped to look at her. I felt so exhausted. "Why are you bringing this up now?" I asked.

"You're not exactly in a place to –"

I clenched my jaw. She stopped.

"Okay. Just use some of that strong, pull-yourself-off-the-reality-show mojo, to be your own person at work."

Unsure what she was talking about, I shrugged and zipped up my suitcase. I lugged it into the living room and Adam took it from me out the door.

"Thanks for everything, Andrea, you were my life saver today," I said still whispering. A littleness seeped over me because I had needed her to combat Julian, but I tried to look appreciative because she had done it.

"It's fine. Hey, let's plan on watching *The Whole Package* together next Thursday, okay?" she said.

"Ethan asked me not to," I said.

"That would be convenient for him, but are you sure that's what you want?"

"No. It'd kill me not to see what happens next," I admitted.

"Thursday then," she said, giving me a hug.

"Thursday," I repeated.

I followed Adam down the path to his car.

"Oh, my car's here," I said, turning back around.

"You look really tired Carrie. Just let me drive you. I'll bring you back Thursday."

"I am exhausted," I said. And then I wondered how Andrea would feel about me bringing Adam back to her house.

"You know, since your mom is your legal dependent, you could take sick leave next week to be with her. It might be a good idea."

"I'll think about it," I said, too drowsy to think about anything.

4

"Here, let me text Karl for you, then you can call him Monday," Adam said. He opened my door for me, pulled out his cell phone and started texting.

This irritated me, but I was so tired and couldn't wake up no matter how I scolded myself. I probably did need a week to get back to myself. Adam always made me feel protected, so I let it go.

Adam drove me straight to the hospital. Cameras waited outside for me despite the late hour. I didn't know how to wrap my head around all the attention people wanted to give me. Mom was incredibly surprised to see me. She thought I would again spend the night at Andrea's. I tried to explain I was fine, but when I could barely slur out the words, she insisted I go home.

I took the next week off work as Adam suggested. I wanted to help Mom, but I slept through most of it. Sleeping was better than thinking

CHAPTER TWO

Sitting on Andrea's couch a week after I left *The Whole Package,* I felt her palpable frustration. She grimaced at Adam. Andrea hadn't meant for me to bring him along, but he came to see me an hour before I needed to leave and said he'd drive me. I didn't want to take the train all the way to New Jersey packed with people who might recognize me. Everywhere I went, someone recognized me.

I felt surreal sitting on Andrea's couch, between her and Adam, while I watched my own velvety red-brown eyes that held a joke come onto the television screen. How funny I found *The Whole Package* when that picture was taken. The joke died. My picture ran by with a big X over it. I wanted to sob. I lost him.

Instead I set my jaw and held my breath. I wouldn't give in to this.

The contestants still eligible to be crowned "*The Whole Package,*" ran across the screen. Lance's voice-over gave the details of the contestant's life as if running off the stats of a professional baseball player. The screen shifted to Veronica.

"You think Veronica's gone tonight?" Andrea asked.

"Sandra and Tess have been haggling over the title since the beginning. I don't think Veronica has it in her to compete with them. Not to mention I pretty much talked her into giving up the million dollars," I said. Immediately, I felt saturated with guilt.

"She may still be playing; she seemed to get along with Ethan at the table-setting challenge," Adam said.

"Yeah, but she didn't bother trying to win like she had been," Andrea said.

6

"Because I talked –" I started.

"You talked her out of going after a man you thought was loyal to you. You were trying to protect her. Don't feel bad," Andrea said.

"It... It wasn't just that. Veronica stayed loyal to me the whole time, and I manipulated her for it. I need to apologize to her."

"I don't think she expected to make onto the show. You took her farther than she would have by herself," Adam said touching my arm and rubbing it. I smiled for him.

Last in the line of pictures came Tess, her golden-brown eyes spewed mismanaged sexuality and just a touch of "come take advantage of me." I listened carefully to what she overcame, like it may have changed in the last week.

"Tess overcame being severely bullied and abused for over two years. After she came forward, her tormenters were prosecuted. Tess finished high school on her own through online classes. She still managed to earn a double major in accounting and economics. She earned her Certified Financial Planner –"

"I wonder what severely bullied means?" I asked.

"It doesn't matter, she's that girl. A total a back stabber to all of us," Andrea said.

"She didn't know I... She didn't know he was kissing me when she –"

"She still would've – you know, even if she did know," Adam said.

"Maybe so, but she's broken in a way."

"Still, I don't think you had to apologize to her," he said.

"I apologized to prove I'm not a reality show star."

"I'm proud of you," Adam amended quickly, "Ethan's the one who should have apologized to you. Did he?"

7

"Maybe he couldn't, maybe he still wants to be with her," Andrea answered as she scowled at Adam.

"No, he chose Tess," I said feeling the muscles in my neck tighten and my arms close over my chest.

"He's still in love with you," Andrea said, "Don't give up on him so soon. The reunion show is only three weeks away."

"Are you insane?" said Adam. "Don't encourage her; he's an actor. He told her what she needed to hear to get her to perform. That's how they do it."

I turned surprised to Adam. He glared at Andrea, extremely provoked.

"That's right, you know all about this, you even know Julian don't you, Adam?" Andrea asked.

"I talked to him a little."

"How come Veronica had to wait two years before she went on the show and I got on in six months?" I asked cutting in.

"Oh, well I know one of the private detectives from –" Adam started.

"You fast-tracked her application didn't you," Andrea snapped.

"It was late –"

"Okay, you fast-tracked me, but how was I chosen before Ethan if my application was late?" I asked.

"What do you mean?" Andrea asked.

"Ethan was told I would be on the show at the time he signed his contract. How was I a year and a half behind Veronica, but still chosen before Ethan?" I asked.

"What?" Adam asked with very little breath, like I wasn't speaking English. I examined him. He seemed far more on edge than normal.

"Ethan told me the head of the studio, who Addie said she knows vaguely from the club, but apparently he keeps trying to talk to her now."

"Carrie, focus," Adam said. He seemed to need to hear what I said.

"Okay," I said.

"Ethan was chosen after you?" Adam asked.

"I don't know. Ethan knew I was going on the show when he signed his contract. But if I was late applying, how is that possible?" I asked.

I thought about this obsessively over the last week and couldn't be sure what happened. I felt so targeted. Adam said nothing for a minute and I could see him processing this. Then he cursed.

"What?" I asked.

"He found someone who could get to you," Adam said, "There is no way, the two of you just...."

"Clicked, you and Ethan clicked, quickly," Andrea said filling in where Adam left off.

"We had a lot in common, even down to religious mothers," I said.

"His eyes were amazing; he's self-made, which is your catnip. Julian expected you to win," Andrea said quietly looking at me.

"I had the best designer. Julian only made me look bad in one episode and that was to force me to get in line – canter... Maybe I would have won," I said.

"Why did you leave, I mean, a million dollars?" Adam asked.

"There's only so far you can allow yourself to be manipulated before you –"

"Carrie, manipulated or not, this means your connection to Ethan is real. You can't fake chemistry. Julian found someone you have chemistry with," Andrea pointed out.

"Andrea, you can't really be encouraging her? To pursue a reality show romance further than the TV show is insane," he said. He turned directly to me. "They never last."

"Is that the rationale behind sending her on a reality show? It'll never last and she's a million dollars richer?" Andrea asked.

"I... I knew she could use the money – you work so hard Carrie. Since Gordon, you haven't –"

"Dated, you haven't dated anyone," Andrea filled in.

"No. Well, yes, but she hasn't lived either," Adam said, growing flustered.

"Did you think she would learn how to live, locked up in a house while being hand-fed non-stop romance? Or did you want her to come home ready to date someone?"

"It didn't seem so ... tacky when I heard about it," he said.

"You didn't think it was tacky when you heard about it from your detective friend who digs up dirt on these poor contestants."

"It's fine Andrea, it's over. Let's just forget about it," I said, making a mental note never again to invite Adam to hang out with me and Andrea. Looking back to the television screen, I found Ethan and realized the commercials ended.

"Last time on *The Whole Package*," Lance's voice said as it showed me storming out the door, "In a startling turn of events, socialite Carrie Carnegie, after her mother's car accident, eliminated herself in a dramatic showdown with Ethan."

"Hey Ethan, Carrie left you something," Veronica called from the television. Both she and Ethan were dressed in different clothes, as though a day had passed. They were getting on a plane early the next morning. They must have changed and filmed this scene sometime the night I left.

"What is it?" Ethan said in the plastic way that meant he may as well be reading from cue cards. She showed him the canvas I left on my bed. I flinched when Veronica placed her hand consolingly on his back.

The camera showed Ethan's face up close. Julian captured one of the rare moments of true reaction. That must have been the first time Ethan actually saw the painting.

"Poor guy," Phil said looking up at me from the floor where he sprawled.

"Julian caught his reaction," I said, "He must have edited it in after Ethan and Veronica did several takes to get the wording right. Nothing happens in the sequence shown."

"Well he looks –"

Andrea stopped. Ethan's silver blue eyes scanned the canvas, blinking a little. I couldn't attempt to keep my pain hidden witnessing his.

"He loves you," Andrea said. I blushed. I could not look at Adam. He merely grunted.

Maybe Ethan did love me? Julian left the camera in his face for an uncomfortable amount of time, and I knew he did it to torture me.

"That's weird," Andrea said.

"What?"

"They've never spent so much time reviewing when a contestant left *The Whole Package* before. People must like you," Andrea said. Her eyes grew big and her smile derisive. I forced myself to smile.

"Julian probably filmed this when he still thought I'd be back on the show by the next morning."

11

"Yeah," Andrea agreed. "He tried to get me to leave a few times. He would have kept trying to get you back even after your interview if I hadn't been there."

I nodded, trying to swallow the embarrassed lump in my throat, trying not to feel weak and childish.

"What's the picture of?" Adam asked.

"Just something I painted."

The camera finally showed my painting of the ocean. With all the hope I could muster, I left it for him. Praying he'd understand why I had to go.

"Wow, Carrie. That's beautiful," Andrea gasped. "You're talented. I didn't even know you painted."

"You need to start painting again," Adam insisted.

"Like I have time between my family and work," I said.

It felt like an obstinate, separate individual lived within my mind as I obnoxiously scanned the evenings I spent alone in my apartment. I often watched TV or read when I could've been painting.

Oh, alone. How alone I'd been for years. I couldn't go back to it – I couldn't. I leaned toward Adam. His dark eyes examined me, trying to read me.

"I painted that one in my bedroom after Mom's accident."

"Did you leave all your supplies?" Andrea asked. She demanded my attention away from Adam's puppy dog eyes.

"Yeah, not much fit in my suitcase but my stuff. I kept the dress I was wearing when I ran out the door. That's about it."

"Only the clothes off your back. That sounds a little like the concentration camps," Phil said.

"Don't worry. I'll get you some more," Adam said.

"Clothes?" I asked trying to joke.

"No. Painting supplies," Adam said, "you should definitely keep up on your painting. You're talented."

"Oh no," I said. No man would ever buy me something so personal again. "I have more than I'll ever use at Mom's. Whenever she goes through the craft store, she buys me something, just in case... well, if I find time."

I pulled my greasy auburn hair into a ponytail and then looped it to get it off my sweaty back and shoulders. I made little effort to bathe over the last week. Andrea reached over her head mimicking my action trying to fit her short blonde hair into a ponytail. It looked more like a puff of a bunny tail fixed to the back of her head.

"Hey, Karl was a little confused if you're coming back to work Monday," Andrea asked.

"Yeah," I said. I had to go back to work. I lost the million dollars. No. I gave it away. I would not be a reality show star. I could take care of myself. I worked hard at a good job. I didn't want Ethan's dowry.

"You know you don't have to if you need another week. I can talk to Karl," Adam said. "In fact, why don't we work from your mom's next week?"

"No, I need to get back to work," I said. I had already spoken to James Hall and his contract ended two weeks ago. He was a free agent and I couldn't afford to lose him.

"We can work out of your grandpa's study, all that equipment was state of the art a few years ago, it would –"

"Adam, leave it! She's done playing house with you," Andrea snapped.

"Uh..." I stammered, narrowing my eyes at her.

"Anyway, I was wondering something else about Ethan," Andrea asked. "Adam thinks you guys didn't hang out unless the camera was around?"

"You can't have a real relationship like that," Adam said.

"But it sounded like Ethan hung out with you guys most the time, plus the two of you really connected, running alone in the mornings, right?"

"Andrea, she doesn't want to talk about that. You're embarrassing her," Adam snapped looking stern. "Don't talk about it. It's better to move on."

"No," I said to prove I didn't care, "It's okay. I already told Andrea everything. We were almost always filming. Julian needed extra footage if he had extra time to fill."

"Sounds nice," Andrea said, "All that down time."

"It wasn't exactly down time. It's a lot more stressful than you'd think," I said, "Although when the group became smaller – we played a few massive all-night board games—that was fun."

I enjoyed those games because Ethan often found little ways to show a preference for me, not because it was fun fighting with the other contestants over a board game.

"No wonder you were attracted to him," Adam cut in. He slid his consoling arm around me. "There was no one else to be attracted to. One guy with all those women – who by the way, are also attracted to him – it's no wonder you got so confused."

"She wasn't confused until you started working on her, and if you think that's consoling—you're being a jerk," Andrea snapped. Andrea gave me big eyes again and a nod like I needed to understand something. I couldn't put my finger on what, but it dragged me down.

CHAPTER THREE

Ethan reappeared on the television screen. I leaned into Adam's arm a little. I wanted an arm around me so badly, but his cologne didn't smell right.

"Well, he sure doesn't look sad now, does he?" Adam asked.

"Nope," I said. Ethan grinned as he and the other girls boarded a private plane.

"Going to the Big Apple. We'll be close –," Ethan said, leaning down to get Veronica to look up at him. She grinned.

"Yeah, I miss my parents," she said.

"Something was edited out. He cut Ethan off," I said.

"I guess it only took Ethan the few minutes in the opening segment to get over you," Adam said. We all stopped. I turned to him, my eyes clearly showing my surprise.

"Seriously?" Phil asked.

"Sorry, Carrie," Adam said, "I'm just... sorry."

He tipped his head back and exhaled to the ceiling. Andrea brought out the worst in Adam; I really shouldn't have brought him.

"Veronica must be happy to have a newspaper; it drove her nuts not to know what was happening in the world," I said turning away.

How isolated we'd been for a month and a half – how smothered. I hated feeling smothered. The cameras moved to Tess and Sandra's bantering. This told me Julian didn't want his audience to know how badly Veronica wanted to go home. She cried at night sometimes for wanting to go home.

"Could you move your arm, please," Sandra asked Tess politely. She looked pointedly at the arm rest.

15

"She uses her manners to get what she wants," I said as if I were translating a foreign film without subtitles.

"No, my arm was here first," Tess shot back. Sandra gave her a look, and Tess glared back.

"Oh, that's Tess's last straw face; Sandra's probably been driving her crazy all morning," I said. "Tess doesn't get mad that easily. This isn't real."

None of it is real. Julian pushed us until we reacted. He filmed it all. It didn't show how hard we were pushed until we reacted, it just showed the reaction. I left. I left so he couldn't create and then exploit my weakest moments any longer. I should be allowed my weaknesses without having them constantly thrown in my face, or judged. As if they were anyone else's business.

A warmth passed over me. Hope trickled back in. I didn't want to be on that show. I was free. I shrugged away from Adam's arm that was right next to mine. I missed Ethan so bad it ached, but I would see him at the reunion show. Three weeks. Then he'd be free. Free of Julian's creative editing. He loved me. He had. He would again.

Tess would win the million dollars, but I'd get Ethan. I was free. Sandra and Tess weren't free.

"It won't be so bad," I said.

"What?" Andrea asked.

"Veronica leaving tonight; at least she'll be free," I said. "I wish I could pick her up from the airport – I never thought to get her phone number."

"You'll see her at the reunion show," Andrea said.

"In three weeks," I answered.

Then we'd all be free.

Sandra complained Tess was picking on her and made Veronica feel guilty enough to switch seats with her. Then

Sandra snuggled into Ethan, to tell him a short story about when she was a little girl. Ethan listened attentively to Sandra, staring at her pretty face in a way that made me flare.

I reminded myself he was captive; a man being held. He didn't know what he got himself into – none of us did. Sandra leaned in and kissed his check. Nope – I couldn't hold it. I hated him.

"I don't know, Sandra might be able to steal him from Tess. He doesn't seem too interested in her, anymore does he?" Adam asked.

I stood up abruptly from Andrea's soft overstuffed couch. Adam sunk. He'd been close to me.

"Hey gorgeous, where yah going?" he asked.

"I'm starving," I said forcing my voice not to crack as I stepped over Phil and left the cozy side room. Andrea only let people she was friends with back in this room. I brought Adam in there. I'd have to do something nice for her.

I went into Andrea's large open kitchen colored to match the grey-black granite countertops. I kept forgetting to eat. I had no reservations at Andrea's house pulling out a plate from the cupboard and a piece of pizza from the fridge. By the time I heated my pizza in the microwave and returned to the living room, the show resumed. Nobody watched it.

Andrea glared at Adam. The argument they clearly had while I was gone lingered between them like a toxic fume. Each hugged one side of the couch and my vast spot stretched between them. They were very much like children I had to keep separated or an onslaught of contention would break out.

"So, Carrie –"

"Shhh, Andrea," Adam interrupted, "Carrie's watching the show – she needs to see this."

17

"You just don't want her to –"

"She doesn't have to be involved. It's your argument," Phil snapped. He sat up on the carpet, "A person shouldn't have to referee when they're in a hard place. It just makes things worse." "

"Phil's right. Especially since Carrie's mom has been in an accident. She needs her daughter in Hartford," Adam said, more like he was getting in the last word than agreeing with Phil.

"She can stay here if she wants. She's a grown woman. You aren't her babysitter," Andrea said.

"Oh, sorry. I forgot my overnight bag," I said. Or actually, Adam said he would grab it, but he forgot. I didn't mention this.

"I have stuff –"

"Andrea please let her be," Phil said.

Andrea relinquished. She did nudge me. She felt it important I understand what I was content to ignore. But truth be known, I couldn't remember anything but Ethan – on the television – the twenty-nine-year-old pediatrician from the Boston area. I left him behind, but he wouldn't get out of my head. What else was there to understand?

"Look how Ethan pays close attention to each girl," Adam said.

"Leave her alone," Andrea snapped.

"She needs to see what happened to her."

"What you did to her."

"Let her alone, both of you. She's not ready to face it," Phil snapped. Andrea put up her hands, and Adam leaned back on the couch red-faced.

"What?" I asked confused. Did Phil think Ethan played me? I looked at Phil.

18

"You need to mourn," Phil said touching my foot.

I wanted to crawl up in a little ball and disappear from off the face of the planet. Phil was right about one thing. I couldn't handle Andrea and Adam fighting over me, as if every aspect of my life was up for grabs.

I felt like a human buffer between the two.

I focused on the television. They were on a dinner cruise aboard what looked like a small cruise ship. While I zoned out, Ethan met the friends of Tess, Sandra, and Veronica.

The group ate rolls from the center of a huge table while people filling balconies watched in the background. Julian must have sold tickets to watch the show live.

"Right," Ethan said, nodding to Sandra, and her best friend – whose otherwise flawless face, contorted in a constant pucker, looked like she sucked on lemons. He looked amused. Half asleep, I'd missed something – or something happened they couldn't show. Sandra must have done something.

If only I could be there, laughing with him. No, Julian would have used me – manipulated me. I left. I would not be manipulated. I reminded myself I was cauterizing my wound and forced my eyes to focus.

"You went to college together?" Ethan asked Tess's friend. She answered playing with a necklace at her deep neckline.

"No…" Tess started to explain. Ethan nodded, but pulled his hand from her. He turned to Veronica again asking if she could see out the window.

"He's focused on Veronica, this time, isn't he?" Phil asked.

"She kind of needs someone to look out for her," I said feeling grateful. Ethan saw that with me gone, Veronica

19

needed help. Maybe he did still love me. He helped my friend because he loved me.

"Sandra, will you walk to the top deck with me? I want to see the statue," Ethan said. After they walked away from the group, Ethan took her hand.

"Never let the other women see," I whispered.

"I fantasize about knocking that guy out," Adam said.

Andrea laid into him. "Adam, seriously…."

Nothing either of them said could affect me. The television had already slapped me across the face. I dropped my eyes so I didn't have to watch. I was free. I didn't have to perform. No amount of cauterizing was going to stop the bleed in my heart, though.

I glanced up and saw Ethan on the television screen pressed against Sandra, an arm wrapped around her waist. I dropped away again. Loyalty wasn't Ethan's strong suit. Sandra would get her turn – she'd assured Ethan he'd never want anyone else after her turn. I hated Adam. I leaned away from his arm that was sliding into my space. No, it was Ethan. Ethan I hated.

Adam apologized. Ethan never did.

"Who's that with Veronica?" Andrea asked, indicating the make-out session was over.

I refocused on the television screen and said trying to sound pert, "Her cousin Helen."

Helen wasn't a nervous wreck like Veronica. She added to the conversation here and there, but mostly she watched everyone else – she looked amused, as I had. I wished I could laugh again. I wished I could naïvely believe I would never be sucked into behaving like a reality star. I had. Wrapped up in my humiliation, I vowed I'd never be that again.

"She looks nice. She's the only one who really sees how ludicrous Ethan is being," Phil said, "He seems a little leery of her. She sees through him and he knows it."

"Yep," I answered.

The television showed Ethan pulling Veronica from her seat by the hand. He held her hand – in front of everyone. He'd never held my hand in front of the other contestants. They walked away from the group – hand in hand. It showed him putting his arm around Veronica's waist as they exited the main dining area. In a dark foreboding way, my chest curled in on me.

I couldn't watch when Ethan pulled Veronica out onto the windy bow of the ship. How could I pull my eyes away? Veronica was my friend. She was loyal, even when Ethan was not. She was my sidekick. Everyone said she was my sidekick.

Veronica's pretty hair swirled around her face as she laughed so much more comfortable than she ever had before. She was coy. Perfect. I tried to get her to be coy in the beginning – when she wanted Ethan so badly – but she stopped wanting him, hadn't she? Ethan's eyes, with light beaming from them, watched her mouth move. He pulled Veronica into his long, strong arms.

Ethan started kissing Veronica. Veronica! She wrapped her long, perfectly formed arms around his neck and kissed him back.

I couldn't breathe. I didn't notice the others talking to me. Heat hit my throat and I couldn't swallow. Veronica was my friend – was. I tried to stammer, but nothing came out of my open mouth. Hatred for Ethan flared. Tess hadn't known – Sandra would get her turn – but Veronica? I told her how

21

much I loved him. This was shot within two days of my leaving. Betrayal seeped over me.

Apparently, the island did cry. Tears streamed down my face. The shakes began behind my neck and ran along my shoulders to my hands. Ethan looked like he couldn't get enough of Veronica's mouth. His hands ran along her spine down to the very bottom of her back. I stammered. Andrea turned the TV off.

"Who wants to watch that anyway?" she said. I barely heard. I tried to focus. Through my daze I heard:

"Come on Carrie, let's go," Adam spoke in a tone that I couldn't put a finger on. "I'll buy you some biscotti on the way back to Hartford."

"Okay," I said forcefully wiping the tears from my wan face. Phil jumped up off the ground. Standing in front of me, he elbowed Adam out of the way. His voice broke in desperation,

"No, Carrie you should stay tonight. We could order Chinese and watch some English comedies."

Adam started arguing with Phil. I considered for a moment – my discernment evaporated in confusion. Did Phil seem – what? I'd rather stay with Phil. I hated the idea of trying to sit still in a car for over two hours – Adam would try to talk to me, distract me. For some reason, with Adam around, it was hard to forget how stupid I'd been.

Oh, to face my mother after having been so stupid. I hated the quiet, unsure stance she and Addie held around me last week. My grandmother's house in Farmington, just outside of Hartford, had never been the repository of comfortable peace that Andrea's house afforded. I was about to agree with Phil's offer when Adam broke into my muddled considerations.

"Carrie, your Mom's expecting you," he tilted his eyes toward me, "in her condition...."

"I know you're right. Thanks anyway, Phil," I said nodding to Andrea and Phil. Phil showed Adam out of his room, while Andrea held me back a little.

"In a way Adam's right. Ethan is just an actor. For him to kiss all those women in front of a camera may not mean as much as you think it does."

"Yeah, but that's where he was kissing me, too," I said.

Andrea kissed my cheek and I sobbed a little. I couldn't hold it in. Andrea knew me too well. Maybe I did want to leave. I walked through her posh, perfectly Asian-influenced sitting room, toward the front door. Andrea put a hand on my shoulder and stopped me.

"And this too shall pass," Andrea said immersed in my pain as I stopped before her front door.

"For life, as it were..." I answered.

"I knew I shouldn't have let you join my book club. First, you highjack the discussion, and now you're quoting Washington Square at me," Andrea teased, and I couldn't help but laugh a little. She added, "You can gain control of your life and soften again. It doesn't have to be either-or, Carrie; you just have to watch who you let into the softness." Here she looked pointedly at Adam who stood just out the door with Phil.

I took a deep breath. Why couldn't she be civil to Adam? I nodded to appease her and then walked down her sidewalk into the warm night. The glow of the summer sun hovered as dusk settled quiet and still over the neighborhood.

"What was that about?" Adam asked Andrea after he thought I'd walked out of hearing range.

"None of your business," Andrea said. I turned, shocked by her extremely provoked tone.

Adam studied Andrea. I couldn't bear to get involved. Lost too deeply in my mortification and wrenching ache, I turned and walked away. I just couldn't deal with Andrea and Adam. I walked down the path toward Adam's car. It startled me when, only moments later, Adam put a hand on my lower back to guide me down the path to the street.

"See you, Phil," he called over his shoulder with a hint of triumph in his voice. I turned to give Phil a real parting, but stopped. The look on Phil's face was that of a fifth-grade teacher with an unspoken reprimand on his lips.

I wished Adam hadn't provoked Phil. Phil was loyal. Adam would never be invited back to Andrea's house. But then, Adam and I never did much outside of work. I couldn't imagine we would hang out here again, anyway.

CHAPTER FOUR

Adam drove away from Andrea's curb with a screech. His voice rolled around in my head like gibberish. He belittled conceited doctors and reality show producers, feeding my anger. A few tears dropped from the hatred building up in my chest. I raged inside, but I swallowed hard, wiped my tears, and forced myself to perform.

The car felt like a cage. I had nowhere to go. Still, I smiled, and laughed outlandishly – more like gasping for air – at everything Adam said. I would not cry again.

It wasn't until after we shifted off the 684 to merge with I-84 that I realized that I should have been in my own car. The radio should've been blaring. The windows should've been rolled down, instead of being overwhelmed to a headache by the new car smell of Adam's vehicle.

"Oh, I left my car at Andrea's," I uttered, "I'll have to ride the train all the way back to Andrea's house, and pick up my car before Monday."

"Yeah, but you didn't want to be alone right now. Plus, Carrie, what will you do in New York if I'm out here?"

I shrugged. I couldn't tell him why I needed to be at Monday morning staff meeting.

"It would be better…" Adam talked at me about working out of Mom's house again.

I didn't have enough emotional strength left to fight the feelings of regret that grew in my chest. Regret easily united the raw battering of my soul, with betrayal and mortification leading the riot. Heartache and hope, having been pushed so far back by anger, left plenty of room for regret to join the internal mutiny threatening to show on my face. After what felt like a battle in living hell, I won. I stared out the window appearing calm – nothing more, nothing less. Well, calm with a slight shudder in the deep breaths I took.

. Finally, Adam pulled off I-84 and stopped at a little Italian bakery.

"It looks closed," I said relaxing back into my seat with a deep, grateful breath. Squinting through the darkness at the building painted like an Italian Flag holding hostage Adam's biscotti, I finished, "I've been here, though, and you're right. It's really tasty."

"That's just great," Adam said disappointment creasing his face. He got out of the car and walked to the glass door. Peering through the darkened window of the bakery for a minute showed how upset Adam felt. When he climbed back into the car, he slammed the door.

"Hey, there's a cute little café up the road from here if you really need something to eat," I said half-heartedly, trying to take the edge off Adam's disappointment, but praying he wouldn't want to go.

"I guess if you want to," Adam agreed.

"No. Not for me. You can drop me off at home. I thought you needed something to eat." I tried to back out.

"You need to eat. You keep getting food and leaving it all over the place," Adam said. I pointed toward the café and off he drove.

We were seated by a big window. The young waiter at the quaint little café fumbled to hand me a menu. He apologized to me by name. I turned red at the recognition, and the boy nearly tripped over his feet to get away.

By this time, I battered my emotional turmoil into a death-like nothingness. I wanted to go home. I wanted to sleep. I wanted to die inside. Pretend nothing was wrong.

In the process of killing off my pain, heartache wriggled up through the powerful, but fleeting anger. I kept telling my heartache it wasn't that big a deal – it was a show, after all. Nobody should be blamed. If I could just make it home, I promised my heartache I'd allow her to pulse through me in the privacy of my bedroom. I begged her to just wait until we were alone with misery.

I glanced at my menu and picked out a salad, then set the menu on the table so the waiter knew I was ready to order.

While we sat and waited for the waiter to come back, Adam told me about the new business he generated in the last two weeks. I'd heard his exuberance on this subject multiple times already. I hardly listened and watched the headlights of cars pass through the darkened world outside.

"Carrie, did you hear me?" Adam asked.

"I'm sorry. What?"

"I said that considering how much business I've generated here, I may ask the partners to give me my own team in Hartford. Even if it's just you and I at first, and we worked out of your grandpa's study…. I didn't even know you had a working office in your house until I had to send that fax yesterday."

He glanced at me and I nodded so he continued: "I mean just until the partners can find us a…."

I couldn't focus. I must be dreary company especially when Adam was trying so hard to help me, like always. Adam's interest in the world began and ended with work. Oh, he asked me something.

27

"Oh right," I forced myself to answer, unsure if that made sense. I smiled and even managed a nod. Adam looked appeased.

Did time slow down, or was our waiter just exceptionally slow? I bounced my leg nodding at everything Adam said. Finally, the waiter came back to take our order and bring us water.

I ordered my salad. Thankfully Adam just ordered a bowl of soup. My tense shoulders relaxed knowing neither would take long. I was wrong. The table next to us was seated, served and then cleared before our food came. Perhaps the young man picked the vegetables from some backyard garden? Then to wash and chop them by hand must have taken an extraordinarily long time.

I pictured the waiter stumbling around in the dark pulling off the tops of carrots without the edible root attached. Having to find another must have been difficult– because something took forever. Adam fumed, and asked for the manager twice, but the boy couldn't seem to find him.

When I finally got my sodden salad drenched in cranberry dressing, I ate it anyway. The food hit my grumbling stomach. I was starving – to the point of being lightheaded. I stabbed a weed and as I brought it to my mouth dressing dribbled down my tee-shirt. I wiped it with my napkin.

As I straightened up a bright flash hit my eyes like a fist to the face. I blinked at a man with a camera. Adam stood up and pushed the man. He helped me up, throwing his arm around my shoulders. Another flash of light hit my eyes. I wondered if the nightmare would ever end. Adam didn't even bother paying the bill. He pulled me from the restaurant.

This was not the first time in the past week I had a random camera in my face. Taking Mom home from the hospital, a few cameras had been there. Fortunately, my grandmother used my father's life insurance to gate her property before she died. Most of the reporters respected that. Charles, Addie's boyfriend, dealt with the others. The local photographers knew not to get on the wrong side of a Goodrich.

When Addie dragged me to the club to play tennis, a camera had been there. A camera was in my face when I picked up Addie's dry cleaning. I fumed about that one. I did it on a pretense, but still, I picked up Addie's clothes for a political fundraiser, after everything else I had to endure.

Her boyfriend's father used my little sister as his publicity slut, and I picked up the conservative evening gown from the dry cleaner so he could do it. Addie swore she wouldn't be going if it weren't so important.

I vowed, after watching myself quietly ask the man to get out of my way that morning on TV that I was done with the media. Even so, I wished I showered between my last two photo shoots. Maybe put on something aside from my faded "Got Milk?" tee-shirt, holey jeans and flip flops. Ethan was out kissing women and I looked pathetic and dumped.

As Adam opened the car door for me, the cameraman yelled, "Hey Carrie, how did you feel tonight when Ethan stuck his tongue down Veronica's mouth? That was pretty surprising, right?"

I tried to ignore this, but then the man said, "Hey Carrie, why do you think Ethan booted Tess off?"

I stopped.

"He kicked Tess off?" I asked the man. I felt disoriented as I grabbed for the door frame.

"Yes, why do you think? Do you think he decided to be the player you accused him of being?"

I laughed a little too bitterly and accused, "You read way too many of the magazines you sell, friend."

Then I quickly climbed into the car with Adam.

"That kid better have made some money off that photographer, because he is going to lose his job."

I nodded to appease him, but couldn't focus. Ethan booted Tess off? Ethan hadn't picked Tess after all. What did that mean?

CHAPTER FIVE

"Ethan got rid of Tess?" I asked Adam out loud.

"Just goes to show you he isn't even loyal to her." Adam ranted on about some men not having any self-control. I tuned him out. The question kept revolving through my head. That only left him, Sandra and Veronica.

Hadn't Veronica said she would bow out – let him go? Well, obviously not any more. With an angry, hurtful pride, I was glad I hadn't apologized to Veronica. I helped her. Veronica relaxed would be more compatible with Ethan than Tess or Sandra. When Veronica relaxed, she became funny, compassionate, and overwhelmingly pretty – even prettier than Sandra. Ethan seemed to really respond to beauty, but being jumpy and nervous camouflaged Veronica's beauty. Relaxed, laughing, sweet – her beauty couldn't be denied.

Because we went the long way through town we came to the little-used front gate of the house instead of the back drive with a coded gate. Adam rang, but we didn't have a doorman anymore. I had to call Mom to buzz us in.

We drove down the lane where massive sugar maples hovered over us like guards ready to pounce. The lane opened up and we came upon the white and grey stone mansion surrounded by sixty-three acres. The massive three-story structure stretched out symmetrically on each side of the white columned entrance in a perfect example of England Federal-style.

Stained glass fanned over the door and glowed from the chandelier in the two-story entryway. Mom always left the chandelier on whenever one of her girls went out. I tried to

31

think the gesture sweet and not of the electric bill I had to pay as we drove toward it. The flagstone driveway curved around the house to the back where the detached garage stood.

"Here, just park in front," I instructed Adam who then pulled up to the roundabout.

I jumped out of the car and stomped over the hens-and-chicks ground cover that grew over the path to the door because I couldn't afford a grounds keeper. The kid who mowed the lawn almost broke me. These thoughts always flooded in when I came to see Mom.

I tensed when Adam's door slammed shut from behind me. I made a silent resolve to tell him I needed some space.

One of the large mahogany double doors in the entryway swung open. My mother pulled me into the house. She held me in a hug and knocked the air out of me patting my back with her cast-covered wrist.

My mother tucked her chin-length auburn hair behind her ear and the white streaks at her temple stood out. I hated it when she surveyed me with an older version of my velvety reddish-brown eyes.

"I didn't like that Ethan anyway," my mother, Irene Carnegie, finally said. I nodded and pushed past her.

Addie stood slightly behind her. She examined the split ends of her long sleek light brown hair with blonde highlights. She preferred this to looking me in the eyes.

"Hey, how about we play a board game?" Adam said. He popped his head into the house he hadn't been invited into.

"That'd be great," Addie exclaimed.

I stopped in my speed walk toward the stairs to look at my little sister. Her naturally red face glowed, giving her away.

"I'll invite Charles," she said glancing at me and biting the side of her cheek.

Charles Goodrich was the son of Parker Goodrich, a wealthy businessman running for Connecticut's open House seat. In the last week, Charles asked me a couple times to come and campaign for his father. This did not help my opinion of him thus far.

Amused with Adam's lack of creativity I watched as he turned to Addie eagerly, "You should invite him. Let's get some Chinese food coming."

To my surprise, Addie agreed. She looked away from my probing eyes quickly. Adam put an arm around my shoulders and led me back to the dining room where he felt we should play, despite the lovely gaming table in one of the sitting rooms. Then again, he'd never before been in the old place.

I sat exhausted in a chair while Mom and Addie set up my grandmother's favorite game. In her life, she didn't play board games, but she happened to buy in London a vintage copy of Sorry carved into gorgeous wooden pieces. She certainly couldn't own a game made of cardboard.

Mom turned on the dining room chandelier and it sparkled over the shiny waterfall dining room table. My finger followed a swaying beam of light on the table bent into a rainbow that moved and curled with the African Bubinga wood. I couldn't imagine Grandmother setting up even a vintage game on her sixty-thousand-dollar dining room table.

Zoned out like a high hippie, I jumped a little when the doorbell woke me from my daze. Charles must have been en route to the house because he showed up five minutes later. When I realized Addie never called him, I started putting the obvious pieces together in my head.

Addie must not have been expecting me home. She didn't usually roll over when Adam invited himself into the house. And I didn't like Charles around as much as he came. She only welcomed Adam in so she didn't have to hear me complain that her boyfriend didn't need to be over all the time. I forced myself to wake up.

I watched Charles carefully for the first few minutes waiting for him to slither. He had blond, curly hair with almost the same blue eye color as Addie. Broad at the shoulders, his body tapered into his waist.

I thought him cobra-like. If I watched him long enough, he'd shed his pale skin to reveal something more sinister inside. He must have noticed my less-than-warm appraisal of him because he tried especially hard to entertain me.

For my part, I pretended nothing happened. My heart wasn't broken and aching. However, in a hysterical desire to push it away, my sarcasm took a few nasty turns that made Mom's soft, pudgy face tighten in disapproval.

Mom went to get snacks even after I assured her we didn't need them and she should be sitting. She wouldn't, but did leave me with a warning in her eyes.

"Are you a poli-sci major, Charles?" I asked less combatively.

"Poli-sci? Not a chance. MBA, same as you," the impossibly patient Charles said. He leaned over the dining room table to look at the board game we were playing. He appeared wholly amused answering the questions I shot at him. He expected my interrogation. After finishing his turn, he said:

"I'm going to run United Skills. My dad's going to step down as president while he's in the House. That's why we have to campaign for him. We've got to get the old man out, so I have a job."

"You're living off your Grandpa until then?" I asked.

"No, he's a vice-president at United Skills," Adam informed not catching my sarcasm.

"I'm Executive Vice President and General Manager over research and development of commercial planes," Charles admitted.

"How did you... I mean that's an impressive title, isn't it?" Adam asked, and I could tell he was only acting impressed.

"I graduated from Yale," Charles said. He carefully eyed the game. He did not look at me. He must have felt the "oh-yes-you-are-a-spoiled-rich-kid" look I spewed in his direction.

"Yeah, and I'm a corporate head hunter for Kimber and Stophers. Yale gets you an entry level management position at best. It doesn't make you a vice president over research and development at a multibillion-dollar corporation," Adam said.

"My undergraduate is in mechanical engineering," he said.

"Still," Adam said.

"I did mention my Dad's president of United Skills," Charles said.

"Right, but you're still pretty young," Adam said.

"Must be nice," I said. My tone sounded openly hostile.

"Yeah, well the company was acquired in a takeover by my grandpa thirty-five years ago. Before I was even born. "

"Barely," I said.

"I've grown up with it," Charles said.

"That's great," Adam said kissing up, in a way that told he wanted the contact. Digging his head toward the game, Adam started going after one of Charles' pawns. We both preferred self-made people.

"United Skills, so that's airplanes," I said.

"Yeah, Aeronautical technology," Charles said.

"Grandpa worked with planes," Addie said. Charles flinched.

"Not on the same scale. Shades, is worth pennies comparatively," I said noticing his discomfort.

"Your family wasn't always in airplanes, right?" Adam said. It felt obvious and grating how he redirected the conversation to Charles. How did he know that little detail? In fact, he seemed to know a lot of little details about Charles. Adam seemed determined to befriend Charles. United Skills would be a huge client, but he didn't seem to understand this was personal. I couldn't recruit for United Skills after I unhinged Charles from our lives.

"My family started in financials. Over the years Grandpa swallowed up smaller companies, like United Skills. My Dad took an interest in it just as he graduated from Yale. It's been his baby for over thirty years. Today it doubles the profits of any other companies Grandpa ever acquired."

"Your dad owns it – or your grandpa owns it?" Adam probed.

"Well 'owns' is a naive word in this world."

"Obviously, but the concept is the same considering you're what, thirty, and a vice president of a multi-billion-dollar company?"

"Thirty-one. When my grandpa died years ago, my dad leveraged everything to buy out my aunt and two uncles. Dad owns over forty percent of the stock."

"That kind of a majority is almost unheard of these days. Good for you," Adam said.

Charles squinted at Adam; even he must have noticed his sincerity left something to be desired.

"How much is your dad worth personally?"

"Adam," I said.

"It's okay," Charles said. "There are about eight or nine family owned businesses on the Forbes 400. You can look him up."

"Yeah, Goodrich-comma-Parker," I said looking troubled at Addie. The word gold-digger ran through my head before I could stop it.

Addie turned her whole slender frame at me and threw me a knock-it-off glance. Despite her efforts to block it, Charles saw the look. Unaffected, he smiled at her and said, "Really, though, I need to bring the company up to date or we'll start losing money soon. Since 2000, everything's gone online. It's crazy not to. If we didn't have a name, and government contracts we'd be losing money."

I laughed and said in quotes, "Ah 'up-to-date.' You'll have to be careful in your business practices. You know they watch you a little more carefully when you're related to a politician. Or was that a larcenist? I never can keep it straight."

Adam and Charles laughed. Addie dove into her purse for a piece of gum so she didn't have to watch the scene before her.

Mom came through the square entryway with a huge bowl of popcorn clutched in her cast-free arm.

"Hey Mom, let me get that," I said, jumping up.

Just then Adam forced my piece back to the start for the third time. It rubbed me the wrong way. I said with a bite not even trying to hide my annoyance, "I'm done; it's such a stupid game."

Sitting at the end of the table away from the game, Mom consoled, "That's okay, Sweetie. It'll give you a chance to hear how Adeline met Charles."

"The Christianson's annual Lighting of the Christmas Tree Party," I answered, "They started dating before I went on the show, remember?"

"Did Adeline tell you how she asked him out?" Mom asked, trying to help Charles into my good graces.

The popcorn going down my throat came back out as spittle at Mother when I exclaimed, "What?"

"Hey, we were never supposed to mention that," Addie said. She also lost what little interest she had in the tiresome board game. She moved to the end of the table with us.

"I was eyeing her. I just wasn't brave enough to talk to her," Charles said smiling, his grin broad across his flat face.

"That's not true," Addie pursed her lips demurely. The poise of her extremely pretty Carnegie face reminded me of when we were little. Addie with small shapely crimson lips, creamy skin, and rosy cheeks had given me hours of amusement pretending she was my porcelain doll. We weren't allowed to touch our actual dolls.

Suddenly Addie piqued my interest and I refocused. She said, "He turned me down because I was a Carnegie. He thought I only liked him because he had the right last name."

"You turned her down?" I snapped, turning to Charles. I tried to fight the vindictive pleasure of my sister's rejection. "Do you know what it means to associate with Adeline Carnegie?"

This may have carried more weight if I hadn't been pulling a strand of lank greasy hair behind my ear because it escaped the messy bun on the back of my head.

"You have to understand," Charles defended, "She's really young."

"Yeah, she is," I agreed. He quickly continued:

"I've dated a few charm school graduates. Most of the time women who approach me are only interested in... you know my dad's company, or who I'm related to. Well, and the age difference was a little.... It just didn't seem on the level she was asking me out."

The muscles in my neck twitched. Addie never paid attention to the budget I constricted her to; she wasn't a gold digger.

"Anyway," my mother said, refocusing, "Charles said no to Addie over a misunderstanding."

"I can't believe my little sister, the lady, asked a man out," I interrupted. I put a little too much emphasis on the word "lady."

"Addie, tell your sister why you did it," my mother prodded.

"Well, I really didn't even know him, but I noticed he had a pocket watch...." Addie shrugged unable to make eye contact with me.

I humbled instantly. Then I grew angry at Charles for refusing my little sister under such a circumstance. Charles, who started playing the board game aggressively since we exited, made a move and sent another one of Adam's pawns back to his color's starting place.

"I'm done," Adam groaned. "This is a dumb game."

Then with a little more feeling than he would have put into it if Charles hadn't just out maneuvered him, Adam said, "Seriously? A pocket watch – aren't they a little outdated?"

"My dad hated to have a watch on his wrist when he dressed formally," I explained. "Cuff links and a wristwatch were too much. He always carried a pocket watch when he wore a tuxedo."

"Oh, that's cool," Adam said. Embarrassed, he looked away at a painting of sunflowers over the serving table on the other side of the room. He looked annoyed with himself like he'd studied for this test, and should've known that answer.

"You turned her down? And yet how are you dating?" I asked. I tried to discreetly pick a popcorn kernel wedged between two of my back teeth.

"I saw him at a private showing of the Arctic Exhibit a few weeks later. He followed me around and started talking to me about the Saunter's New Year's Eve party. He was fishing and since I wasn't used to being rejected, I was not taking the bait. He finally asked if I wanted to go with him," Addie supplied, walking over to Charles who pulled his chair closer to us. Addie leaned against the arm of his chair, and I bit back my grandmother's response to be careful of the nearly extinct wood of which the chair was made.

"What changed your mind?" I asked.

"Oh … a …" Charles stammered looking uncomfortable. He was hiding something.

"I just felt like I'd been rude so I … um … asked her out. We went out every few weeks. Our dates were polite – formal. But then after you got on the show, you started cracking jokes. I wondered if maybe Addie had a sense of humor," Charles admitted.

"I thought only women watch *The Whole Package*," I said.

"Mom watches it," Charles returned quickly.

"Likely," I said.

"Anyway," Charles said, putting his arm around Addie's waist, and glossing over my amusement, "you had a sense of humor. Most of the women at the country club think you're having a seizure if you try to be funny." Charles

40

paused. I wondered if the way he leaned into his laugh with his broad shoulders had something to do with that impression. Then I wondered why Charles had to be touching Addie all the time.

Charles drew breath and continued, "After you got on the show I sat and talked to Addie at a luncheon. She laughed at all my jokes."

"She even laughs at the ones that bomb," I said. "I totally have her trained."

"Well, from there I learned why she asked me out. The whole pocket watch thing. Anyway, I felt like scum." Charles took Addie's hand in his and kissed it sweetly. I glared at Charles. He let go of Addie's hand, but she held tight to the arm he had around her waist so he couldn't drop it.

"She isn't the same as most of the women you meet at those functions." As he said this last bit, Charles looked up at Addie in a way that made my jaw tighten.

"Well, that's sweet; I'm sure you two can show each other out. I'm exhausted," I said. It wouldn't be hard to drive Charles off – later. I walked around the table and kissed Mom on the forehead and Addie on the cheek.

"Hey, where's mine?" Adam asked his handsome face looking up at me full of charm.

"Nice try. Good night everyone," I said. I laughed just to keep my voice from sounding panicked.

Adam had not been kidding. The earnest look in his eyes could no longer be ignored. I left the dining room headed for the steep mahogany stairs. As I climbed the stairs, I had no idea what to do. Adam gave me way too much to think about.

I paused on the long landing between staircases to look up at the old stained-glass window above me. My father loved that window. How I longed for him every time my

41

Grandmother grounded me. She said I was not as dedicated to my studies as I should have been. The real reason being I wouldn't go out with creepy Tanner just because his family finally hit the hundred-million-dollar mark.

My Grandmother taunted me until shame drenched me like a thick wool sweeter in heavy rain. My Grandmother groomed me to find a wealthy man one day.

And I did.

Addie had been groomed in the same manner. She couldn't really be in love with Charles. I had to protect Addie. I had to re-teach her like I re-taught myself. Out of nowhere, an unexplainable resentment toward my father overwhelmed me. I pushed it away and ran up to my room.

CHAPTER SIX

"Did you see this?" Mom asked when I came in for breakfast the next morning. She sat at the small cherrywood kitchen table reading the newspaper.

"That's the entertainment section of the newspaper." I stared at a picture of my unkempt image and Adam impeccably dressed with an arm around me. The headline read: 'CARRIE MOVES ON.'

Thankfully I showered and brushed through my hair before I came down to breakfast. If only I'd done so before going to Andrea's the night before. I scanned the rest of the article and stopped when it spoke of my surprise at Ethan's choice of elimination.

"Look at this Mom, he booted Tess off."

"I know. If you read down the article, people on the website are really upset with Veronica. They voted her designer completely out of the contest for this week."

"Good. Becky can win still."

"I don't know."

"I can hope."

"Then I will hope, too," Mom said. "Do you want to see them interview Tess?"

"When is she on?"

"I'm sure she's on with Samantha Prowers right now," she said.

"Yeah, turn it on," I muttered.

Mom stood up, pushing off the table. She turned the remote to a mounted TV next to the stainless-steel refrigerator. I poured myself a bowl of cereal and played with it absent-mindedly. Impatiently, I wondered how many ways the weatherman could say it's going to be hot again. Finally, a promo told Tess would be up next.

I tuned out the commercials.

"Is that Addie?" I asked, hearing a car pull up to the back door. Mom nodded and I watched the door.

"Where you been?" I asked when Charles and Addie entered the kitchen.

"Tennis," Addie claimed, swinging her racket. Charles, comfortable enough in his surroundings, helped himself to some orange juice from the fridge. I would have said something, but Tess came onto the TV. She walked through the plaza with Samantha Prowers. The onlookers booed. Tess looked confused until a woman called, "You're a slut. Carrie should've hit you."

"Poor Tess," I said shaking my head. I looked from my mother to Addie who leaned against the white with swirls of gray marble countertop.

"She was the villain in your melodrama," Addie said.

"Look at her. She doesn't understand why they're so mad," I said. I felt physically ill. My soggy cereal didn't look appetizing.

After another commercial break, Samantha asked Tess a lot of hard questions. Tess snapped answers back, every word dripping with sarcasm. Tess said nothing to improve her image. The interview ended when Samantha cut Tess off.

"We're out of time. Tess, I believe you've agreed to sit down with television psychologist Dr. Corbon later this morning?"

"Yes," she said, slumping.

"Tune in next Thursday before the next episode of *The Whole Package* to see Tess discuss what went wrong. Is the bullying of her youth still affecting her decisions?"

"Why is she doing that?" I asked, looking to Addie. Nobody said anything. I didn't think of Tess kissing Ethan. I just thought of her sad face when Ethan hadn't even seemed to prefer her after she'd thrown herself at him. If she hadn't been in his bungalow to stop me, would he have discarded me so easily?

I couldn't let her go on that show.

"What are we going to do?" I demanded.

"You could call in," Addie answered.

"How?" I asked.

"I don't know – why would you bother?" Addie answered.

"Despite everything else, she's my friend."

Addie raised her eyebrows at me.

"She didn't know Ethan was kissing me. The show makes us look like we know what's going on behind our backs, but we don't." I added angrily, "Veronica knew, but Tess didn't. She's innocent in all this."

"The way she dresses and behaved on the show – she's far from innocent," Charles said.

"Look, she's just sarcastic, and her designer dressed her. I know it probably looked bad, but she's really cool. Not to mention, she threw herself at Ethan. He allowed her to do that. Then he dumped her like she hadn't meant anything. Shouldn't we be mad at Ethan? Tess was just playing the game."

Charles looked like he wished he hadn't said anything.

"We could drive down to New York and take her to lunch. Get our picture taken," Addie suggested, trying to distract me from scowling at Charles.

"Brilliant," I said.

"I'll drive. My dad lent me his car so we could all meet for lunch at the club today," Charles said.

"That's too bad. You'll give him our apologies," Mom said. A relieved smile played around her lips. We both knew whatever the son's admiration for Addie, the father's agenda included me publicly supporting his candidacy.

"Don't you have to work?" I asked. Shouldn't Charles be busier if he was a vice-president at a huge corporation?

"Nah, Dad gave me the day off." Charles blushed.

"Well, that's convenient," I said.

"Can we have the top down?" Addie asked sweetly pulling at the bottom of her tennis skirt.

"Of course. Do you want me to make a few calls? I bet my secretary can get us tickets into the filming of the Dr. Corbon Show." Charles looked at Addie in the same sickening way, which tweaked my last nerve.

"That'd be great. Thanks," I said. His poor secretary – probably Self-Made must get a lot of personal requests. Charles must have noticed my annoyance because he grew more businesslike when he asked, "Should we call Adam? He's staying in town at the Marriott."

"No. We should let him work," I said.

"You know," Addie said, "In the long run, it's nicer to let him know he doesn't have a chance than to let him believe he does."

"We work together," I replied.

"I don't think he cares," Addie answered. I drummed my fingers on the table and asked, "Considering how he's been there for us, I can't understand your dislike of him."

"We didn't ask him to keep coming around, Honey," Mom said, putting the milk back in the fridge. Then she snapped the door shut too hard and everything inside clattered.

"Mom, I asked him to look after you guys."

"I didn't. In fact, quite a few times I've tried as politely as possible to ask him to back off." Mom knit her eyebrows in frustration.

"Do you actually like him?" Addie asked.

"I know he's not your type," I said. "But he's good to me. I like that he isn't kissing all my friends and family."

"Oh well, that's infatuation indeed," Addie said.

"Um... I showered at the club," Charles interrupted, "I'll just call my secretary from the car."

Charles scurried out.

"Oh, right we have to leave if we're going to make the show," Addie said., "I'll bring my make-up. We can do it on the way. Carrie, if you're going to get your picture taken you may want to do something with yourself."

Looking down at the newspaper, I couldn't disagree. Addie smiled at my dismissive shrug. I wasn't usually passive about letting Addie help me become presentable. Addie ran off in the direction of her bedroom ticking off what she wanted to do to me.

CHAPTER SEVEN

Mom lost no time putting her arms around me and laying into her lecture.

"Carrie you're feeling rejected. You're very vulnerable right now."

"I'm fine," I assured, trying to figure out the fastest way out of this conversation.

"No, you're not," she said sternly. "You shouldn't be."

For some reason, my mother giving me permission to feel bad started my eyes stinging. This was something new. Over the last two years, I'd almost become the parent and my sick mother the child. Suddenly I became a little girl again, susceptible, with no way to contest Mom's words.

"It's okay to feel like you've been hurt. You have been hurt," Mom insisted, seeing she'd struck a chord.

"Julian made me canter like a pony after Ethan – I just feel stupid."

"Carrie there is something inside us all, a deep and longing need to be loved. It's beyond hormones or rational. It is this inborn yearning that holds us almost captive in a way," Mom said, sounding almost bitter toward the need.

She had been a widow for a long time. By the time I'd moved for college I couldn't hear her crying through the wall at night anymore. I thought she'd healed, become resigned to her situation.

"I know what you're talking about," I said.

"Honey, did you know I met your Dad the summer after I graduated from Miss Porters? He was on summer break from

Harvard. After we met, we saw each other every summer and break for four years. It wasn't an accident."

"You didn't... you married Dad because of Grandma...."

"I loved him, I still love him, can you really doubt that?" she asked.

"No, but –"

"That need, it made me vulnerable and I fell in love. There's nothing wrong with that. I love your father. And that's okay."

"But Grandma manipulated it," I said.

"Most relationships are helped along in some way."

"Why are you telling me this?"

"Addie is falling in love with Charles," Mom said.

"We need to protect her."

"Is love so wrong?"

"He's an old man –"

"The same age difference between you and Adam at least –"

"Yeah but I'm out of school, I have a good job –"

"Addie is a senior this year."

"Charles wants something from us. He wants our public support of his dad. It all feels too forced," I said.

"Like Adam coming over here every single day, getting in our business, forcing his hugs on you, forcing his flowers on our table. Going to the club and meeting all our friends. That kind of forced?"

"Come on, Mom," I said.

"All I'm saying is Addie is more naturally falling in love with Charles than you are with Adam," Mom said.

"Right and that's okay even if Charles' father does seem to be contriving for the alliance, especially since I became so famous?"

49

"Maybe, but they are falling in love," Mom said.

"It's okay for love to grow out of contrived situations? That's not healthy," I said.

"Most dating and marriage have some contriving on both sides. You have to be sure the contriving isn't dangerous, and the love is worth having, Sweetheart," Mom said.

My obsessed tortured mind shifted to Ethan. Ethan had been pushed into romancing me. Could that have turned into something real? Did he love me? No – he kissed Veronica. Nobody could be so cruel as to kiss openly vulnerable Veronica and not mean it. Did he love her now? I hated the idea of love. It felt like such a fickle, stupid emotion. I needed to banish it.

"The point is, Carrie," Mom said, pulling me from my thoughts, "love doesn't always come in conventional packages. That's why you need to rationally decide what kind of a man you want to date. Then only date those kinds of men. If you date the kind of man you'd never want to end up with, it won't matter. That's who you'll fall in love with. Someone who isn't nice."

"Someone like Gordon?" I asked.

"He wasn't cruel, Carrie, and he loved you so avidly."

"Right, and since Charles isn't that bad, it's Addie's turn to try for a meal ticket."

"Show a little respect."

"You didn't tell her the money's gone did you?" I whispered looking over my shoulder.

"No, Carrie, she doesn't know, but maybe she should," Mom said.

"Please just let's get her through college first, please," I said.

50

"She's not dating Charles as a meal ticket. She loves him," Mom said.

"Then shame on him for playing with her affection."

"He's not pushing her into it, not like Gordon did with you,"

"Gordon didn't –"

"Yes, he did. In fact, his mom is still living in your romance. You know every time you go up there she posts it all over her social media."

"I noticed."

"It reminds me of your Grandma when Dad died. Doing anything she could to get the attention she had with your father around. It would have been better for her if I'd moved on during her lifetime."

"Wait, you moved on from Dad?" I asked.

"I have to live my life," she said.

"What are you saying?"

"I loved your dad so much, but he's gone, and I'm a woman too. This need – it ... well, we all have to keep living our lives."

I stopped.

"What do you mean – did you meet someone?"

"No, no nothing like that," Mom blushed scarlet.

When she couldn't recover from her embarrassment, I demanded, "Mom, are you seeing someone?"

"It's nothing like that Carrie. I'm trying to tell you, you need to stop trying to take your father's place. And even if I did want to date again –"

"You aren't, right?" I asked. I already had one relationship to break up – why did Mom look so embarrassed?

"No, Carrie, but if I were to date, I'm an adult – you don't get to tell me –"

"Oh, right, I wasn't trying to," I said dismissing everything after she acknowledged she wasn't dating anyone.

"Carrie please, Adam –"

"What? Adam, is self-made and doesn't come with a fortune, so I shouldn't like him?"

"That's not the point. He's coming on too strong, and you want to be loved, badly."

"I don't...ur ... well, I didn't care until Ethan said he loved me."

"Did he say that?" She asked surprised. I hadn't been forthcoming with details about the show to her. I mostly pretended I'd been away on an extended holiday to a psychiatric ward when I spoke of my time in the manor house.

"He told me he did. I'm sure he's told Veronica he loves her by now. Love just doesn't mean the same thing to some people."

"Do you love him?" Mom asked, looking hopeful, of all things – seriously like it was Dr. Corbon. Great. I loved a reality TV show star instead of being Jerry Springer twisted.

"It doesn't matter," I said.

"It does to me," Mom said.

"I don't see why. Falling in love on a reality show, seriously how stupid could I be?"

"One way or the other, sweetheart, I want you to be able to love. You turn off your emotions when they hurt too badly."

"I control them."

"No, you suppress them—you force yourself not to feel. That's not the same as facing the emotion head on. You did it after your father died. Sometimes you were yourself with grandpa, but after grandpa died... well, you kind of disappeared. Sometimes I wonder whether you ever reappeared – even for Gordon."

"I loved Gordon," I defended. Trying to convince myself, I said, "I was sad when Gordon died."

"Yes, you were. I'm not saying you didn't love him, but it was a guarded love. He near worshiped you. I'm not sure what you felt was ever equal."

"But I did love him," I said, more relieved. I wouldn't have agreed to marry a man I didn't love. Of course, I loved him, just in a guarded way. At least that was love – right?

"Gordon knew he'd cornered you into the relationship. That man had aspirations, and he needed you to complete a picture for him. You loved him as much as you could."

"He knew?" I asked.

"Of course."

"Why didn't you –"

"Say something? I nagged you to look at whether you loved Gordon."

"I had to...." I blushed. I couldn't tell her. I couldn't say why I let Grandmother set me up with Gordon. I couldn't say why Grandmother made me take over.

I supported the family because she wasn't capable.

I said nothing. My mother said:

"Do you remember the lacrosse player you were always talking about? How nice he was and how much fun the two of you had studying together? Then Gordon would come around and you sunk a little. You weren't happy."

"I... I dismissed you," I said remembering the times she'd questioned my relationship.

"Well, now you can make it up to me. Do you love Ethan?" She asked point blank.

"Yes," I said closing my eyes.

"It's a very normal emotion. It's nothing to be ashamed of, especially if it pushes you toward nice young men."

"Right."

"Does he still love you?"

"Are you kidding me, Mom?" I snapped. I walked away to the table. I grabbed my bowl, fed the disposal my soggy cereal, and slopped water everywhere as I tried to rinse it.

"A week isn't sufficient enough time to change his affections. Andrea said they put all kinds of pressure on the contestants to perform a certain way. Are you sure Ethan isn't being forced to play a part? He may still love you."

"How could he?"

"Well –"

"No, if he's playing a part, then he played it with me, too. Veronica's one of the best friends I ever had, right up there with Andrea. He knows that. He kissed her. He can't love me and kiss her."

"Who cares about him then? I'm just glad you love him. There's no shame in that."

"'Kay, Mom," I said.

"Now all you can do is grieve, and then eventually you move on."

"I don't need to grieve," I said blowing out the breath I'd been holding.

"Right, you don't grieve. You never gave yourself time to grieve after Dad died. You went directly back to school and then to work. You shut yourself off from the world. The only acknowledgment you made, even indicating you noticed Grandpa died, was when you insisted on driving Addie into town once a week for her allergy shots, and then taking her for a treat after like he would. You don't grieve; you try to fill the void—like somehow it's your responsibility."

"We don't grieve in this house," I reminded.

"I always told you Grandma was wrong. You liked the idea of not grieving."

I stayed silent. My father had been gone for almost as many years as I'd lived with him. So what if I didn't mope around and cry at night like my mother did? The money was gone. Some people don't have the luxury of mourning. How can I explain this to Mom?

"Carrie, sometimes we have to feel our pain until we deal with them, and then we can move on. In the old days, people would be in mourning for a year. They felt the unalterable void left in their lives. When certain days or holidays came along, the dead were remembered. The living acknowledged things would never be the same and they had to accept that."

"You want me to mourn for a year – over Ethan or ... what?"

"At the least, you could cry a little, lose yourself in a good book. Listen to the same sad song over and over again. I re-read Apostle Paul's writings about patiently suffering so many times the year after your father died."

"This pain I feel must be nothing compared to yours; sorry Mom," I said. Mom was a woman – a woman who'd lost her husband and become a widow at a very young age. I couldn't be hurt by a reality show. I forced the idea on myself.

My mother's pain – that was real. My pain seemed manufactured. When I didn't respond, Mom continued, "You don't know what it did for me when I saw you painting again. It's the way you express yourself."

Mom paused with emotion. I turned away. She saw my drift and said, "If we don't take the time to face the pain of disappointment, how can we fully recover from it?"

"Mom, I'm fine. It was all a game. Not like losing your husband, the father of your children. I just needed some perspective. Thanks. I feel better."

"Oh, Carrie!"

"I'm fine."

"Let's say you are just fine –"

"I am, I mean seriously, my fiancé died. This is nothing."

"It's at least a breakup. Consider that you just broke up with Ethan. I know it's an abnormal sort of breakup, but you're still going to need time to feel the sting and deal with it." She continued more curtly, "Do me a favor. Don't rush into anything with Adam. If he really likes you, he can wait a little longer."

"Longer? It can only have been a few weeks. He may have realized when I went on the show... I thought he liked me.... He always flirted with me, but this is something more."

"I don't think so," she said.

"What'd you mean?" I asked.

"Andrea said –"

"Mom, they don't get along. You can't take seriously anything Andrea says about Adam."

"Well then, let's look at what we know. Before you even came home he planted himself in our lives? I don't know what he's expecting but I'm worried about you."

"Adam is just trying to help."

"No, he's trying to take over your life."

"If that's true why did he send me away from him to be on a show?"

"Andrea talked to him while you were gone. Adam knew the reality show would be like living a romantic movie. You can't exactly say your fiancé died and you aren't ready to date, can you?"

"I don't want to date anyone."

"You let Adam put his arm around you last night. Carrie, he's your co-worker. Even I can see he clearly believes you have some sort of latent affection for him you're smothering. Men like him, handsome, petted; they believe every woman is in love with them."

"That doesn't make sense."

"Not to you and I who aren't so full of ourselves. Sweetie, I've met enough self-centered men I assure you. They can talk themselves into anything. I suspect Adam is the sort of man who gets a thought in his head, and he can't let it go."

"Mom, that's not fair. Adam has been a real friend to this family – he helped me when we needed help."

"Yes, and now he thinks he owns us. He barges into this house whenever he wants. Which means he was never being altruistic. Carrie, think about it. Who recruited you?" My mother's eyes were drilling into mine. She wouldn't let me look away.

"Adam, but –"

"Who arranged to meet you right as you were finishing up your bachelor's degree and talked you into getting a graduate degree in business? You never had any interest in getting an MBA."

"Adam, but that doesn't make sense."

"He obligates you to him, Carrie! He makes sure you're dependent on him."

"That's not fair," I answered.

"Maybe, but I want you to think about Adam rationally right now, before you get romantically attached to him. The way he's just hanging around lately – forcing his arm around you while you're so vulnerable –"

"I'm not vulnerable!"

"Do you really believe that?"

"I'm –"

"Carrie, you can't live your life in this daze. You have to wake up. Adam is still trying to recruit you," Mom said.

We went silent staring at each other.

I welcomed the smooth purr of Charles' car at the back door by the kitchen. The sound brought Addie running down the back staircase toward the kitchen. Addie entered the room wearing a dark yellow linen dress with a pattern sown into the fabric and a bit of a drop shoulder sleeve, held in the middle with a thin belt and matching sandals. Becky would have been proud. We both glanced at my tee-shirt and cut offs almost as if in sync.

"Do you want to change if we're going on a show taping?" Addie asked.

"'Kay," I said.

"Your black fit and flare with the triangles around the neck," she suggested.

"A dress?"

"Dr. Corbon's web site said business casual, but if you try to wear a suit, I swear –"

I didn't hear her threat; I ran up the back stairs and quickly put on the dress that made me look younger than I did wearing a suit. When I came back down, Addie pulled a pale olive-green silk scarf around my head. She wound it around my neck twice and finished by knotting it at my collar bone. Then she handed me a pair of black rimmed sunglasses.

"What's this for?" I asked.

"Charles is going to leave the top down until my hair is dry. Then we can plug my flat iron into his inverter to do our hair," Addie said, patting her large black bag.

I laughed. I started to follow Addie out the door. I turned to say goodbye to Mom and saw her face full of distress. I walked the few paces to Mom and kissed her soft cheek, just below the wrinkles around her eyes.

Mom didn't notice, but held me tight and said into my scarf-covered ear, "Please baby, I need you to wake up. You're very emotional right now. That's a dangerous place to be. That need you spoke of is coursing through you, being distorted by anger. Wade through all this emotion to find the truth."

I couldn't bear Mom's probing eyes.

"I'll think about it," I said. Then I added as an afterthought, "I'm the one who didn't want him to come this morning, remember?"

"Right Sweetie. On some level, you want him to leave you alone." Mom showed a look of relief on her face.

I wondered why she worried about Adam, of all people.

CHAPTER EIGHT

"Carrie, let's go," Addie called through the door. I waved to Mom and ran out of the house and across the flagstone. Then I climbed into the back of Charles' grey-black Bentley convertible and slid into the seat.

"My secretary could only get us stand-by tickets for the first taping, but they are lined up now so I don't know if we'll make that one anyway," Charles said, glancing at me to see how I took this. "Dr. Corbon tapes two shows and we are in for the second. She's pretty sure, since they're bumping something else, Tess won't tape until the second segment anyway."

"Okay," I said, buckling up. Charles turned around and took off. As we drove the feeling of air rushing across my face stole my breath and picked up the ends of my hair not tied down by the scarf. After pulling onto the interstate I saw a silver Lexus speed past us like a blur. The tail lights braked in the next lane until we were even with it. I barely had time to yell, "What's going on?"

Adam started honking and waving us over to the side of the road. Surprised I waved back. Charles took the next exit. We stopped at a gas station. Adam pulled up beside us, obviously put out.

"Hey! Why didn't you guys call me?" he demanded.

"We saw Tess on TV. They were butchering her. So I thought it would be nice if we went and took her out to lunch. Addie thinks if we time it right, we may even get our picture taken. It may show support," I yelled my answer from across the leather seats to Adam's open window as we all kind of squirmed.

"Your mom told me all that," Adam said, still annoyed, "I'm glad you're a good friend to some people."

"Come on, Adam. It's Friday. We thought you were working," I said, permeated by guilty feelings.

"In Hartford?" Adam said.

"Isn't that what you're doing here?" I asked.

"Not really. I'm here for you! Plus, last night I said I'd introduce you to all my Hartford clients so we look like a team, and you agreed," Adam said.

"Right, but I'm still on leave."

"It didn't have to be... you didn't have to report back to Karl you'd met them," Adam said.

"Well, should I come meet them?" I asked.

"No, I already canceled. Hopefully, we can reschedule, but I can't be sure with new business," he said. I almost felt bad, but stopped. It was before nine. Was anyone even in an office for him to cancel with? I wasn't listening well the previous evening, but I thought he said he would arrange it, not that he had. He left my house after eleven. How could he already have arranged for me to meet his clients, drive out to my house, called to cancel with his client, and caught up with us? He must have come over to the house shortly after we left because I left my dead cell phone at home. No wonder he was so upset. He hated it when I didn't answer my cell.

"We're going to New York, so we'll see you later," Addie called, nodding to Charles.

"Fine, Carrie you come drive with me so I don't have to drive alone, at least," Adam said.

"Just leave your car here," Addie snapped back.

"I'm not leaving a brand-new Lexus in a gas station parking lot," Adam said. "Come on Carrie."

"Did you find out where they tape the Dr. Corbon Show?" I asked Charles.

"Yeah, the same place as the morning show, in the network building. I guess I'll see if I can get another ticket."

"If not, I have Carnegie currency with some executive I've never met, so we can try that," I said.

"Richard Blanchard would give you the studio if you asked," Addie said, "Seriously he hounded me last week at the club."

"Were you rude to him?" I asked.

"He tried to follow me into the lady's locker room," she said.

"Hopefully he'll still want to help us. Let's at least drop his name and see if we can park under the network building," I said.

"Follow us since I know where the entrance to the underground parking lot is," I called to Addie with a little wave.

Addie nodded, but she didn't look happy. Charles glared at Adam. I climbed into Adam's car. I still couldn't stand how brand new it smelled. I quickly buckled my seat belt after Adam swerved out of the gas station parking lot and I almost hit my head on the window. We veered back onto the interstate – speeding.

"Carrie, if this is really that important, I'll drop my business for you. There is nothing more important to me than being there for you. We're a team."

"Thanks," I said because it felt like he paused for me to say that.

"Still, if you insist on running all over the city, I really should be consulted."

"I've been dominating all your time lately; I can't exactly call you every time I leave my apartment."

"Right, but infiltrating a live studio audience? You should have known to call me," he said.

"I guess. Sorry, Adam. I didn't know you'd care so much."

"Where you're concerned, I always care," he said. In one quick glance the intensity glowing through his gorgeous face backed me further into my seat.

This conversation rang oddly familiar. I couldn't place a finger on where I'd had it before. I must have a tendency to wander without letting people know where I was going.

"It's all right," Adam said glancing over and putting a warm, strong hand on my arm to show me we were still friends.

"Ah, right," I answered, keeping my arm still instead of pulling away. Maybe it was something I could get used to.

"Your car still smells so new," I said, knowing this was a subject he could talk about forever.

"Yeah, isn't it nice?"

"Yeah," I said. He started telling me the make and model.

"Do you have a place to keep it in the city?" I asked when he'd finished expounding on its fuel efficiency.

"There's a parking garage near my condo," he said. "Besides, I really think we or... the partners are going to give me a team out here. There's so much business in Hartford. Did you know Charles's company is the third largest employer in the state?"

"No," I said.

"Addie could do worse for herself," he said, glancing at me.

I said nothing. The car went silent. After an awkward silence, Adam asked too casually, "When do you want to go put that money in a short-term CD?"

I shrugged and looked back out the window.

I'd received a check for a little over twenty thousand dollars from the network via Fed Ex. I'd won five thousand of it, but I didn't know where the rest came from. I didn't know what the money was or wasn't obligating me to. Exhausted and humiliated, I confided the amount and my fears to Adam then asked for his advice. I soon wished I kept the matter to myself, because he didn't stop giving it.

Adam wanted me set up a short-term CD, but I had to pay the property tax on my mother's house in another month and if I was going to cash the check I needed it for that. Finally, two days earlier, Adam asked me to go with him to pick up his new car. As an excuse, I told him I couldn't – I had to pick up Addie's dry cleaning. I dropped by Hartford Finance corporate offices to ask Mr. Wilson about the money.

Mr. Wilson, my dad's best friend, knew my burden. He saw my grandma taking advantage of Mom's money and I remember him often asking my dad if he wanted him to be the executive of his will. If he hadn't been, I don't know what would have happened. He just happened to give me the biggest bonus in the history of the company right as the membership dues for our country club had to be paid.

Mr. Wilson briefly looked over my contract with the studio. He assured me the money came prearranged. I couldn't sue the studio for using me in the promotions aired to advertise the show, and for the interview I did after the show ended. After I cashed it, the studio owed me nothing. I couldn't sue them, or talk about the show with anyone unless I received express written permission. Other than that, I

owed them nothing except to show up at the reunion show –
in three weeks. Three weeks until I saw Ethan again. Focus!

I went straight to my bank and deposited the check. If I
saved my next few bonuses, I'd probably be able to cover the
property tax. I glanced over at Adam knowing I needed to just
tell him that.

"I happened to see my dad's friend, Mr. Wilson, on my
way back from picking up Addie's dry cleaning."

"Oh, right. He's a nice guy," Adam said. His grip tightened
on the steering wheel.

"He liked you too," I said. "When did you meet him?"

"He came to see your mom at the hospital, just after her
accident."

"Oh, that makes sense."

Adam's strong jaw line tightened. His smooth face was
shaved, but his dark five o'clock shadow would come on
strong by afternoon. He really was everything I wanted in a
man. Even Mr. Wilson told me not to let that one go. I tried to
tell him it wasn't like that, but Mr. Wilson didn't believe me.

"Did Mr. Wilson say anything else?" Adam asked glancing
at me, his head fidgeting.

"Nah, he seemed distracted. He wanted to know if Mom
recovered from her accident, and if the MS bothered her," I
said.

"That's good of him. You know if you want, we could go
to the bank together," Adam said, changing the subject.

"Right, well when I saw Mr. Wilson –"

"He said hi?" Adam questioned.

"Never mind, don't worry about it," I answered. I went
quiet. He didn't notice and instead said:

"You can't just have a check that large sitting around."

I closed my eyes and drew breath. I didn't let people tell me what to do anymore. If I wanted that, I'd still be on a reality show. Set Adam straight – once and for all. I had to. I hesitated.

Telling him to back off would be... The word "dangerous" popped into my head. I glanced over at Adam. Why would I think that? It's not like he'd kick me off his accounts if I told him to back off. Right? Money didn't rule me anymore. I steeled every last nerve. Ignoring the shake in my hand, and the bubble in my chest, I said:

"Adam, I know you're just trying to help, but I've already taken care of the money."

"What did you do with it?" Adam asked and the car swerved.

"It really isn't any of your business."

Adam smoldered next to me.

"It's a chunk of money, not the million dollars, but a decent chunk. Carrie, you need to be very careful. I would hate to see you put it in your checking account and have Addie spend it on nothing."

"Addie wouldn't do that."

I turned from him, leaning forward. What was happening? Adam and I never fought before. I wished Mom hadn't said anything. It put this tension between us.

"Carrie, I can't see the mirror," Adam snapped. I leaned back and pulled my foot up on the seat.

"Carrie, the leather!" Adam exclaimed. I threw him an annoyed look. A bead of sweat glistened down my forehead despite the cold car. How would Adam react when he found out about James Hall?

The show money would be nothing compared to the heavy fire stance he'd take if he knew. I couldn't tell him.

66

Andrea was right, I had to make some kind of a power play or I'd be Adam's lackey forever. Guilt pierced my chest. I needed to move up in the company. If Adam knew he'd take over completely, but when he found out I didn't tell him... My heartbeat sped up and my stomach tightened painfully. I bit my lip trying to calm down.

If I told him now, before I told Karl maybe he'd.... I opened my mouth. No. I closed my mouth. I clung tightly to the information shoving it back down inside me. This contact meant I could get somewhere on my own within Kimbers & Stophers. I might actually get an account of my own and I wouldn't need Adam to throw me bones every couple of weeks so I could earn the extra money necessary to support Mom.

During the last week I called James from my cell phone in my bedroom, and in two calls I had a meeting set up with him. Adam still wanted me to work from home next week, but I had to get back to work. Maybe Adam would stay in Hartford; it would be easier to branch out on my own with him not around.

"Look, we'll figure it out after we go to lunch," Adam said sweetly, reverting back to his calm normal self. "I didn't mean to snap at you. I felt really bad when you ditched me."

"I'm sorry," I said – again.

"That's okay. I'm just hungry and frustrated. How about I buy lunch, and you can pick wherever you want to go."

He rested his strong hand on my arm again. He smelled so good, like manly gingerbread.

"I am hungry, too. Can we go to Jia Liu?"

"No, not Chinese..." Adam returned. He slid his hand down my arm and then returned it to the steering wheel. I crossed my arms, leaning against my door to stay out of Adam's reach.

"What about Italian?" I asked.

"No. Let's go somewhere I can get a burger."

I took a deep breath and tried to think of somewhere close to the studio.

"Do you want a fast food burger?" I asked knowing nowhere downtown would be fast as lines and traffic loomed before us. Suddenly I hated the weight of the decision on my shoulders.

"Whatever you feel like, but I really would rather sit down – in a clean atmosphere."

"Oh right sorry, um ... I don't know where," I said feeling stupid I couldn't pick out a restaurant.

Even worse, my body shook and I couldn't focus. When was the last time I'd eaten? I remembered heating up a piece of pizza at Andrea's house, but had I eaten it? I had a few bites of the salad Adam bought for me. Adam bought me a salad when I needed a friend. Why was I being rude to him?

"Why don't we just ask Addie and Charles?"

"No, we need to have a game plan," Adam said as he swerved past an old pickup truck.

"Could you just figure it out?"

"Let's look it up on the GPS."

After nearly hitting the car in front of us, Adam used the touch screen on his GPS. He quickly found a certain restaurant. He looked at me a few times, like duh, it's the obvious choice. I nodded and leaned back in my seat.

Without my permission, my mind wandered. Was Ethan was taking Veronica to Doctors Without Borders? If he could, he'd take her somewhere exotic so she could scuba dive. He'd arranged for me to go parasailing when I confided in him that

I wanted to try it. I dismissed this thought. Julian took pictures of all our passports; he must have set Ethan up with Doctor Without Borders before the show even started. Neither could control where they went.

I must have looked sullen. Adam informed as if he had to convince me his choice in restaurants was perfect:

"It's close to the studio. It's upscale enough we wouldn't be embarrassed to have our picture taken there. It has a good-sized menu, so everyone can get what they want."

I doubted they served Dim Sum, but only returned as lightly as I could muster, "Sounds good."

"Stick with me kid, I'll take care of ya," he said with a wink.

"Um-hum," I said as we approached our exit. Then I remembered the task at hand.

CHAPTER NINE

At the beginning of my noble quest, I thought of nothing but a call to action. Now in New York City, I felt apprehensive about meeting Tess again. I tried to mentally prepare myself for the afternoon I'd endure.

"I think 49th is closed, let's take Broadway up," he said.

"Okay," I said.

I clutched my seat as Adam started accelerating even though the car in front of him braked. I drew a sharp breath. Adam swerved all the way to the left lane at the last minute to avoid the bumper of the Toyota in front of us. Then he slammed on his brakes not to hit the Volvo that changed lanes at the same time. He cursed loudly.

"Remember Charles is following us and we're going to want to take the round-about," I said quietly nodding at our exit, trying not to annoy him further.

"Charles is a big boy; he can take care of himself."

I looked back wondering how often Charles drove into the city. He worked in East Hartford. Last night he mentioned a few manufacturing plants in other parts of the country, but he probably flew out of Hartford. No, Adam was right. Of course, Charles knew his way into downtown, even with a road closure. How could he not? Adam was right; Charles was old enough to figure this out.

"Don't you want to get into the right lane," I reminded, feeling tattered. The exit came closer and closer. I glanced from Adam to the exit wondering why he wasn't changing lanes. Charles was in the same left lane as us.

With only a fourth of a mile to the exit, Adam swerved, weaving through cars. He barely made the turn-off. I turned in my seat, stomach knotted, to see if Charles made the exit. To my relief, I saw him two cars behind us. By giving Adam some distance and other drivers being extremely careful of his pretty car, Charles exited with us.

Adam glanced in his rear-view mirror and grunted a little, like he was frustrated.

Did Adam want to lose Charles? I studied Adam. What did Mom mean Adam recruited me? Why did I feel like a human buffer between Adam and Andrea, and now Adam and my family? The rest of the ride to the studio was much the same, alternate routes until by the time we got there I almost wondered if Adam were trying to miss the taping all together.

"I'm a friend of Tess, she just got off of *The Whole Package. We* have tickets to *The Dr. Corbon Show*," I heard myself say to the security guard manning the gate at the parking garage.

"I know who ya are," the man said grinning at me, "We can't find you when you're supposed to come and now here ya are."

"I'm a friend of Richard Blanchard, maybe –"

"Nah, I know who to call." He picked up a large phone on the desk and called back to someone inside the building. After a few more phone calls he finally said, "You'll be met at the elevator."

"Thanks. The car behind us is with us," I said.

"They can just wait outside with the rest of the studio audience," Adam interrupted, "Just tell them to find other parking; there's plenty of public garages around here."

"They need to come with us," I snapped. The man said it should be fine if they followed us in.

71

"I would think that you and I could do some things alone, but whatever," Adam said as we drove away.

"Sorry," I breathed realizing I apologized a lot during the car ride. What had I done wrong? Why did I always feel like such a bumbling idiot when Adam was around? Adam drove around for a while trying to find a wide enough space that his new car wouldn't be nicked. Finally, he pulled up to a free parking space and I jumped out of the car before he fully braked.

"Are you crazy, do you want to be killed?" Adam asked.

"I... You're being a little dramatic," I said.

"Yeah, until you lose a leg under my tire."

I didn't respond. I walked quickly toward the elevator, needing a minute alone. I stopped. Julian came out of the elevator. Caught in this moment, with Julian in front of me in his funky un-tucked shirt unbuttoned a few times so his chest hair hung out, trying to be artistic, and Adam behind me, dressed impeccably in a Polo shirt and khaki pants, trying to be posh, felt similar, but I couldn't decide why exactly.

"I wanted to take Tess out to lunch," I stammered.

"Sorry, Tess's segment will be taped in forty-five minutes; we can't have her lost in the city alone," Julian said.

Did Julian and Adam agree that women shouldn't go anywhere unaccompanied?

"Can I talk to Tess?" I asked.

"On air? I'm sure Dr. Corbon would love to talk to you. As a matter of fact," Julian, who'd shaved his beard, ran a pen over the stubble under his lip vying to become a soul patch. With a quick glare at Adam, he said with sarcasm, "I bet we could get an interview for both of you—you and your new man."

"My new man?"

"That could be fun," Adam said quickly before I could contradict Julian. I noticed Julian watching me, trying to gauge my affection for Adam. Finally, I just responded with a blank face:

"No thanks."

Adam glanced at Julian. They appeared to have some tense, unsaid understanding between them. Watching the two I remembered Andrea saying Adam fast tracked my application – he knew Julian.

"You could go alone," Julian considered. He fumbled with the button on his collar, no doubt because I couldn't stop myself from staring at his chest hair.

"We just want to see Tess," I said.

"Come on, Carrie, let's go together. It could be fun," Adam said putting his hand on my arm.

"No thanks," I said, pulling away and looking at him like he was crazy. Julian smirked at Adam like he'd won something, and I glared at him.

"You're Parker Goodrich's son, aren't you?" Julian stated as Addie and Charles walked up to us.

"Yes," Charles said coolly.

"This must be Addie?" Julian said, "Just enough resemblance in the face to know you're related to Carrie. You have a different coloring to you."

Charles stood a little in front of Addie. He squared himself in front of Julian and said, "Those who are not intimately acquainted with the family call her Miss Carnegie."

Julian laughed a little. Maybe Charles wasn't all snake even if he looked a little ridiculous.

"You know, Goodrich, we're always looking for eligible judges for *The Whole Package.* You interested?" Julian asked.

"Not a chance," Charles said. "I've heard about the way you do business – I wouldn't sign a contract with you for a water source to save my life."

Julian didn't hear Charles. His eyes widened and he stared at me as if he'd never seen me before.

"Come on Julian," I asked. "Let us talk to Tess."

"If you give me a half hour afterward," Julian said. He calculated something in his head. He glanced at Adam who came up and put his arm around me trying to reclaim the position of my boyfriend, but Julian wasn't buying it, because he just averted his eyes.

"What do you need?" I asked.

"If I tell you now, I won't need your time then. It takes some explaining," Julian finally said. He surveyed me with his callous hazel eyes.

That must have disturbed Charles because he shifted to stand between us. Again, he squared himself as though expecting a boxing match. He must not have had many confrontations in his padded little life. But then he was an in-the-closet reality show enthusiast. Maybe he thought this was par for the course – maybe he even enjoyed himself a little.

"I'll come with you; it'll be fine," Adam said pushing me to agree to meet Julian while he looked at Charles overreact.

"No," I snapped. Adam turned his hurt eyes on me, so I quickly said, "Charles should come with me. He has a lot more experience with the business side of things."

Wait, I trusted Charles more than Adam? Adam's complaint that he had his MBA echoed through the parking garage. I cut across him and said, "Show us the way, Julian."

Julian pushed the button to the elevator. Charles shuffled Addie in first. Julian caught the elevator door before it shut

74

and held it open for me, dropping it on Adam who had to catch it.

As the elevator shot up I looked from Adam to Julian and wondered how well they knew each other. The tension between them indicated they were mad at each other…. Or rather, Julian looked dismissive of Adam.

"You know, Veronica is having a lot more fun on the show since you left," Julian said in feigned concern. I didn't respond.

Julian held the door for Addie and me as we walked out of the elevator. Again, he dropped the fast-moving door on Adam. I almost ran into a cart full of props watching him do it. Julian walked with me. He forced the others to follow behind us down a hallway lined with huge pictures of Dr. Corbon and a few other daytime talk show hosts.

"I feel bad about Ethan using you so badly," Julian said, "He seemed so nice when he wanted to."

Out of nowhere, I remember Ethan agonizing when he kicked Erin off the show. He called it a double-edged sword he couldn't get away from. He was nice, wasn't he? But then why had he invited Tess down to his bungalow?

"If I'd gotten to know him better, I wouldn't have chosen him for the show," Julian said. "He can't seem to make up his mind about who he likes the best. As you know, we allow him to judge the contestants without interference."

I said nothing, but remembered Serena being popular. Julian made sure the audience didn't like her before he allowed Ethan to kick her off.

"Carrie," Julian called. I had zoned out of his manipulative droning. He was so obvious; I couldn't even bother making the substantial effort it took to pay attention.

"I don't want to talk about it," I said, unsure what he'd asked.

"Just let me explain. I didn't mean for you to get hurt."

"I didn't. It's all a game."

"I swear I thought he felt you were most deserving of the prize money. I wasn't just telling you that. I try to gauge who my judge likes best so the audience can see why, but with Ethan, he shifted so often."

"I guess he should stick with Veronica. She won the most competitions," I answered.

"Yes, I suppose she did do very well," he agreed. Julian's crooked smile went for sympathetic, but his greasy aura made him rather disgusting. "I am sorry you'll have to start over. You know there are plenty of good fish in the sea. Don't settle for someone less deserving." As Julian said this, he glanced back at Adam with a knowing look. Did Julian know something about Adam?

What was happening? I was in a daze. Wake up! Mom told me to wake up. Since I left the show, or no, had the daze come since I met Adam? I didn't look at my life. What did she mean Gordon knew he pushed me into our relationship? I spent my life desperately trying to keep water cupped in my hand instead of looking for a cup. I needed to wake up.

Julian led us into a much smaller green room than the one I'd waited in to go on the morning show. This one had huge pictures of Dr. Corbon, an older woman with dark curly hair and thick rimmed glasses.

Tess paced the room in extremely high heels. Her dress looked just a touch long for an open backed vest, barely covering her rump. When we walked in Tess rushed to me, needing a friend.

"What are you doing here? Are you going on the show too?" she asked.

"No. I just came to make sure you're all right," I said.

"Oh, thanks Carrie," Tess fell into me, and unused to much human contact I gave her an awkward hug, trying to figure out where to pat with so much skin exposed. Tess pulled away and asked:

"Do you know why people seem to hate me so bad?"

"They blame you for my leaving."

"I don't understand. Were you... did you love Ethan?" Tess asked, turning to me.

"He kissed me a few times. I guess people thought for some reason he ought to be loyal to me, but then Julian set me up to catch you kissing him."

"Oh Carrie, I didn't know ... I mean you guys got along, but I didn't realize you –"

"None of this is your fault. Julian set the whole thing up."

"When I saw your face though; you... do you really –"

"Nope, let's focus on you."

"But Carrie you should know he –"

"I can't talk about it right now," I whispered putting my forehead on her temple so only she could hear.

"I'm sorry, Carrie," Tess whispered back.

As I tilted my head, I noticed Julian standing by the door away from the group, whispering to Adam. He noticed me watching them. He said one last thing to Adam. Adam nodded – like they'd agreed on something in the two minutes I'd been focusing on Tess. Julian left the room and Adam smiled to himself—like he won. And just like that, they appeared not to be fighting anymore. Each man still needed the other, and they only had one common factor – me.

I couldn't figure it out. Just then Tess asked:

"What am I going to do?"

"Here this is my sister Addie, she thinks if we get our picture taken together after the show it'll help your image."

77

"Oh, of course. Hi Addie, I've heard all about you," Tess said turning to her and giving her a hug.

Addie looked embarrassed. She forced herself to be polite to Tess, doing her best to be congenial in a high-pitched voice. In all fairness, Tess's cleavage jetted out of her vest dress, bulging like eyes popping out on a squeeze toy.

"This is Charles," I said, nodding to Charles who proved even more uncomfortable. He barely shook her hand and kept looking at Addie to see if she disapproved him even talking to Tess. Poor Tess looked unnerved when his pale face turned bright red. Adam walked up to Charles and started talking to him. Apparently, Adam didn't notice I was making introductions.

"This is my friend from work, Adam," I said.

"Hello," Tess said enthusiastically leaning forward and moving toward the extremely handsome man.

"Adam," I called. He looked at me. He didn't step forward.

He didn't take her hand.

He did stare at her cleavage for an instant too long and then he dismissed Tess as trash with just a head nod as if that were some kind of acknowledgement.

"We picked out a place to eat," Adam said turning back to Charles, "Maybe you should take Addie ahead so we don't have to wait for a table."

"I hate waiting for tables," Tess agreed.

"Oh, I don't wait," Charles said politely looking at Tess like he was trying to include her in the conversation since she was still in Adam's space. Adam more obviously turned his back on her.

"It'll be better if you arrive first. I'll go with Carrie to see what Julian wants," Adam continued, "You take, uh, Tess with you."

When he said her name, Tess moved in next to Adam so she made up a member of his and Charles's conversation. She looked up at Adam's gorgeous face hopefully. I joined the conversation across from her so she didn't look so out of place. Tess moved closer to Adam like she would nuzzle him if he let her. Adam quickly leaned away from her in disgust, dismissing her again as if he'd had her and was now through with her. Worse, he acted as though she were in the way of his convincing Charles to leave me alone with him and Julian. After way too long, Tess finally saw his appraisal of her and the flush ran up all the way up her skin from her chest to her hairline.

The weirdest thing about this interaction was Adam looked to me like a proud little puppy who needed his head patted. Was his complete disregard and degradation of Tess for my sake? He looked at me like, of course, I would expect him to disrespect her like a prostitute on the street.

That didn't make sense, considering our mission of mercy. Didn't he know Tess and I were the same? Each of us broken; we just displayed our broken differently. My brand of broken was no more impressive or less demanding because it didn't drive me into skimpy dresses desperately looking for the approval of the opposite sex. No, we were the same, both of us broken. When he dismissed her, he dismissed me. Adam and I would never be a couple, not ever.

I couldn't pretend any longer.

I overestimated Adam. What a jerk!

CHAPTER TEN

"Carrie and I will meet you at the restaurant. I negotiated with Julian before," Adam said.

"That didn't end well," Charles said, with an authority I suspected he used in his business life. Adam didn't know how to respond right away.

"Look, I will handle Julian," Adam said.

"I think it best for Carrie to handle her own business, but I'm happy to help where I can," Charles said without flinching. With a glance Adam told me I was supposed to take his side as he said:

"I have the rapport – "

I stepped right through their conversation and, putting an arm around Tess's waist, I said:

"None of that matters right now. Come over here Tess, let's figure out how to help you." I pushed, but she didn't budge. She stood waiting in Adam's space like eventually he'd take advantage of her if she waited long enough. What happened to her? More forcefully I pulled her away from Adam's cold condescension.

"Come on, let's make the public adore you, as you deserve," I said, turning my back on Adam.

Still glancing at Adam, Tess came over to a sofa and sat down while we proceeded to hatch a plan to get Tess in the public's good graces and soften her image. The whole time she watched Adam to see if he was listening.

"I know it's like eating crow when you have no reason to," I said after we decided she would just apologize to the world for kissing Ethan, "but you can't explain you didn't know and therefore did nothing wrong. I already tried that. Nobody heard."

"Oh, I don't care about eating crow, as long as this interview doesn't go as bad as the last one. I couldn't do anything but defend myself, eh?" Tess said.

The next talk show hostess, despite her Ph.D., would be nasty. After all, *The Whole Package* was her brain child. The live audience would be brutal on Tess. Tess, unlikely to attain any level of professionalism, would be traumatized. I sucked in really hard saying:

"Julian said I could do the interview with you. Do you want me to come out with you? We can be linked arms or something?"

"No, I'm going to finish this," Tess glared at Julian who'd just come back in with her microphone.

"You have to do the show, you signed a –"

"I know," she snarled ripping her microphone out of Julian's hands.

"After this interview, you're done. We'll get our picture taken together," I called. She nodded and a sound operator tried to help her figure out where to clip her microphone onto her dress.

Addie agreed in a non-verbal way. She pulled the scarf off my head. I tied it like a headband. She brushed my turbulent hair until it turned to smooth coppery ripples. Julian observed the interaction between us as if we were a rare sight.

Addie forced me to pucker so she could apply some pale rose lipstick. Julian moved in observing. I swear he would have E.T.-touched us if he could have. I gave Julian a dirty look and he backed off.

That's it. I had to be rude. I couldn't be a kind person. Adam often called Andrea overbearing and unprofessionally rude. But Andrea didn't get taken advantage of. Perhaps with some people, rude was the only way to stay on even ground. My mother said kindness was the best route but I wasn't sure I could be kind and not get steamrolled. Tess finally seemed to realize the role she'd been cast in.

"You told me to lose the country girl look and grow up," she snarled at Julian. "Before I even got on the show, you said that I'd have to get with the styles to make it in the top ten. You made me cut my hair like this – give me a whip and I'm a dominatrix at a strip club. You dressed me up to be the slut!"

"I saw your audition tape. You like the look," Julian defended. He glanced at Adam who shook his head in the negative, slightly glancing at me. Julian looked at me. I glared back.

"We've had a lot of interest from many male viewers wanting to know more about you."

"All the perverts," Tess answered, "When I was twelve, and developed young, my father dressed me like that. He brought home all his male clients for drinks served by his pretty daughter. All through high school I ... I ... I'm twenty-five now. I don't have to do that anymore. It's disgusting."

"Oh, Tess," I said.

"Whatever, it's my past, and after this interview so is this. I'm going back to Pennsylvania, I'm packing my bags. I won't be that twelve-year-old girl anymore. I can go anywhere I want. I have savings. I can start over," Tess said.

"Tess, let me go out there with you," I said.

"No thanks. I can do this, and then I'm gone," Tess said near tears. Addie and I glanced at each other, and I noticed her eyes were filled with compassion. In fact, so were Charles' eyes. Julian surveyed the situation impassively, analyzing his next move. And Adam had the same calculating look in his eyes.

Adam didn't even notice poor Tess or her distress – she was barely a person to him. I'd been Adam's personal recruiting project since before I graduated from college. I realized now that he was in a battle with Julian for the role of domination over my life. He couldn't be bothered with Tess.

What should I do? I couldn't just leave a reality show to rid myself of Adam. He entrenched himself into my world. He'd mentored me for over three years– I had nothing without him, possibly not even my job.

Time.

I needed time. I needed to make my own name at work. I could. I had a valuable contact, but was it enough? If Adam stayed in Connecticut and I went back to New York, maybe I would... I needed time. Trying to hide the terror palpitating through me, I turned to Tess.

"Why don't you come over to Mom's house tonight?" I invited. "We'll have a girl's night, no boys allowed."

"What?" Adam objected.

I turned back to Adam. He found his distress. His eyes pled with me. His gorgeous face contorted into a need only I could fulfill.

"Oh please, Adam," I said, "We have everything under control at Mom's house. Besides, I have to move back to New York by Monday. And it sounds like you have a lot going on in Connecticut."

"I thought you would work –"

"Nope, I'm ready to move back into my apartment," I said.

"I'll help you move back. I'm almost done in Hartford anyway," Adam said.

"I thought..." I stopped. Didn't he just tell me he wanted to start his own team in Hartford? I wasn't going to argue with him.

Adam tilted his forehead confidently, even sweetly toward me. He turned his large grainy molasses-brown eyes on me. His handsome face grew as appealing as it had been so many times before. My stomach lurched. He lost his charm. No. It couldn't be gone. I'd give it back if I could. I'd grown so dependent on him – I needed him. I was alone. I had to take care of my family.

"Were you going to say something," Adam asked the full force of his gorgeous face on me.

"Maybe...."

"Spit it out," he said playfully.

"Never mind," I said.

I couldn't do it. I couldn't take his hand again, even to save Addie. The idea suffocated me. My safety net had fallen and doing acrobatics high above the crowd without one proved debilitating from fear. No. I smothered that thought. I had to fight. I glanced at Julian. I knew how.

Finding my interview face – devoid of real emotion I refocused serenely on Adam. I pretended to be politely distracted and not stuck, a captive in my head.

"What is it, Carrie?" Adam asked.

"Adam you've done so much for me. You need to figure your own stuff out. Andrea and Phil already offered to help me move back. Andrea has been feeling neglected."

"I will –"

"Adam, let it go," Addie interrupted sternly, putting dangly earrings on me. Adam backed off. I'd hear about spoiled entitlement next time we were alone, but Adam gave a side look at Charles. He wanted something from him because he did. He just let it go.

Addie put people in their place. Our grandma passed this trait down to her. Often it humiliated me, and I wondered how she'd get along in life incapable of working with people. Over the last week, I listened, and even gave value to Adam's arguments when he degraded my little sister's attitude.

Yet, her being strong enough to stand up to Adam was useful, and heaven knows no one ever told my grandma what to do, but then did I want to be that kind of person? Did I have to be abrupt and rude to people to be left alone?

I forced a smile, and then turned to Tess and said, "Farmington isn't too far out of your way. Let's have a girl's night tonight."

"Only the opposite direction, Dipstick," Tess said.

Everyone in the room stiffened. I laughed heartily and said tartly, "Whatever. At least I'm not lame, with no sense of adventure. I'll drive you there and back. I'm driving into New York Sunday night, anyway. Where's your car?"

"At my house in New Holland," Tess said.

"Oh, even better. I can stick you on a train in New Haven. That'll be faster than fighting traffic."

While Addie teased, then smoothed my hair in places, I added: "We'll have fun. Plus, Mom is full of really good advice – if you're humble enough to take it."

Tess laughed. I was serious. Mom was right on.

CHAPTER ELEVEN

"Tess, your adoring public awaits," the production manager said, showing her where to go.

Tess nodded and walked out of the room.

"Carrie are you ready to go?" The man looked at me being primped, then looking to Julian.

Julian nodded at the man. He looked confused. Then they both looked at me.

"I suspect she'll go," Julian finally said.

I turned my rusty colored eyes on him in disbelief. As Tess walked out on the stage someone yelled a crass name at her. I turned to watch a television screen fixed to the wall of the green room. The crowd clapped their approval and it echoed in stereo because I could hear the actual audience clapping Tess's degradation. I glanced at the man and then Julian. The production manager held out a microphone pack to me. I walked over and took it.

While he helped me attach the lapel microphone I looked over some paper work I had to sign. I could have been signing away my firstborn, but I couldn't focus with poor Tess on the defensive. Tess did not look sweet on the defensive.

Tess refused to answer when asked "Do you feel comfortable wearing that dress?"

Her encounter with Julian right before she went out made her raw, and it wasn't fair to feed her to the wolves alone. I resolutely walked to the stage door and charged out in front of the cameras like any good reality star would.

Jogging across the stage, I threw my arm around Tress' bare shoulders.

"Tess is a human being. You can't treat her like this."
Everyone went silent to hear me, including the hostess.

"Tess apologized to me and I forgave her. I apologized to her about the sundress and she forgave me. You can choose to hold a grudge and be angry or you can forgive. I hope you will all let this go, and let Tess move on – I have!" I said.

No one said anything. A stage hand rushed out with a stool for me. Dr. Corbon didn't appear surprised enough to see me, and I had my suspicions as to where Julian disappeared to earlier. Acting like the whole thing was all a part of the plan, she started throwing questions at both of us about our time in the house.

"Carrie, when you told Ethan he didn't get to kiss you and the other women, you set a boundary. He violated that. He broke that trust. You were in the right to take yourself out of the situation," she said.

"Maybe so, but Tess didn't know anything about the boundary I set, so no one can really blame her, either," I said.

"That is fair," she said.

Tess leaned into me, like she had many times on the show.

Dr. Corbon talked to me about trust, and I admitted I didn't want to babysit a grown man who was supposed to love me. I also admitted trust was a tricky thing for me, and she told me to seek out the people I could trust.

"While on the subject of trust, Carrie, how do you feel about Veronica?" she asked. "We all thought she was loyal to you. I, for one, was shocked she turned on you – making out with Ethan only a day or two after you left."

"Yeah, that was precious of her, wasn't it," I snapped.

Of all the things I did that day, publicly turning against Veronica was the one I'd learn to regret the most. The audience turned on whomever I told them to. They applauded my censure of Veronica. I didn't think – hey, one-day Veronica's going home to live her life just like I am. Perhaps being a kind person in this instance would have served me better. Instead, I allowed the audience to feed my anger.

"Of course, you'd feel betrayed. What did you think about Ethan asking Veronica if she wanted to go with him and some friends to a pumpkin festival? Do you think making plans for after the show means Veronica's won?" Dr. Corbon asked.

"I didn't see it."

"How far does friendship go, Carrie? Are you going to try and steal Ethan back at the reunion show? You lost the million dollars, but that doesn't mean you have to lose Ethan if he can manage to gain your trust back," Dr. Corbon said.

The audience screamed their approval.

I'd been asked this so many times when I first got off the show. It seemed comical then. Now, I was different. Was there any chance this could work out for me? How did a person rebuild trust after a reality show? No. That wasn't my life. Adam using me – that was my life. Die inside, I ordered myself. After the audience calmed, I said:

"I never got the impression Ethan even wanted a girlfriend from the show. I got confused a lot; it's not really a dating show, right?" I said.

"It's not supposed to be," she said. Her eyes flashed with something like loathing and she glanced behind the camera crew; that's the first time I noticed Julian standing there, watching us.

"Anyway, you behaved just as you ought to have, and the way you've overcome is brave. Is your disinterest in Ethan perhaps too resilient?" Dr. Corbon asked.

"Huh?"

"Who's the man in the photo with you? Have you found a boyfriend already?"

I puttered a few times with near repulsion – I pushed the anger down. Oh, how Adam weaseled his way into my life while I'd been sleeping.

"No! That's my co-worker. He's actually the one who nominated me to go on *The Whole Package*. He thought I'd end up with Ethan, no doubt. We're business associates; our company doesn't allow fraternization, so the more people saying we're a couple the more likely I am to get in serious trouble," I said. I looked right into the camera hoping Adam got the point. How many times did I have to fight to live my own life?

"Oh, that does make more sense," she said.

Then she pretended to take a break for commercials.

CHAPTER TWELVE

Next, Dr. Corbon turned on Tess and my heart started pounding, ready for a fight.

"Tess, first of all let's talk about relationships. How many long-term relationships have you been in?"

"One... well, sort of," she said.

"Are you out to have fun, one-night stands and partying? Is that satisfying enough for you?" she asked.

"No... Not anymore," she said looking at me, like I could answer for her.

"Then we need to work through what resiliency looks like for you."

"Okay," she said tentatively.

"Let's start with forming a simple emotional bond. Your friend, the one who appeared on the best friends in New York segment of the show with you –"

"Vi," Tess supplied.

"Yes, Vi, she was pretty catty to you. The viewers will only have caught a hint of this, but I've reviewed the raw footage. She was cruel to you," Dr. Corbon said.

"She likes to be the center of attention."

"Okay, so let's call her a relationship that is not emotionally satisfying, is that fair?"

"Ah," Tess said glancing nervously at the camera.

"Clearly you've created a real bond with Carrie. She's here today to defend you."

Tess smiled at me. I grinned back at her.

"You trust Carrie. She always looked out for you and is worthy of your trust. Do you feel she's someone you'd like to always be friends with?"

"Always," Tess smiled at me.

"Always," I agreed.

"That's because the two of you have what I like to call an emotionally satisfying connection. Tess, I'd like to help you find that kind of emotionally satisfying connection with a man."

"Okay," Tess said.

"What do you bring to the table as far as a relationship goes?"

"Um, look at me," Tess said. The audience jeered.

"No, no," Dr. Corbon said to stop them, "She is very beautiful. Tess, I love how confident you are, and that you like your body. That's something many women never achieve. Every woman should feel good about the way they look. What else?" she asked.

Tess looked at her. She looked at me and I smiled with a head nod, letting her know it was okay to brag some.

"I'm um..."

I saw the panic in her eyes.

"Your job," I prompted her.

"I've always been good with numbers, and budgeting. I'm good with money," Tess, said doubtful that's what the doctor meant.

"That is a huge benefit in any relationship," she said.

"Is it?" Tess said, looking at me to laugh with her.

"It would be really hard to be with someone who couldn't figure out their money situation," I said with a shrug.

"Oh yeah, I guess so," she said.

"What else?" Dr. Corbon asked.

Tess looked around, bouncing her leg, panic building in her eyes again.

"Carrie, can you help her out?"

"Sure. Tess is fun. She's great to be around. She doesn't sulk—after the sundress thing she could have been pissed, but she brushed it off. I really appreciated how cool she was about it all. She's always popping off, making me laugh," I said.

"Those are all wonderful things to bring to the table. Who wants to be with someone who drags them down," Dr. Corbon agreed. Tess looked at me and I saw her blinking hard.

"Are you okay?" I asked.

"I just didn't know..." Tess shrugged.

"Tess, today's society" – here she glanced at Julian, "teaches women all she has to do is be sexually available for a man, and he will be her boyfriend, but what about your needs Tess, are they being fulfilled?"

"I'm not sure I understand what you mean."

"Tess, sexual desire in men is stimulated in the limbic system of the brain. This is considered the oldest part of the brain. Every animal has these desires. The area in the amygdala responsible for hormone uptake is significantly larger in men than women. Men need to overcome this desire to evolve."

"Okay," Tess said.

"I think she wants them to be gentlemen, you know, care more about you personally than they do about sex," I said, because Tess looked to me.

"That's one way to put it," Dr. Corbon said, "Tess, when you show off your body in such a provocative way all the time, men can react in one of two ways. They can brush off the hormones flooding their brain and use self-control to move past your sexuality, or they can move into fantasizing about you."

"I don't mind if they fantasize," Tess said. She seemed flattered by the idea. The audience hooted.

"Research tells us that the man who moves into fantasy mode will then cast you in a role; you will become objectified. These men will not be interested in how good you are with money. They may never acknowledge how much they appreciate the forgiveness you easily give. Instead, they will have unrealistic expectations about how you are supposed to perform a certain role in their lives. They will often project shame or negativity felt because of their bad behavior onto you. They will blame you for not performing your role correctly. Have you been in a relationship where you couldn't do anything right?"

"Yes." Tess bit her lip.

"This is emotional bullying, or emotionally unsatisfying, isn't it?"

Tess only nodded but looked away quickly.

"Right now, I would estimate I can see over ninety percent of your body," she said. Tess looked down at most of her breasts and legs exposed and nodded.

"You know that being naked doesn't automatically lead to intimacy, right?"

"In my case being naked always leads to sex," Tess laughed.

"Okay, well then, you can have sex without intimacy; intimacy is an emotional bond you share with people. And when you have intimacy with a man, Tess, you will have much more satisfying sex."

Tess didn't know what to say to this.

"When you first meet a man, I suspect you start picturing your life together."

Tess bit her lip.

"Meanwhile, dressed like this, if he is nice, he's fighting to keep his mind focused on you as a human being, and if he's emotionally unavailable, his brain has been hijacked by the sight of your body and he's thinking 'Wow, I'd like to hit that.' This is a common phrase, and it doesn't even allow you to be a human being – he wants to hit that."

"So she deserves what she got?" I asked furiously. "Just because he decides he wants her, that doesn't mean he has the right to –"

"You misunderstand me, Carrie. Nobody has an automatic right to her body! No matter what you wear, no matter what you do, no matter what he feels, no means, no," the doctor insisted.

Tess nodded with a desolate look in her eyes. For the first time I started to think maybe I didn't want to know exactly what happened to her. I put a hand on her shoulder.

"In this case we're not talking about the unwilling being forced into sex, but rather an over willingness in Tess that has and will again put her in bad situations."

I looked at Tess; she looked away.

"Like I said, I watched hours of Whole Package raw footage. Tess knows what I'm talking about," Dr. Corbon said, drilling her eyes into Tess. Tess nodded reluctantly, but neither explained.

"In the last year I started a series working with sex addicted men who unscrupulously take advantage of women. It is an epidemic that needs to be addressed among these men, not the women who trust them." This time she glared at Julian to be sure he knew she was talking to him.

"Okay," I said also glancing at the camera and Julian, thinking Tess and I may have been caught in an argument extending far beyond our season on *The Whole Package*. Dr. Corbon was aggravated.

"What I'm saying is a woman needs to define what she wants from any relationship and not accept anything less than that. There are men who debase woman until they accept whatever scraps they are given. That's not okay," Dr. Corbon said.

I had nothing to say to that.

"Tess has admitted she wants a boyfriend. Tess, you need to make an emotional connection to form a healthy relationship with a man. There is an epidemic out there. More and more men are becoming emotionally unavailable, and completely sexually motivated."

"What am I supposed to do?" Tess asked.

"Emotionally connect, date until you find someone who fits your needs. There is a man out there who will devote himself to the beautiful woman who can budget, forgive easily, and uses humor to lighten up tense situations."

"I..." Tess stammered.

"You are *The Whole Package*, you are worthy of that kind of love," Dr. Corbon said. She looked so insistent.

Was she trying to undo the damage further inflicted on Tess by Julian? How responsible did she feel for Julian and *The Whole Package*? She must have started out with good intentions at some point. Dr. Corbon talked on like this, trying to build Tess up. She truly wanted her to find a friend in herself, as she called it.

I started taking a few mental notes trying to decide how Adam happened to me. At times, as with Julian, it felt a little like I played a certain role for Adam, only I'd never shown anyone as much of my body as Tess did. Perhaps it wasn't as much what she wore as the way she opened herself up to certain men while wearing it. She would have done anything to be with Adam, not knowing anything about him. But then my financial success was intertwined with his. How much did I really know about Adam?

Despite all the differences in how we were raised, what we believed, and even the way Dr. Corbon viewed us, weren't Tess and I essentially the same? Each of us, in our own way, were vulnerable to being taken advantage of.

Finally, Dr. Corbon started to wrap things up. I unclenched. It wasn't as bad as I thought it would be, though I couldn't see how televising one's therapy session could really be more beneficial than humiliating. Dr. Corbon turned to me and said:

"Carrie, you really should have won, in my opinion, but I'm proud of you for taking care of your widow mother."

"Thanks," I said feeling something in my chest swell. I did take care of her. I would keep James Hall to myself. I would find my own place within my firm and continue to take care of her. Adam would have to suck it up.

A light above the camera started blinking. Out of time, she turned to the camera and said, "Carrie, who we all know and love, has forgiven Tess. She asks that we all do the same. That is mental health, people."

She stopped and adjusted her glasses then continued;

"What a great surprise for us. We helped two instead of one! Carrie, Tess, remember your mental health is just as important as your physical health."

The cameraman nodded. Dr. Corbon turned from the camera and leaned into us to talk:

"Thanks for your time ladies. I really do hope you both recover from all this," she said quietly.

"Ah, we're resilient," I said. She laughed.

"I'm taping another segment after this. You're welcome to stay. I'll be talking to twin brothers who dated the same woman."

"Did she know?" I asked.

"No, the younger one emotionally engaged her for his older brother who was only interested in the sexual relationship. She chose not to see it, but in many ways, it was a form of rape. She was not consenting to the man she was having sex with. I've talked to law enforcement; they won't do anything for her."

"Oh, she knew. How could she not?" Tess asked.

"Sometimes it is very hard to face the betrayal of someone we love," Dr. Corbon defended.

"I think women want to be loved as aggressively as men want to have sex," I said, looking away.

"Both of those things are very natural, and in a healthy relationship will only bring two people closer together. Don't lose that vulnerability, Carrie," Dr. Corbon said, examining me sadly. "When a relationship has failed you, it's hard not to give up on the whole gender. I know it doesn't feel like it, but vulnerability is braver than closing off. There are men out there worthy of it; you must know a few of them."

"Phil," I said nodding.

"Yes, we all have a Phil who can give us hope. You maybe even still have an Ethan –"

"Right," I said puttering.

"Like I said, I've reviewed hours of *The Whole Package* raw footage. The way he looked at you, the way he moved toward you when you entered a room, not to mention how you lit up when he gave you that half smile of his. I wouldn't be so quick to write that off my dear. Believe it or not, he's fighting Julian," she said looking up at Julian.

97

"Fighting?" I laughed, looking to Tess to join my amusement this time. She looked confused.

"Just like you fought," she said, "Though I don't think any moment will compare with your asking Julian if the million dollars would only be half a million after taxes. I watched it five times and even showed most of my production crew."

"Carrie, Tess," Julian called quickly, like he overheard her. I turned to see he was edging his way toward us. Dr. Corbon looked up and glared. Julian made a half circle passing us, moving toward the stage exit. He really was a coward.

Tess stood up obediently, adjusting her vest dress. Dr. Corbon took a hold of her arm.

"Tess, you need to get some kind of weekly therapy."

Tess looked at her like she had the plague.

"Okay, thanks," she said, averting her eyes.

"At least tone down your wardrobe so you aren't such a target," the doctor nearly pleaded.

"Fine," Tess said like a teenage girl to her mother. Julian waved her over; she cantered toward him.

"Carrie, getting back into life is going to be extremely hard for Tess. She's going to get ... aggressive attention from the kind of men who stalk porn stars. I've seen it in the last three seasons. Tess needs a therapist or for the rest of her life she's going to be a revolving door for emotionally unavailable men."

"What can I do?"

"She listens to you. You've built trust with her. You're probably the only one who can help her," Dr. Corbon said.

"Okay," I said standing. A sudden wave of dizziness threatened to knock me over. How did I take care of one more person? I had nothing left. I needed to get off the stage. I gave her a little wave.

"Carrie," Dr. Corbon said.

"Yeah,"

"It wasn't supposed to be a dating show. Myself, and two other psychologists were supposed to be the judges."

"I know Julian. I don't blame you for anything," I said trying to console her, but I felt so dizzy. I stumbled toward the green room and caught up with Tess. She stopped in front of Julian wordlessly waiting for instruction. I took her arm and shoved her past Julian without stopping to let him get in another word to her.

I threw a dirty look at the identical twin men sitting on the couch near where we walked in. One of them caught my eye and smiled. Tess smiled back. Oh, how did I help her?

I couldn't tell when I started spinning. Charles talked to Addie in a low voice, but I couldn't be sure why he had to keep looking at her like that. My grasp on Tess's sweaty arm slipped. Adam knew Julian. I made the bulk of my living off Adam's clients, without him, I had nothing.

My fingers couldn't hold on anymore. I lit up for Ethan, and he couldn't make up his mind – he couldn't decide who he liked better. Why do we bother with them? My head started reeling. I aimed for a chair. I needed a soft landing. My eyes blurred. Addie asked if I were okay. Ethan kissed Veronica. I reached the chair, but there were three of them instead of one.

Something happened in my pulsing skull like sand emptying out of an hourglass. I began teetering. I grabbed onto a table spilling a vase full of assorted flowers. My safety net failed. I hit the ground. When I came around, Tess bent over me. Charles, deceptively strong, pulled me up while Tess put her arm around my waist.

"Here, I can carry her," Adam yelled amid the confusion.

"No, no I'm okay," I said from somewhere outside of my head trying to pull myself up. Adam could not support me. Panic curled up in my stomach; Adam could no longer support me.

"Charles has her – back off Adam," Addie snapped.

Addie took control of the situation. Addie took care of me, instead of the other way around.

"Do we call an ambulance?" Tess asked.

"No," I said. "I'm fine."

"Did she eat this morning?" Adam asked.

"Carrie's ill. I need to get her home. Tess is coming with us," Addie told Julian. I felt someone tug the microphone pack off my back, "Carrie will keep her commitment to meet with you another time."

Addie didn't wait for an answer. She pulled Tess's suitcase through the halls while Tess supported my weight. Addie must have felt I'd done enough to say I didn't want Adam around. At the car Adam said I should ride back with him, Addie laughed without even bothering to respond. She sat me in Charles' car and helped when my shaky hand couldn't buckle the seatbelt.

In the car, a cold bottle of water came from Julian. I heard him say something about waiting a few minutes to see if the water would revive me. Grabbing the bottle from him, Addie gave it to me, making it clear we were leaving. Addie murmured comforting words to Tess who sounded like she was crying, but I don't know when that fit in.

I must have fallen asleep. I had little memory of the drive aside from being awakened and force-fed a soft taco. We acquired it from a drive-through window outside the city. It took all my willpower not to throw it up. I slept in the front seat – Addie must have insisted I sit in the front seat at some point – definitely before the bottle of water. I closed my eyes and opened them.

I was home.

I walked through the back door with Tess's arm around my waist. I trust Tess; she and I went to Hell together.

"Come in, come in," Mom said, walking behind Charles who helped me to a chair by the kitchen table. She sounded scared. Addie must have called her.

"This is where we say goodbye to the boys," Addie said firmly, smacking Charles with a kiss on his way out.

"But I have to make sure Carrie's all right," Adam said jogging up to the door from his car. Addie merely shook her head in the negative.

"Carrie," he called to me. I said nothing.

Adam must have followed us every step of the way. As I sat amid the chaos I laughed. Adam ate a taco instead of a hamburger. For some reason I found this extremely funny—I doubted we got it from somewhere he wanted his picture taken.

Adam stood on the doorstep fuming, but Addie wisely didn't notice. She did not let him push his way into the house again. I wondered if Addie could give lessons. As a last-ditch effort, Adam called,

"Carrie, I'll see you Sunday for brunch?"

"Oh, no," Addie answered, "We've invited Andrea, and the baby, down. We know how Brea gets on your nerves so we limited our guests to just the Clovers and Tess. I'm sure with all Tess has been through… We only want those who are intimate with the family on hand. Of course, you understand. Another time – perhaps."

Then she sweetly smiled at Charles, shutting the heavy door in their faces.

101

"Seriously that guy was getting on my nerves. You and your sweet little hints, but when you announce on national television you're not interested? For heaven's sake, it's time to back off," Addie said.

I stood up and hugged Addie in total gratitude. She rubbed my back like she understood. Could a woman get to the age of twenty-one and be whole? I'd been at Harvard during Addie's high school years. I ought to ask her about them, maybe sometime – after I figured myself out.

Tess threw her arms around us. She was bawling. Addie and Mom were even misty eyed. I should be crying, but I couldn't. I wouldn't. I'd broken something inside me and it wouldn't let me cry. Instead of being glad about it, it scared me. I started to laugh a strange frightened laugh, wondering why I couldn't cry with them. Tess started to laugh too.

"Julian would love to film this," Tess said.

"Yeah, but when my bracelet got caught in your hair he would've made it look like we were fighting."

"Was it really that bad?" Tess asked looking up at the ceiling as a few more tears fell.

"Julian tweaked pretty much everything you said. America spent an hour a week watching the Tess whom Julian created. I'm sorry," I said.

"So am I," Tess said.

"Neither of you did anything wrong. Let it go now," Mom said pulling a chair out for Tess. "How are you feeling Carrie?"

"I'm better," I answered, coming around. "Napping all the way home must have helped."

"Maybe you should go up to bed and we'll entertain Tess down here," Mom said.

"No!" I said. "We're having a girl's night."

Mom analyzed me. I tried to look healthy.

"All right. If this is going to be a girl's night, you have to eat something, Carrie."

"Sounds good to me," I squeaked, sounding unnaturally shrill in my effort not to sound groggy. "Mom, will you call ahead to Emery's, and get a Greek pizza?"

"I want a whole-wheat with smoked turkey with the olive oil rub," Addie said.

"Rich people, you know most of the world goes for pepperoni," Tess said.

I laughed but then stopped. I needed a new game plan, one that didn't include Adam. An idea started in my head. The rest of the world would think, duh, but it never occurred to me before. Mom gaped at me. She saw it too.

Simply put, why buy lobster, when chicken breast will do? I didn't have to pretend to be a socialite. I wasn't one—not anymore, especially after my debut as a reality star. The thought screeched to a stop. Fear took over.

Addie had Charles right where she needed him. He could continue to buy her lobster. I had to get rid of him first. Then perhaps I would explain about the money being gone. Could I chance it? Would I even have a choice? When I made it clear to Adam he didn't get a say in my life anymore, what would happen?

CHAPTER THIRTEEN

I fell asleep on the couch during the movie. When I woke the next day, patches of light fell across the room through the row of windows behind the house. I felt rested. It was easily the best sleep I'd ever had in my grandmother's house. I also felt hungry. I must have been hungry before, but I hadn't felt it.

I could hear Mom and Tess talking softly through the open door to the kitchen. I sat up. At first, I couldn't tell what was being said. Then the words came into focus and I heard Mom say, "You have a degree. You could get a different job. At any rate, you could move, and find a different clientele than the one your father left you."

"It's all I know how to do. I have fifty-seven clients all over Lancaster County, and they're real loyal to me. Plus, moving from a small town is like disowning my family. Plus, my father will kill me," Tess said.

I hurt for Tess. I wished Ethan kept her on the show. I wished he fell in love with her. Ethan would have been so good for Tess. I caught myself. Ethan, the hormone crazed jerk, was the enemy. Especially after what Julian said about him.

The rational in me rolled her eyes. What did Dr. Corbon mean that Ethan was still fighting? Ethan wasn't the horrible person Julian was describing him to be, I knew that. Julian wanted something from me, and it required me disliking Ethan. Even when I left, I knew Ethan was being forced to play the game. Or was he indecisive – unable to decide which woman he wanted? Did he see us as desserts set out on a platter for him? Or worse, did he just get whatever he could no matter the cost to anyone else?

Then my mind flickered to Tess putting herself onto that platter.

"If he were that guy," I asked myself quietly, "then why did Ethan kick Tess off?"

A voice from beyond said, "I think he loves you, Carrie."

It took me a moment to realize this answer came from the quieted voices in the kitchen. I flinched, crossing my legs under me on the soft velvet sofa and pulled my white-knitted afghan up to my chest. Tess came into our family lounge through the door propped open to the kitchen. She sat next to me so I gave her part of the afghan.

"Sorry, Tess, I didn't mean to disturb you. Or bring up anything painful."

"Nah, you're so good, Carrie. You couldn't mean to hurt anyone. Even when you joke around you always watch me to make sure you're not hurting my feelings. I know that, ah," Tess said curling up next to me.

Was this how she saw me?

She continued, "When you caught him... you know kissing me – "

"No, you don't – "

"Listen to me – you should've seen his face after you walked out. He didn't want me. He hadn't even wanted to kiss me. He wasn't into it."

I shook my head, no. I didn't want to hear. I preferred growing numb and pushing Ethan out. Tess either didn't have the tact to stop, or perhaps felt I needed to hear what she needed to say.

"He wouldn't come near me after that. I thought he and I had some chemistry – you know?"

"You guys did; it made me... crazy," I said.

"Well, not enough. I thought if I could get him to joke around with me again, it'd click. When you left, I thought it was my chance, but he wouldn't even..." Tess drifted off.

"He liked you," I said.

"Not like he liked you," she said looking so rejected. "Even on the dinner cruise, he flirted with every woman in sight – obnoxiously so. But he wouldn't flirt with me. He wouldn't pretend with me."

I said nothing. She continued:

"I think he's pretending with Veronica and Sandra."

"Did he say something?"

"No, he couldn't. Julian has him wound up tight. But I can tell. He became plastic and cold when you left. He would sit and talk to Veronica sometimes, but he always seemed quiet and thoughtful. He was moody, never happy like before."

I sat and listened. I didn't know what to say. I hadn't noticed Mom come in the room until she sat across from me in a wingback chair.

"I told you yesterday. Andrea thinks Ethan is under pressure to perform in a certain way."

"He did say Julian was getting weird about his contract," I remembered.

"What else," Mom asked.

"After your accident, he wanted to support me through it, but he said he would get in trouble. Something about his contract –"

"He said that?" Addie asked coming in the back door from a run in a tank top and spandex shorts. Most of her hair stayed slicked back perfectly.

"He always said things like he hadn't understood how it would be. He hadn't known what he got himself into."

"What does that mean?" Addie asked.

"I don't know," I answered with a shrug. "He couldn't explain."

"Julian was so hyper about everything," Tess said.

"Right. He threatened me with a lawsuit if I left after mom's accident," I recalled.

"He did?" Tess asked. I nodded.

"We all thought it was weird you were so calm about it. Then after it happened, you spent almost all your free time in your room painting."

"Ethan has his own practice, doesn't he?" Addie asked, shifting gears. "Could Julian go after that?"

"I doubt it," I answered. "I'm sure it's protected. In the medical field, he'd have to be."

"Is it different if someone brings a suit over medical issues, versus personal issues? His insurance isn't going to cover that, would it?" Addie asked.

"I don't know," I answered.

"I'm sure it's a gray enough area that Ethan wouldn't really know," Tess said, catching on and snarling, "Julian's a jerk."

"I asked Ethan questions about insurance claims once. He said he would ask his nurse Beth after the show ended. He had no clue about the business side of his practice," I said.

"I didn't know that. We never talked much about anything real," Tess admitted.

Everyone felt the tension in the air until Tess asked, "I don't know if I ever knew him well enough to be in love with him, did I?"

"It's a manufactured situation. You were competing for a handsome man and a large amount of money. Of course, you'd convince yourself you were in love with him if you could," Mom said. Addie and I nodded.

With a charity that surprised me, Tess said, "For good or bad, though, he's a nice guy. He even seemed nice to Serena, and by the end, she drove him nuts."

"I'll bet they target guys like that. The nice ones they can manipulate," Addie said.

"But hot so the every female lookin' at him wants some," Tess added.

"Julian did seem interested in Charles," Addie said. Tess gave me a half glance. I made as discreet a shrug as I could manage. Neither of us found Charles that good looking. Mom looked at me significantly, but I didn't know what point she wanted to make.

"I'm glad Ethan's going to be with Veronica," I said, willing myself to believe it. "She was always the best of us."

"Granted he did hover around Veronica quite a bit, but he didn't seem interested in loving anyone. Well, except when we were filming. Then he was interested in everyone. He even flirted with the camera crew at one point."

"I wonder if that's how he's fighting," I said, and quickly explained what Dr. Corbon told me.

"You could fight for him," Addie said.

"Seriously? He humiliated me on public television," I said. "If he wants me, he's going to have to come fighting for me."

Everyone was quiet.

Mom broke the silence with, "Carrie, hopefully in three weeks that will be the case, at the reunion show you can just ask him. Until then you need to lend your focus elsewhere."

"But if he –"

"He isn't here, and trying to decide what he is, will drive you guys crazy. Besides, I'm not sure...."

Mom looked over at Tess. I noticed for the first time how battered Tess looked. What had they been talking about before I woke up? Trying to figure out if Ethan loved me wasn't a fair conversation for Tess.

"Anyway," Mom continued, "we need to talk about this household. I feel like I failed you, Carrie."

"Hey, now?" I replied but before I could say anything Mom turned to Addie.

"Addie, we have no money."

"Mom!"

"No. Carrie she needs to know. Carrie hates her job. She makes just enough money to keep us going. She's never complained to me, but I can see she hates it. From this point forward, we will not spend Carrie's hard-earned money as if it flows from the faucet."

I stopped. Addie stammered. I could see the truth taking hold as her face cringed and she tried to understand. How long would it take her to come to my grandmother's solution in the form of Charles Goodrich?

"Carrie, why didn't you say anything?"
Addie flushed, embarrassed, tears welling in her eyes.

"I just wanted you to live the life you were born to."

"Addie's twenty-one. She's old enough to cope with the reality of this."

"Ah, maybe I should go," Tess said, scooting further down the couch uncomfortably, leaving the coziness of my afghan.

"No sweetheart, it'll be good for you to understand every family has drama. Carrie, I left you alone too much after your father died. I saw you laughing at your Grandma most of the time, and I thought you were safe. But you weren't."

I remembered the reality show: I remembered laughing at first. I thought I was safe then too – but nobody breathing in toxic waste stays healthy.

"Look I'm fine. This is not the way to deal with…." I turned, concerned, to Addie.

"You totally withdraw when you're hurt," said Mom. "You don't ask for help. You refuse to try again. You are ashamed of feeling love –"

"Mom," I stammered.

"You're not healthy," Mom said.

"How can you say that?" I asked, growing heated, "I'm stable. I'm the one who has a master's degree from a highly-accredited university. I'm the one who holds down a great job. I'm not screwed up!"

"Come on, Carrie. You've always been capable, but you have a cloud over you. It's like you gave up on yourself and went into survival mode."

"Didn't I?" I screeched standing up and dropping the afghan to the floor.

The room stopped. Everything quivered around me as though the tension made my sound waves visible. I screeched again, not even trying to stunt my anger, "Didn't I give up my life the day you were diagnosed with MS? I stepped up. I got good medical insurance. I got a high paying job so I could take care of this family. So Addie could go to all her functions, and so you wouldn't have to worry. I stepped up and did what I had to!"

I turned to storm out of the room.

"Who asked you to?" Mom called after me. She stood with squared shoulders.

"What?" I snapped and turned back. Completely embarrassed, Tess tried to look small on the couch. Addie got up, nervously backing away from Mom and me.

"Who asked you to do that? I didn't. I'm the parent here. I never put that burden on you. You just did it," Mom said, taking a step toward me.

"Grandma told me we were out of money after Grandpa died. She said either you had to work, already exhausted from the MS, or I did. What could I do? She used Grandpa's insurance to send me to Harvard. I found a high paying job! I stepped up! And I'm still stepping up."

"She said that?" Mom whispered.

"Six months into my sophomore year she introduced me to Gordon. I was nineteen years old. Where were you then, Mom?"

The second I said this I wished I could take it back. Mom took a step and sat back in the chair. She looked like I slapped her.

I hadn't ever wanted Mom to know this. It was supposed to be my burden. I couldn't stop now. The pressure built up for so long inside my chest, it all burst out in one geyser of confession as I spewed:

"You had to know that's why she sent me to Harvard. I thought it was to support us, but she let me major in art. Then she introduced me to Gordon, like Harvard was my personal dating service."

"Oh Carrie," Mom looked at me, sickly white, her face crinkled up, crying. This drew me out and I whispered:

"I'm sorry mom. You're right; you didn't do this to me. I did this all on my own. I wish I'd never met him. I hate how Gordon loved me so much. I hate that I convinced myself to love him so he could take over."

111

"Why didn't you say anything?" Addie asked tears streaking her face as she sat on the couch.

"I didn't want you guys to feel bad," I said and sat back on the couch, putting my arm around my weepy little sister.

"Carrie, you know we have options, right? Other than living in this house and incurring all this expense?" Mom asked.

"Like what?"

"We don't owe anybody anything. We used your Dad's insurance to pay off the lien and all the debt. We own this house free and clear. This is your Grandma's house. We live here – by her rules – she's dead and still running our lives."

"Caroline, let's not fall asleep on couches when our beds are only up the stairs," I mimicked.

"I know," Mom said closing her eyes, "Let's sell this place. I wouldn't mind moving to an affordable suburb somewhere – we could move by Andrea. Get in close enough to New York that you could live with Addie and me so we don't have two households to support. You know I could get a small fortune for the house."

"It's been in our family for forty years," I said.

"Yes, but with all the renovations Mom did, it's just like new. Not to mention the sixty acres some developer would love. I'm sure it'll sell," Mom said.

"Oh, Ma, that isn't what I meant," I groaned. "It's the house that Addie will one day pass along to her children."

"Not over your broken back, I won't! Quit your job! I can take care of myself!" Addie sobbed a little. I squeezed her shoulder.

"Oh sweetie, you know I didn't mean it. I love making it possible for you to live your life. I love you."

At times I wondered about this, but saying it out loud I knew it was true. I loved Addie so much. And even more, I felt it. Feeling something was better than feeling nothing.

"I would have understood," Addie said.

"I've always been proud my career allowed you to live the life you were born to," I said.

"I was born to this – Grandma's debt," Addie said, "The life I'm living is the lie."

"Who let you into those philosophy classes?

Addie made some sound like "humph."

"You were a junior in high school when grandma died. You'd never have understood back then. How could I rip you from private school and all your friends?"

"Maybe then, but –" Addie said.

"You enjoy the life Addie, you know you do," I interrupted.

"Not over your broken back I don't. I don't need it," Addie defended.

"I love you, Addie," I said again mostly because it relieved me to feel something so warm.

"I'm moving with Mom to a small house where we can raise chickens," Addie said.

"The suburbs aren't a farm, Addie. We live in the country now. It would be like us moving closer to Hartford. It doesn't mean redneck either, no offense, Tess."

"Close enough to redneck from where I've been sitting my whole life," Addie said, nudging Tess.

"If you want, you can come home with me. Plenty of wide-open spaces, chickens, cows, and Amish people," Tess said "Addie, just so you know: Where the cows have been, you gotta watch where you're steppen'."

"It isn't much better with our friends. At least with the cows, you can actually see what you're wading through," I said. Mom threw me a look and Tess laughed nervously hoping the yelling was over, and said, "Too true, too true."

"Oh, look what a holy mess I've made of things," I sighed shoving my knuckle in my eyeball. "I should've kept my mouth shut."

"No," Mom said. She stood up and then sat back down squeezing onto the couch between Addie and me, "This is what we needed. This is where we begin again."

"We could move by Andrea and I can commute with her," I said.

"Addie, you could become an interior designer, like you wanted to," Mom said.

"You do?" I asked not realizing her degree in sales wasn't working out.

"Yeah, I'd only have to take a few extra classes to change my major. I'll still need sales, but then double major in interior design. I could take out a student loan," Addie considered.

"No, I'm going to work you through school," I snapped.

"We'll all start over. Carrie, you don't like your job. Quit. I'll sell the house. We can finance everything with that."

"If you're determined to do this mom, we have to do it smart."

My mind went crazy with planning.

"I'll give Addie five years to finish up college and get established professionally."

When she turned my age, twenty-six, her life was in her own hands. She would be a fantastic interior designer. A warm loving feeling told me I could sacrifice five more years. I would see Addie happy. Then Mom and I would figure things out. A lot of jobs would provide me with decent insurance. If

114

we sold the house, it would cut a lot of expenses. I could support Mom doing a million other things.

I had a timeline. I could endure what would end. My cage opened to a long dark lonely tunnel. Just a speck of light pulled me forward. But a speck of light to someone whose world has been shrouded in darkness, I might as well have been sitting on a beach lying in the warm sand feeling the sun thaw me out.

"Five years," I repeated, "I'll get us settled. I can do it. Please, Mom."

But five years was still too long for Mom. Or, she was trying to finagle her way back into the role of parent.

"You can work until I sell the house," Mom said.

"Mom, what happens the next time you have to spend a few weeks in the hospital? We need insurance."

"We could pay— "

"Mom, I don't really mind the work. We need insurance. I'll start researching insurance options, and look at what I need to do to get another job, okay?" I said.

"Okay," she said.

Noticing Tess hugging the end of the couch uncomfortably, I finished, "I'll find Tess a new job. I was thinking of Mr. Wilson, but ... he couldn't sign a contract with Kimber & Stophers last time. I don't know if I can place a candidate with him again."

Mom looked at the ground self-consciously at this suggestion, and the head shift allowed me to see Addie look away quickly. Neither made an effort to comment. I wondered if they were fighting with the Wilsons. Mrs. Wilson was always looking for a fight so I shrugged it off. Mr. Wilson wouldn't be involved with society tiffs, but he couldn't employ anyone who hurt his image. I said:

"What if we send you to the West Coast?" I said. "Where the people are liberal, and your being on TV will just get you clout."

"Really?" Tess asked.

"Sure, Tess, it's what I do. I may not love it, but I'm good at it."

"Will you come with me?" Tess asked. "You could leave the East, too."

"Charles has to stay on the campaign trail with his father," Addie said, looking down a little. Up to this point with all the wildly free plans taking over my thoughts, I'd forgotten Addie and her budding romance. Charles? I didn't trust him. I didn't trust anyone, honestly, but I felt him closer to a snake than man. But then he'd embraced his inner dork standing up to Julian. Still, something about him felt off.

It didn't matter. It wouldn't be long until he deserted. I'd seen what happened when people left the fold. They were cut off – hard and fast. When Charles found out we put the house up for sale, he'd bail on Addie.

"I really like this plan. Seriously, it feels good, doesn't it?" I asked

"Yes," said Mom.

"Yes," said Addie, after I knocked the back of her head.

"Hey, Carrie," Addie said.

"Yeah."

"I'm sorry I was so... sorry I always overspent my budget. I thought it was you trying to raise me, being bossy, you know. I didn't realize you were the one funding me, or I would have tried harder to live more... moderately."

"I was so afraid you'd go find someone else to finance you if you knew."

"I may have," Addie admitted.

"Please don't. Please work harder in school. Launch your own interior design business. I'll help you. With Dad's friends you will make it, I promise."

"Kay."

The rest of the day Addie taught Tess how to find the good deals as they went shopping, for Tess's toned-down wardrobe. Apparently, Addie walked through the stores with a little shake in her hand like an addict coming off crack, but she didn't spend any money.

I spent my time on the computer. I investigated how much we could sell the house for. How much interim insurance would cost if I had to go back to school between jobs to get a teaching certificate. Only a few times did I investigate schools in Boston. Every time I did, I felt mortified and easily recalled the image of Ethan kissing Veronica.

CHAPTER FOURTEEN

The next morning at brunch we showed up fashionably late. I'd been held up when a horde of elderly women at church cornered me in my straight-backed pew. These women wanted to tell me how I reclaimed my place among them by insisting the world forgive Tess. Thankfully Andrea texted she already made it to the house, so I excused myself.

"Wow! You look great!" Andrea whistled when I finally made it to the dining room where Tess set out brunch on the serving table.

I shrugged, tugging on my wrap-around dress. I smiled at Mom, who woke me up early because she thought it important for me to feel good about myself and look nice. Tess made a feast while we were at church and brunch never looked so good.

"Tess, you must have been really nervous," I said.

"I started thinking about the conversation I'm going to have with my father when I get home on Monday."

"If you need to get the wording perfect in your head I've been craving Chinese food," I returned.

"Nice try, Red."

"I invited Charles," Addie said, "I hope no one minds. He'll be a little late."

"Of course not," Mom said cutting me off.

"Is Adam not coming?" Phil asked.

Everyone grew silent. I said in my best imitation of Addie, "Phil, Adam is getting a little aggressive for our tastes. You will excuse us, but he probably won't be invited back for some time."

"Thank goodness! He was getting really weird about you Carrie," Phil said, handing half a piece of toast to Brea.

"He's had a crush on her since he recruited her three years ago," Mom said.

"No, they only met a year ago," Andrea corrected.

"No," I said. I'd been living in my own personal reality show since I met – no, my grandma. I'd been on *The Whole Package* since my dad died.

"Carrie," Andrea snapped so I'd refocus, "you met Adam three years ago?"

"Let's see. He met me before I finished my bachelor's degree, a month or two after Gordon... he died in October. January of my senior year, so three and a half years ago, I think. That time is all kind of a blur," I said.

Mom nodded.

"Wait, can I tell you this? He's my recruiter. It's a part of the privacy clause in my contract," I cringed.

"You've got to learn to read things before you sign them. It's really not that big a deal," Andrea said.

"Adam made it sound like I couldn't say anything."

"We can't talk about your salary, but who recruited you isn't confidential."

"Yeah, he made a huge deal out of me not saying anything to anyone."

"This actually makes sense." Andrea said, "None of us could figure out ... he'd never let a recruiter work for him exclusively, he'd always rotated through the youngest women. Then he invites an intern to be his private recruiter the week you start. Do you think that he's been...?"

"Recruiting me?" I said.

"It kind of sounds like that, doesn't it?" Andrea said.

"I'm his personal recruiting project," I said as the doorbell rang and Addie left the formal dining room to answer it. I picked up my crystal stemware and made to take a drink of my orange juice. I couldn't swallow, so I spit it back out in the glass.

"Eew," Tess said. "Why are we so freaked out that Adam is recruiting Carrie?"

"How did he meet you?" Andrea asked, completely ignoring Tess.

Addie and Charles sat down and I passed the quiche so I didn't finish it by myself.

"Tess, are you sure you don't want me to find you a job as a chef?" I said, stalling.

"I was thinking about it, actually," Tess said.

"Okay. Polite conversation later. Tell the story, Care Bear," Andrea said.

Mom smiled. She loved having Andrea around. She never pushed me for information, but obviously didn't mind when others did.

"All right, but stop me if I say anything wrong."

"It isn't that technical," Andrea said.

"Okay, after my fiancé, Gordon, passed away, I was in a state of confusion. I didn't know what to do with my life. I had an amazing education, so I decided to find a job to go with it." I smiled at Addie. I stopped before I said something about having to support my family. Her relationship with Charles was tender and she would never forgive me if I destroyed it.

"Carrie," Andrea snapped refocusing me.

"Fine. My Career Coach set up an appointment to meet with me. She introduced me to a representative of the prestigious recruiting company of Kimber & Stophers. Adam promised if I got my MBA, he'd get me a paid internship at Kimber & Stophers and find me a high-paying job."

"But I don't remember your name coming up. How did he hear about you?" Andrea asked.

"No clue," I said not bothering to shovel my way through Adam's sugar covered crap about being on the radar like I usually did.

"How did he convince you to get your MBA?" she asked.

"He offered to get me an internship making over six figures in the first year. He said I'd get a hundred percent return on the investment of my own education in a year or two tops. I jumped at it."

"I still can't figure out how he even heard of you. We don't even glance at people without a graduate degree of some sort."

"I don't know, but he knew everything about me. Who my dad was – every one of his buildings. How his business tanked after he grew sick, because he poured so much money into those blueprints he couldn't finish. He even knew about my dad's friends who tried to save it. He knew all about Shades, the company Grandpa started. I thought he was just being thorough. It turns out he was recruiting me. Not for a job."

"What for?" Tess asked.

"That's the question, isn't it?" I answered.

"You know," Charles said, "he asked a lot of questions about how my Dad got support to run for office. I wouldn't be surprised if he has political aspirations. Plus, he never found my jokes about politics very funny."

I shook my head at Charles while everyone laughed.

"Seriously, though," Charles added, "Adam's really interested in what kind of political pull a person has to have. And you definitely have it."

"He would know," I said.

"He makes it feel like he's just interested in you, not like he's plugging you for information."

"He wants me to be his political pull?" I asked.

"The way he's been networking in the area. I wouldn't be surprised if he has been building his own base," Charles said. The table went silent.

"We won't have any political pull for long," Addie said, "Carrie, you should just quit Kimber & Stophers." The tears in her voice evident, "You don't like it. We'll put the house up for sale tomorrow. You've done enough to support us since Grandpa died."

"Your job supports this family?" Charles asked, surprised, then looked embarrassed, like he broke some unwritten rule.

"Thanks, Addie," I whispered in awe.

"You aren't going to quit, are you?" Andrea asked.

"In four or five years. I'm going to find something I like better. I see you, Andrea, and you love what you do. I don't feel like that. I want to teach, like Phil."

Tess then turned on Phil, who'd been extremely nice to her, as he was with everyone, asking him what grade he taught. Andrea zeroed in on them, monitoring any interaction between the two. Meanwhile, Addie looked at her hands that shook in her lap. My sister knew Charles would bail when he learned we were financially strapped. Addie announced it. Addie did it so I could be free.

How must it be among Yale business graduates – dating a woman whose family struggled to stay fed? Addie gave

122

Charles a heads up – a chance to free himself before we were found out and publicly snubbed.

After all the sacrifices I made for her, she did this for me. Charles looked to be thinking. Was he looking for the fastest way out? Charles took a few bites of a sausage link. After he finished chewing, he said, "Your Uncle Brock isn't –"

"He made it very clear we were to be self-reliant when my dad died," I said.

"Still," Charles said looking at me, then turning to Mom he said, "I'm going to need my own space eventually, and I love this place. I'm sure we'd give you whatever you wanted for the house, Irene."

Was he trying to keep us from the public shame of putting the house on the market?

"That's kind," Mom said. She, too, had been observing Charles, but looked at me as she finished, "We haven't set anything in stone yet."

While Phil and Andrea tag-teamed Tess's questions, Charles tried to get Addie's attention. She still looked at her hands. He leaned over and grabbed one of them until she looked up at him. He kissed her hand, and appeared startled to find a tear trailing down Addie's face. Charles looked at her with such... I'd see that look before, that level of devotion, but couldn't place it. He wiped away the tear that I put on Addie's face. I liked him a little better for it.

Andrea, with no understanding of Yale men's pride, interrupted my observations saying; "I don't mean to draw the subject out. Did you leave Adam with the understanding that you will not be his political footstool? If you want me to, I'd be happy to convey that message to him."

123

"I haven't seen him since I figured this all out," I said, my shoulders and neck tensing.

Phil, in the true style of a fifth-grade teacher, ranted about how he'd give Adam a little lecture. I listened, knowing he was right. Adam was bad for me. He was using me. But on whom would I depend if I didn't have him?

I spent every paycheck before the next came. Sometimes I floated bills into grace periods before I could pay them. I couldn't lose my job without planning, without savings. I had to keep our medical insurance current for Mom. My stomach churned. My throat burned from swallowing down the acid that kept coming up.

Adam taught me to depend on him. He pushed me out onto the tightrope, convincing me to spend what little money I had left in savings on an MBA, banking on the fact that I'd never cut the cords to my safety net. Rational or not, I'd been trained like a puppy to need Adam. And now, I couldn't even see the path I'd plotted the day before. I couldn't see anything but my mother and Addie's needs I couldn't fulfill.

Joke – keep it light I commanded myself, it made everything seem easier. I'd been here before, I could handle it.

"Phil, I have to say, we'll sic Andrea on him."

"Oh, please let me," Andrea begged. "If he's put years of work into this, he won't give up that easily."

"Ah, maybe I'd better fight this one for myself, Andrea," I said a little taken back by the gleam in her eye.

"Can you?"

"I think so. He kind of slipped the last few days. When I told him, I'd taken care of the money I got from the studio he unraveled. He thought I had to do whatever he wanted – like I wasn't even my own person anymore."

"You have to look out for the pretty ones," Tess said.

"Hey! That's not fair," Addie said fawning over Charles. Unguarded, Charles leaned into Addie clearly overwhelmed with adoration for her, and kissed her cheek. He wasn't deserting. Maybe I misjudged him.

"You have to admit Adam has his charm," Mom said, comforting me.

"Huh?" I asked refocusing.

"Adam, he's very handsome, charismatic –"

"No, Mom you're always saying how everything has a spirit to it, that's how you know what's right. Adam always felt dark – confusing – overwhelming – heavy. Plus, he tried to push everyone else out of my life."

"He's charming when he wants to be, and he always turned on the charm for you," Andrea pointed out.

"I saw myself as his muse, because he treated me so special. I spent all my time trying to make him happy, but I'm never happy around him."

"And you're always making excuses for him – it drives me nuts," Andrea said.

"I apologized for not being able to read his mind and pick the restaurant he wanted to go to yesterday."

"Yeah and at work, you follow him around. You've never taken the time to get to know anyone one but me. That was all my effort, not to be rude, but you were hard to get to know."

"I know. I can't help it."

"It's fine, but if you want to make it four or five more years at Kimber & Stophers, you're going to have to make money without Adam. If Bailey leaves after her maternity, you can recruit for me."

"I don't think she will. She's been pretty feisty to me the last six months," I said.

"Your numbers are still high. I'll bet Brooke will let you recruit for her."

"You think," I said trying not to show how my fear petrified me. "I kind of have a plan...."

I stopped. I couldn't tell Andrea about James Hall. If I didn't have Adam, I only had one card to play at work. The business James would give me. I had to do this by myself. Andrea didn't notice I trailed off while she was saying:

"...anyway, everybody is more interested in you since you followed through on the bet. Especially Brooke."

"Wait, Carrie," Tess snapped her head up.

"Yeah?"

"You lost a bet?"

"Huh?"

"Julian told us after we all flew into New York you only came on the show because you lost a bet. You were just having fun at our expense. Is that true?"

"Uh," I squirmed, "I did lose a bet. That is why I went on the show. That's why I was always more relaxed than everyone else. I never laughed at you, though; I just never would have gone on if not for the bet."

"Still, I'm kind of glad you didn't win. It wouldn't have been fair," Tess said looking away.

"You're probably right," I said smiling at her as she glanced at me.

"Does that mean you don't really love Ethan?" Tess asked looking at me with a tension in her face.

"Tess, I was able to be myself for the first time in years. It made me vulnerable. I fell – hard ... I didn't mean too," I said. I averted my look as Tess searched my face.

"Poor Ethan. He must have taken it hard," Tess said.

"No, he knew the whole time I lost a bet. That's how we became such good friends. That's why there wasn't the pressure between us," I said.

"How did Julian know?" Mom asked.

"I don't know. Uh, oh, Adam," I said.

"What?"

"Adam said something about it when we talked on the phone after your accident. Julian listened to my call." I remembered Julian's face. His betrayed demeanor after I hung up. To punish me, he made me walk in on Ethan kissing Tess.

"Veronica seemed the most hurt by it," Tess said.

"Which would make her an easy emotional target for Julian. Might be why he announced it," Phil said.

"She definitely turned on you after that," Tess said.

"Yeah, she did," I said wondering if I could leave the table. After a few moments of awkward silence, Charles said:

"If Julian knew you had to accept the key, then he may have thought he could force you two into a love triangle."

"Probably," I said.

"Nobody's ever walked off the show before," Charles said. "I'd bet anything he thought you'd stay on the show and he could toy with you."

"Wow, that's a lot of detail for your mom just watching the show, huh Charles?" I said.

"Hey, my girlfriend's sister was on it."

"On past seasons," I said. Charles shrugged. Addie should have been upset with me. She looked nothing but pleased Charles openly called her his girlfriend after she dropped her bomb on him.

"We ought to try watching *The Whole Package* again this Thursday, my house?" Andrea asked. I nodded my head.

"You're all invited," Phil said warmly in his kind-hearted nature. "In fact, come early, we'll barbecue."

We all agreed.

That evening, Tess and I rode back to Andrea's house squeezed in the back seat with Brea who, after a long and exhausting day of chasing frogs out by our pond, screamed the whole way. Tess tried to act like she didn't care.

"I'll see you Thursday. Will you be able to find your way back?" Andrea called.

"I programmed you into my phone. Thanks for everything," Tess waved. She quickly jumped into my car.

We drove away before Andrea invited us in with her screaming daughter. Tess jumped just as quickly out of my car at the train station. I apologized again and again for not putting her on the same train in New Haven. She just waved and pulled her suitcase quickly away.

I understood.

Neither of us had been alone for a long time. I wanted to be alone. As I drove away from the train station, I didn't turn on the radio. I just listened to the sounds of the city. I was alone for the first time in two months.

I finally walked into my studio apartment at nine. Everything looked exactly as I left it. My bedspread pulled back, still messy from getting up late. My mugs hung on the hooks over the island designated for pots and pans.

I didn't mind being alone, in fact, I really liked being in my own space.

CHAPTER FIFTEEN

"Staff meeting in ten minutes," Karl called into my office the next morning.

I nodded. I finished writing my e-mail and carefully logged off my computer. A rumor circulated around the office that someone was hacking into computers that hadn't been logged out. I had information I needed kept private. I grabbed my laptop and locked up my tiny office, wondering if I'd be in a cubicle with the other recruiters after this meeting. The only other recruiter that had an office was Andrea's and I'm pretty sure she actually earned hers. When I asked Adam how he got Karl to give me an office he winked at me and said not to look a gift horse in the mouth.

I made it through most of the morning without seeing Adam. He was giving me the cold shoulder. According to his message, "Carrie you should have insisted Addie let me come to brunch," despite my being half asleep. And "when you didn't even call back to check in... we could have at least discussed Sunday Brunch ... well, that hurt."

I fought down the impulses of guilt that naturally flooded over me.

"Ahh, nothing like Monday morning to pump you up."

Andrea walked up beside me as I walked toward the conference room.

"Hey, my future's not really stable yet. You're going to keep that between us, right?" I said quietly.

"Yah think?"

"I know, but I just had to say it out loud. I'm having a hard time trusting lately for some reason."

"Wonder why," Andrea said as I pulled open a huge wooden door to the conference room. Then louder she said, "Hey Adam! Missed you yesterday at Brunch, boy can Tess cook. You really missed out."

Hidden by the door my jaw dropped. Did she really have to provoke him? No, it didn't matter, I wasn't the buffer between them anymore. They could talk to each other however they liked. I stepped into the conference room self-consciously. Tinted windows acted as the far wall. This was the working board room. We had a grander lounge area with smaller more private tables set up for meeting clients.

The picture of Walter W. Kimber was the only ornate décor in the conference room. It hung behind Karl's seat at the head of the table. The rest of the walls were covered in charts and graphs of projected earnings for the entire company. My name still sat at the top of the bonuses received chart. It slid a few positions on the retention rate column because one of my first hires, who needed to be coddled, quit while I was on the show.

Karl's team consisted of nine other people, only two were recruiters who worked exclusively with him. Everyone already sprawled their stuff around the large table. My co-workers dressed in polished gray-scale business attire appeared lifeless after all the bright colors and appealing clothes in the land of television. Adam purposely ignored me, so I quietly walked next to Andrea toward the head of the table instead of going over to him and groveling for forgiveness.

Karl, my boss, looked up and smiled at me. Then, while clapping he said:

"Let's hear it for our blossoming star."

Everyone turned to stare at me. I bowed a little, shifting my laptop under my arm not to drop it.

"Carrie, was Ethan really that good looking?" Brooke, an older, slightly plump woman, asked from across the table. I stopped for a minute. Brooke rarely talked to me. My nerves coupled with my last name made me appear stuck up. Now I'd become nothing more than an approachable reality TV star.

"The TV doesn't do him justice," I acknowledged and smiled. Adam audibly sulked. I took this as my cue to sit down next to Andrea. The seat next to Adam, where I'd sat since my first day of work, stayed vacant. Instead of looking over at Adam I organized my stuff next to Andrea. I acknowledged Bailey, the woman who recruited for Andrea's businesses. With a tight mouth she lifted her head to me. She'd never been warm toward me, but since she'd become visibly pregnant, she'd grown even more wary of my friendship with Andrea. No matter how I tried to prove I wasn't out to steal her business, she didn't warm up.

I sat much closer to the head of the table than I'd ever been.

"Carrie how was your vacation?" Karl asked.

"Long – are you done yet?" I nodded, laughing it off.

"Probably not, Care Bear, that's cute," Karl said grinning at me and holding my gaze. His straw blond hair spiked off in every direction, his eyes were electric blue. His face held an unnaturally red quality to it. Karl looked like an Anime character brought to life. He pulled out agendas and started passing them around with a slip to order lunch.

132

"Karl, did you get that e-mail from me regarding that matter we were discussing," Adam said pointedly. I glanced at him, but he ignored me.

"I did, thanks for being so prompt about it," Karl said. He glanced at me.

What matter? Were they talking about me?

Was Adam done using me exclusively? Would Karl fire me? Would Adam ask him to when I stopped rolling over for him? I had James. I could save myself. Karl seemed to like me. In the last year, I made him a lot of money with business contacts only I had. Would that be enough?

I stopped myself. I would be confident and not live in the "what ifs."

My first goal was to interact with my boss and co-workers without Adam's interference or help.

"Are we going to have staff meeting, or can I go back to work?" Adam snapped annoyed, making sure I noticed.

"All right, Sunshine," Karl said coolly to Adam, "I'm giving you the Stanford job fair in two days. Be on a plane this afternoon. The meet and greet is tonight. I'll send you a list of the entry level positions we need filled. There are a few promising business graduates we need to fight Silicon Valley for."

"December graduates?" Adam started to complain, "I can't just leave the new business –"

"You said you could this morning when you came back to the office, and it's your turn. Brooke, how are you coming on the Spicker account?" Karl interrupted.

"If we can get them to go another five thousand on the salary, he'll jump," Brooke answered. She spoke proficiently, not a trace of the gushing tone she used when asking about Ethan.

"Good work. Keep on it," Karl said.

Karl paused to hand his secretary our food orders, noticed me watching him, and he smiled at me. I smiled back. Karl didn't revere Adam, not in the way Adam implied he did when I first started. Karl put Adam in his place. Did Karl already see Adam the way I started to? The office had a very competitive atmosphere, and Karl was always in charge.

"Andrea, what do you have going this week?" I heard Karl ask when I refocused.

"I've been preparing for Gytech this afternoon." She begrudgingly eyed Adam.

"I should go to that. I can fly to Cali tomorrow," Adam broke in. Then in a waspish voice he finished, "Or Carrie could go. She's acclimatized to San Francisco."

I started. Adam openly lashed out at me. He didn't miss a beat. He continued: "Besides I have a much stronger background in the scientific use –"

"Nope," Karl broke in. Then without glancing up he said, "They're geeks, though. Carrie, you should go with Andrea. What, at four?"

"Yep," Andrea said eyeing Adam just to be sure he knew he was not invited.

"In fact – tell them we want to buy them dinner tonight. Andrea set it up, and I'll join you, email me the details. I haven't met them yet."

"I'll find out where they want to go," Andrea said using a common tactic of aversion so she didn't have to announce to the group where she'd be.

"Carrie, we're going to ride this *Whole Package* train as far as it'll take us. I've talked to the partners. Depending on how much business it drums up is how much we pay you for the leave, so work it, and we'll pay you for all of it." Karl smiled at me with a gleam in his eyes.

"I have the vacation banked, and I assure you I'll recover the cost of the rest," I said grinning back.

Adam must have noticed I wasn't crumbling under his "pitch a fit" coercions because he said:

"She'll need last week covered too; maybe she can come to my meeting with PO next week."

Everyone stopped. No papers rustled, not a single tap to the computer. Adam – invited me to meet with his biggest account? What? I turned to him, but stopped myself from saying anything. I couldn't stop my head from spending the money I could make.

"That's ... nice," Brooke said but her eyes said, "that's weird."

Adam looked at Karl like he bested him. Karl looked back like Adam was ridiculous. In the second they glared at each other, a totally separate idea struck me. Did Adam see Karl as competition? Karl was single, but he was almost thirty-eight and not at all my type. Then again, why had he told me he was thirty-eight a few months ago? Adam was almost thirty-five. Maybe if he could see himself with me, Karl was only another little step up?

"I look out for Carrie." Adam smiled at me – his handsome face took good looking to a whole new level. In total surprise, I nodded with my mouth slightly open. Wasn't Adam mad at me?

"Yep," Karl answered, looking down. How long had this been going on?

"Although... you know, Carrie, we should stick you in every meeting, everywhere we can. Get out your calendar.

Tomorrow you can go with Jenkins to his meeting with Powderhill at ten."

"Hey!" A good-looking black man in his mid-forties looked up. He showed little interest in the meeting, except the ordering of his lunch. He snapped, "I don't have to share my commission if I get the account, do I?"

I looked up from my calendar. As the newest member of Karl's team, I'd never competed for commissions on an account. I'd only ever received bonuses for recruiting. Jenkins started two years before I did and Adam said he didn't have enough business for a recruiter. Yet, if that was the case, he'd be worried about the bonuses I'd take, not just his commission.

"We as a company will give you a slight bonus for each account we sign as a result of your guest appearance," Karl answered. He tilted his head to consider.

"That bonus will come out of the company's percent, not yours, Jenkins. However, after the meeting she can recruit for Powderhill if she finds a qualified candidate."

I stopped. What would Jenkin's say? Was Karl trying to help me pull away from Adam? He definitely dangled something in front of me. But what, and why?

"Great. I'll e-mail you their openings and where we're meeting," Jenkins said. I couldn't believe it. Everything Adam told me dissolved because everything he said manipulated me toward him and away from any kind of self-preservation.

I nodded at Jenkins with a confident smile, – I would not let him down. If I could recruit for Jenkins, I could get away from Adam entirely. Then the strangest thing happened. Jenkins, with half a smile like he really didn't mind me or at least my incredibly high employee retention rate, said:

136

"Oh, I was supposed to tell you that Paula will have someone beat up Veronica and kidnap Ethan. Just let me know where you want him delivered."

"Great," I laughed. "Tell her I say thanks and kiss the kids for me."

He nodded, then started typing something in his laptop. I could recruit for Jenkins. He didn't have anyone. He was coming up in the company and needed someone. He could move into the commissions while I worked for his bonuses. I didn't need Adam as badly as he made it seem. I pumped myself up the best I could. I took a deep breath, and forced myself to say:

"Karl, actually I don't want to book myself too full. You should know I've made seven contacts while on the show. It was like they put these amazing, well-educated, driven women in one room for me to pick off one at time. One of them is a graphic designer for LEDS. She's been there two years – graduated from The Art Institute of New York City."

"What?" Adam and Andrea snapped in sync. Everyone went quiet. And my vacation paid for itself.

"Have you made contact since you got off the show?" Karl asked.

"I have a meeting set up," I said.

"When?" Adam asked, a little too eagerly.

"Ah nice try," I answered. The beating of my heart palpitated up my throat. I turned so I could only see Karl. "You said whoever can get a candidate for Vantose got to contact, right?"

"I put that out there mostly because I figured with your dad and all you'd find the perfect candidate. However, that's a really big contact for your first account," Karl said. He stared me down intensely. What was he looking for?

137

Karl looked from me to the leather binder open in front of him as if he was trying to gauge something. I refused to break my stare – mostly because I needed this. Also, I didn't want to look at Adam or Andrea both staring hotly at the back of my head.

Weighing carefully, Karl finally said, "You can choose who you want to work with. They'll be the lead, but you'll split the commission fifty-fifty. You can be a part of everything, so next time you can go solo on a lesser account."

I nodded. I needed experience that Jenkins didn't have yet, or I would have chosen him. How fast did I severe my ties with Adam? If I gave him this account, we would be even? Could I walk away from him completely?

I owed this to him. He would take over. I wouldn't have anything to worry about. No, I didn't need that. I needed to be guided so I could do it by myself next time. Besides, Adam dissolved. He was the sand washing away under my feet and I need substance. I needed to land on my feet without Adam, no matter how jarring it felt. There was only one person in the office I could trust to teach me instead of just taking over.

I turned to Andrea.

"You on board?" I asked before I could lose my nerve.

"You're kidding, right?" Adam snapped from across the table.

"What," I asked. Everything inside me screamed that I owed it to him.

"You're my recruiter," Adam said.

"But this isn't recruiting. I need to … you're busy. You just signed three new companies –"

"Not one of those was Vantose –"

"But what about your plan to move up –"

"You wouldn't even have this job if weren't for me. I took care of your sick mother. I did that for you!"

I stammered in shock.

"The rest of you should've been canvassing LEDS if it was really that important to you," Karl cut in. He stared Adam down. Adam fumed and I could see something being repressed in his eyes. I turned back toward Karl so I didn't have to look at Adam. Karl shifted and smiled at me. I still couldn't say anything.

"We'll discuss the details of this deal later," he said, then more excitedly he finished, "That's what I'm talking about Care Bear, good work."

"I prefer Carrie," I said.

"Fair enough," Karl said more professionally.

I could feel the heat rising in my face. I tapped the keys on my laptop in front of me, praying for divine intervention, that the pricking at my eyes wouldn't spill over. Thankfully Karl turned to talk to one of my co-workers.

I couldn't look at Adam, or I'd lose it. What had I just done? This pull, this wrenching, horrible pull in my chest told me to give him whatever he wanted. This pull wasn't new, it was deep and significant and it took every self-preserving nerve in my body to ignore it. Somehow, somewhere along the line, it became my job to make Adam happy, but I couldn't. I couldn't be responsible for his happiness. The only thing that seemed to appease him for a while was me, handing over my life.

I bit my lip. I refused to give into the smoldering tension wafting in my direction because I'd pissed him off. Out of nowhere Karl stopped talking. I hadn't been focusing on the meeting, and couldn't be sure what was happening. He left the room.

"What's going on?" I asked.

"Who knows?" Andrea said typing quickly in her notes.

I opened an email I'd been working on, and pretended to type, but it turned into nonsense. Adam glared at me from across the table. I worked very hard not to notice him. He would corner me in my office later.

He'd done it before when I pissed him off during staff meetings. Working with him would always be very uncomfortable – five years... maybe four... Addie was a senior. Though to be an interior designer she'd have to start back as a junior. I'd endure Adam for Addie.

I hated myself for it, but decided to stay around Andrea after the meeting ended. Adam wouldn't confront me in front of her. I couldn't explain why, except to say that if he cornered me right now, I'd probably fold.

Finally, Karl came back in.

"Here's your itinerary Adam." He handed him a piece of paper.

"I'm leaving at three? I have things going on this week."

"The meet and greets is tonight."

"I need to get going then," Adam said.

"I'll have my car service pick you up. You'll have plenty of time when we break for lunch," Karl said. He tilted his head forward daring him to refuse.

"Fine," Adam said, like he didn't care either way.

An hour later when the meal cart came, I sat typing in all my commitments for the next week. I opened myself up to recruit for anyone. My co-workers were not only okay with it, but Jenkins took Adam's silent treatment as an opportunity to let me know about positions he needed filled as soon as possible. Brooke gave me a few very specific job descriptions and said we'd talk later.

As a clear plastic container carrying my salad was put in front of me, I heard Adam clear his throat.

"I've got to go pack if I'm going to make this flight, Karl."

"Oh, yeah. The car'll be downstairs in ten minutes," Karl said. Adam scowled.

Did Karl wink at me? Had Karl gotten Adam the soonest flight to San Francisco to protect me?

Adam picked up his boxed lunch. He started walking toward the front of the table, though the door was closer in the other direction. I ducked into my computer like a shield. I felt his eyes drill into the top of my head. He would try to extract me from the room.

As Adam passed around Karl's chair, Karl quickly stood. He clapped Adam on the shoulder in a friendly way.

"You didn't CC me on the response you must have sent to PO, let's go out in the hall and get it," he said.

"I don't –"

"It's policy," Karl snapped, "Besides, this way I can walk you out and introduce you to my driver."

Karl stood between me and Adam as they passed. He walked Adam out while everyone else ate their lunch. I took a deep breath, one day down 1,460 to go – no, I chided, I'd give Addie the full five years.

We all finished our lunch watching the door, waiting for Karl to come back. Everyone had work to do, so when Karl got back a little over half an hour later, a few people stood up to leave. He shut the door and asked them to sit down. He looked somber.

"What's going on?" Andrea asked, checking her watch for the third time, "I've got to get going if I'm going to rearrange with Gytech."

"We need to talk," Karl said, watching me carefully. "I've had security investigating Adam for a month now."

"What for?" I asked.

"We found out how he's been stealing everyone's clients. He's been hacking our computers. He's been so involved in everyone else's business, belligerently so, we figured it had to be him. Especially when the computer malfunctions stopped while he was in Hartford."

"That's how he beat me out on the JP Morgan kid? He hacked into my computer?" Andrea asked her eyes blazing. Commotion erupted. Everyone joined her outrage.

"Yes, he's stolen clients from everyone," Karl interrupted. "We traced it back as far as the client you lost, Carrie. The bet you lost to get you on *The Whole Package*. We think he was so desperate to win the bet he brought a friend in after hours and they hacked into your computer. Then after he saw he could hack with no repercussions, he started doing it to everyone else."

"Why, he has enough business," Brooke said.

"We think he's trying to start his own company. We believe he found someone to back him when he was in Hartford."

"What?" I asked, growing angry. He hadn't only used me. He'd used ... "He used my sick mom as an excuse to pimp my neighbors for money?"

Karl cracked a smile. My heart palpitated, and I began to shake, outraged.

"We didn't act last week because we didn't know what role you were playing for Adam," Karl said matter-of-factly.

I shook my head in disbelief, barely able to utter the word, "No."

"Well, that's what we figured when you told us about the Vantose candidate, and picked Andrea to head it up."

Oh, thank goodness, I learned to stand up for myself. What would've happened if I'd chosen him? I couldn't afford to lose my job. I couldn't pay Mom's hospital bills, her doctor appointments, let alone the utilities on the house.

Trapped in a vortex of what ifs, I said nothing. Karl continued: "I never suspected you but the security guy Darrin said it had to have something to do with you. We didn't understand why he's been hovering around you. When he wanted to bring in someone with no experience I couldn't see why. You had the education, last name and connections, so we gave you a chance. We think Adam has been trying to . . . well . . ."

Here Karl paused. Everyone around the table leaned forward a little to hear what he didn't have the nerve to say. Karl's face turned redder than normal. I finished for him so he didn't have to.

"Trying to recruit me?" I said.

"In a Bill and Hillary sort of way," Karl said.

"We figured the same thing when my little sister threw him out of the house last Friday because he wouldn't leave," I said.

"Well, our tech guy planted a bug on his laptop this morning. That's why I walked him out; I was waiting for it to crash." I gave him a look which had nothing to do with the laptop. Still Karl, out of his comfort zone, defended, "It's company property. A couple thousand dollars in a laptop is nothing compared with what the company could lose if he walks away with all our information. Anyway, I stayed with Adam until it crashed and then switched it out for a brand new one."

"Does he have our clients' information?" Jenkins asked.

"I'm not sure. Everyone needs to touch base with every one of your clients before he gets back Thursday night. I told him due to security measures, until we can get the new computer protected, his passwords are revoked. There's not much else we can do. Until then all in this room are to change your passwords. Never leave your computers logged on; he may be able to access them remotely if they're left logged on. If Adam calls you," – here he looked at me – "Try to be busy and get off the phone with him as soon as possible. Don't tell him anything."

"I have a few things to say to him," Andrea snapped.

"In the last few months, Adam stole and defrauded this company in ways that may lead to our pressing charges. I suggest none of you even acknowledge him. He'll get his."

I chanced to look up. The stunned faces of my coworkers all looked in my direction. My heart beat wildly. I couldn't tell what happened next. If hadn't played my Vantose card right, would I have been fired? Or, perhaps I would still be after I introduced James to Andrea. My throat felt dry and my stomach twisted in knots.

"I know he got upset sometimes," Brooke broke the silence, "but I would never have thought him capable of this."

I nodded in nonverbal agreement. I let him into my life and I didn't know him at all. What was I thinking?

"Okay, well let's get back to work. None of this information leaves this room. It's a disciplinary offense if it does," Karl said. No one doubted his sincerity. He stringently followed company policy.

CHAPTER SIXTEEN

"Carrie, will you stay a minute?" Karl asked as the room cleared. I nodded, pressing the back of my wrist to the trickle of sweat at my hairline. I was safe – right? I had the Vantose candidate.

My co-workers shuffled toward the door whispering, glancing at me. I stared straight ahead looking down on the city, trying not to notice. My face burned. What could I do? I had no defense. I'd been so blind.

It didn't take long for Andrea to be the only noticeable lingerer left in the room with Karl and me, despite Bailey trying to hurry her up. Andrea looked like she wanted to comfort me.

"Carrie," Karl interrupted, quickly diverting us from our chat session, "we're going to need to move on your Vantose candidate as quickly as possible. Andrea, you go make the changes necessary for Gytech. I'll start prepping with Carrie."

"Okay," Andrea said. She had no choice but to pass me a "we-will-talk-later" glance and then moved to the door.

"Are you okay?" Karl asked me.

"I'm feeling really stupid. He kept talking about the partners wanting him to start a branch in Hartford, and I didn't even suspect he meant to –"

"I know Carrie, you shouldn't blame yourself. Adam must have been planning this a long time. He would've moved on it sooner, and gotten away with it too, but he had one little hiccup."

"I wouldn't go out with him. I wouldn't even respond to his flirting because I was in mourning," I said.

145

Karl looked a little surprised at my insight, then he nodded and said, "That's what we figured. You helped us out. For all it's worth, you're a great employee and we're glad to have you."

"So, I'm not fired," I said, trying to pull off flippant but my voice broke.

"Of course not."

I nodded but couldn't say anything as the vise on my chest spread and I could breathe again. Blinking hard I tried to be thankful for my job – but in a disappointed conflicted way. I hated my job. I needed it, but if I'd been fired, it meant my freedom. No, I thought of my mother. I'd work as hard as I could for five years.

"Are you going to take away my office, at least?" I asked.

"No. You earned that fair and square," he said.

"Did I?" I asked.

"It goes by the chart," he said, pointing but confused. "The top three performing recruiters get offices; the rest are in cubicles. Bailey, you, and Hansh from Joel's team. Didn't Adam explain that to you?"

"Nope, he made it seem like he pulled strings to get me an office," I said.

"I should have explained it better," he said. Then he paused awkwardly, so he didn't seem callous forcing me to get back to work.

"So... When are you meeting with this woman?" Karl asked.

"Thursday at lunch," I answered.

"Can you move it up? I'm sure as soon as Adam has access to the internet, he'll be cross-checking the women from the show with LEDS employee lists."

"Well, she was a he," I said.

"That's reality television for you," Karl said.

"He's the brother of one of the contestants, so Adam's going to have to decipher that. Same last name, though. Her brother's a fan of my dad's work. He actually wrote a paper on him. This, of course, perked my interest instantly –"

"Carrie," Karl interrupted.

"Right. Sorry, you know he takes his contract pretty seriously. I don't think we could have moved on this any sooner if I'd have gotten off the show a month ago."

"I guarantee a month and a half pay for this opportunity will be an easy sale," Karl said as if he hadn't wanted the whole explanation. Relief spread. I would be paid for my time, away. I wouldn't be fired with Adam. Karl interrupted again more impatiently.

"Okay, try to move it up."

"Right, sorry."

I pulled my cell phone toward me scrolling to his contact. I tapped the table a few times then I said into the receiver, "Hey James, it's Carrie, can you talk?"

After the pause it took him to become available, I said, "Hey something's come up, could we meet for lunch tomorrow instead of Thursday? I'm still buying, and yes, you can bring your wife."

I listened a moment and answered, "Yes, she can question me all about the whole Ethan thing. I listened again. "Great, see you tomorrow, same place and time."

"You won't be able to go with Jenkins tomorrow," Karl said as I hung up, "I'm sure he won't be heartbroken. Every free minute you need to be researching Vantose."

"I did some last week while I was hanging out with Mom," I stammered. I wasted so much time sleeping. I should've been more prepared.

147

"Who has the Vantose contact?" I said pulling up the information I'd carefully hidden on my laptop.

"You should have told me about this. I would've paid you for last week if I'd known," Karl taunted.

"You still could," I said.

"You claimed sick leave, but I'll see if I can't use the plugs you gave us as a business expense and stretch your personal days to cover it… only for last week I mean," Karl fumbled and looked away from my probing eyes.

"Thanks … so, when will we meet with Vantose?" I asked again.

"I'll set up the meeting with them. All three of us will attend that one," Karl said.

Karl started writing something down. I said randomly, "Charles, my sister's boyfriend –"

"Goodrich – yeah I know who he is," Karl interrupted.

"Right, well, he thought Adam's trying to get into politics. But turns out he's trying to start his own company."

"Who knows with that one?" Karl said, looking at me. He grinned at me again his eyes moving back and forth between mine like … like … I stopped, confused. Karl dove back into his work abruptly. I took this as my dismissal, so I closed my laptop and got up to leave the room.

"Hey, Carrie," Karl called.

"Yeah," I asked.

"I was talking with Adam this morning, distracting him while my IT guy uploaded a bug onto his computer. He said that Ethan was handpicked for you. Adam knows the producer of that show. I'm not trying to be a … just, Ethan was probably an actor. You may have been… targeted."

"I know, this whole thing was just one long con," I said. I bit my lip and waved, speed walking out of the room.

CHAPTER SEVENTEEN

The next day I met James and his wife, Sophie, outside a French bistro in Brooklyn.

"Carrie," James called.

I waved and moved away from the cab I was exiting. He was no taller than his sister, Alexis. This made him average height for a man, where she was taller for a woman. His tawny hair contrasted with dark eyes that crinkled when he smiled. In complete contrast to his sister, he drew me in instantly. He seemed familiar and comfortable to me. I had the strangest feeling of Déjà vu.

"It is so good to meet you." I gave him my hand. I paused, feeling his energy. He examined me as well, and I felt we were already friends.

His wife, a small dark-haired woman, broke the spell. She quickly pulled me by the arm pushing through the restaurant door in an overly intimate way that made me uncomfortable.

I introduced Andrea as my partner, and she, in her engaging way, kept Sophie in conversation while I went over the paperwork with James.

"Our attorneys are only waiting for a signature to start a motion to dismiss LED's non-compete agreement. You held no company trade secrets so for them to ask you not to work is unfair. Not to mention it's way too broad for the change of information your new job will cover. It will easily be dismissed."

"I know you'll take care of me," James said watching me. I grinned at him unsure why he trusted me implicitly. He signed the contract tying him to me as an extension of Kimbers & Stophers.

As I put the paperwork away, I said:

"A man named Adam may contact you –"

"Adam Pell?" he asked.

"Yeah, did he...."

"He was my recruiter two years ago. I fired him. I would never work with him again. He called me all the time until I finally blocked his number."

"Oh, great. No worries then," I said surprised. I wanted to ask more, but Sophie, seeing our business concluded, jumped in.

The rest of the meal Sophie pelted me with questions about *The Whole Package.* She talked through mouthfuls of pork tenderloin while James tried to rein her in. Every question opened me up to a deeper level of stupidity.

"Did Ethan focus on you while the other women were around?" Sophie wanted to know.

"No, he was really nice about paying attention to everyone," I answered. Internally I noted he always tried to please me without offending anyone else. He played all the angles.

"Did he single you out right away?"

"Yes. He seemed to find a way to be alone with me at times," I said. The challenges always accommodated our run every morning, except once. The afternoon Ethan invited Tess down to his bungalow. We hadn't run that morning.

"It felt like he started to lose interest at the end," Sophie observed.

Yes – But I couldn't say it out loud. I merely nodded.

"What happened?"

I had to search my mind. What happened? I didn't know – yes, I did.

"Veronica relaxed," I choked over the words. Veronica started smiling her huge friendly grin naturally. I talked her into giving up Ethan. She'd lost all pressure to perform when I informed her Ethan was mine.

"He stopped being nice to Veronica to please me. He started being nice to her because she's amazing when she isn't psyching herself out."

"Is that really why you left?"

"No, but I may have been damage controlled if I hadn't."

"What?" she asked.

"Julian, the producer. He would likely have made a fool of me before I was kicked off," I said.

"I'm not sorry Alexis didn't make it in," James said. I turned to him, wanting to be... near him. Did that even make sense? I'd never met anyone who drew me in like he did.

"She didn't miss out," I said to him, "My last night on the show, Julian manipulated me in every way possible."

"But why?" Sophie asked leaning forward, her eyes contracted in pain, like she learned her dog bit someone and would have to be put down.

"Julian controls the show by manipulating people into behaving a certain way. If he can get me to react angrily, or vindictively, then his viewers wouldn't mind my leaving the show."

"You never reacted badly," Sophie said straining to contradict my statement.

"Thanks," I said flatly. I searched my mind for any other subject.

"Still, I think he's more into Sandra than Veronica," Sophie said. She spoke with such conviction that I couldn't possibly know better than she.

"I guess you never really know," I said.

"No, he couldn't keep his hands off her. I –" Sophie made to persist.

"How long have you guys been married?" Andrea cut in.

"Almost a year," James answered.

He blushed and looked from me to Sophie nervously for some reason. He looked guilty, though neither of us had done anything wrong. Did he have a little crush on me? We'd talked for a couple hours about my dad's work over the last week and a half. I read James' paper that was published in an educational journal. It was beautiful, and made him family in a way. Maybe this confused him – maybe it confused me. Maybe that's where the feeling of Déjà vu came from.

The way James looked at me – it felt so familiar.

Before I could ask, Sophie interrupted Andrea's "how did you guys meet," to again explain why Ethan loved Sandra. I made my face into the polite mask only a true socialite could have perfected. I lifted a finger to the waiter and handed him my credit card without even looking at the bill so I could leave. James ended up shaking my hand around Sophie, pulling me to the door he held open, trying to give me a path to leave. He mouthed, "Sorry."

I smiled and nodded like it was nothing, saying: "It was a pleasure. Thanks so much, James."

"I'll see you soon," he said, as Andrea waved me over to the cab she held.

"You don't believe, that do you?" Andrea asked as soon as I slammed the door shut.

"What?" I asked.

"Ethan is in love with Veronica?"

"Oh ... I don't know," I said. "I was targeted; Ethan knew he was supposed to... get along with me."

"I doubt it was that obvious. If Julian knows how to manipulate you, then he manipulated him, too," Andrea said.

"Then we were both manipulated. That doesn't mean Ethan really loves me," I said.

"It doesn't mean he's not in love with you, either. Give him a chance. You're so close. Just wait until you see him again before you decide," Andrea said.

"Okay," I answered because I did love him; not even basking in James's warmth changed that. Did that mean I'd give up dating and the attraction I felt for other men to be with Ethan? Only he hadn't been willing to do the same. Ohhh. What was I supposed to do?

CHAPTER EIGHTEEN

Meetings and events packed the next few days, but no one asked more than a few trifling details about the show. Most people were excited to meet me but thought they knew everything about my life. The extreme few acted like my best friends and not complete strangers.

Some people snubbed me to let me know they weren't all that impressed with me. I cracked a few jokes and easily won most of them over. A few older men refused to work with me. I had to be sent from the room, because they conducted business seriously, without reality stars.

Adam called me several times. I didn't answer my cell.

"Carrie," he said to my voice mail, "I know we were disagreeing about the twenty thousand dollars. But to choose Andrea for the Vantose account was too dramatic. I forgive you, but we need to act quickly to fix this."

Adam must have realized somewhere along the line he'd been found out. He bought his own plane ticket home and flew into New York Wednesday night. He put in his resignation early the next morning before he could be fired.

As per company policy, due to the competitive nature of our business, when someone put in resignation, they were automatically paid out for the two weeks, and cut off.

I caught sight of Adam being escorted to his office to retrieve all his personal effects. He looked pissed. He never looked toward me in my glass office. I hid behind the fake tree that filled one of the panels, anyway. He went quietly. I felt free of him – which was very naïve, of course.

By the evening, I couldn't think about Adam or work. I was about to see Ethan – well not really, but kind of.

When I arrived at Andrea's house, I recognized the Ferrari as Charles' though I'd never seen it before, next to Tess's Pennsylvania State-licensed Toyota. I parked out on the street and walked up the front pathway. Before I reached the doorway, I heard someone calling my name. I turned around and saw Adam running across the street toward me.

"Hey Carrie, how are you?" he said, jogging up to me in his most friendly manner. He leaned in to kiss my cheek, but I leaned away. He pretended not to notice and kissed the air like that's what he meant to do.

"You shouldn't be here," I said.

"Can you at least give me a chance to explain?" Adam said, partly pleading, partly confused – almost like he couldn't decide how to play me.

"Where would you begin?" I asked.

"Look. We have to talk. I know you've been told some bad things about me, but you know me. How could you believe I'd do anything wrong?"

"Are you drunk?"

"You tell me what you're angry about, and I'll explain what happened."

Adam was getting ready to manipulate me – and not even well. It was like we were playing a child's game of imagination. "Let's pretend like you're mad at me because I took over the last three years of your life. I'll tell you why you shouldn't be, and then you can forgive me."

He was a child – a grown up child. And he was going to sell me whatever I would believe, to get back in my good graces. He wanted to. I could see it in his eyes. An eagerness, a glow burning inside him, ready and excited for his next challenge. But I would not be his plaything any longer. Cut him off before he confused me — that's all I could do.

"I'm done with you. We're no longer associates. I don't want you in my life anymore. Please leave me alone."

Adam looked as if I struck him. I turned from him and bolted for the doorbell. Adam reacted faster. He grabbed me by the wrist and pulled me back.

"You owe me," he insisted. "You would have lost your house last year if it weren't for me. Just let me buy you lunch and I'll tell you everything. How about tomorrow?"

Frightened, I wrenched my wrist painfully away but he didn't let go of his strong grasp.

"I'm booked."

"Saturday, Carrie. You know you owe me," Adam persisted.

"Are you serious? I could have been implicated in this. I could have been fired! What would I have done without health insurance?" I asked.

"Oh, come on, I wouldn't let that happen. Karl is pathetic."

Adam glanced toward the door squinting, perhaps his overly inflated ego told him if he squinted hard enough he'd develop x-ray vision and see where Andrea was inside the house. He definitely didn't want Andrea – and all the clients he stole from her – involved in the conversation because he said: "I can't explain right now. Saturday let's do lunch. I promise you won't be mad once I explain."

He pulled tighter on my wrist, drawing me into him, an intimate longing in his eyes. He nodded yes, as to force me to say it out loud. Petrified, I didn't say anything. How did I get rid of him without provoking him? My wrist hurt.

"Carrie, give me an hour. I swear I'll leave you alone forever if you don't appreciate what's going on." Adam gently caressed my name with his most alluring voice as he let go of my pulsing wrist.

"I can't even...."

"Come on. After everything I've done for you, just do this one thing for me," he said.

I considered. He would never leave me alone until we hashed this out. If he hadn't ambushed me like this perhaps I could make him believe he had no chance of smoothing things over with me. Instead I was tongue-tied and frightened, coupled with the idea of Andrea coming out and fighting making me feel silly and little.

I would face him. I would have my Moment in the Wilderness. I would be taken to my pinnacle and then I would show him he had no power over me. I would not allow him to control the situation. I would not meet somewhere unfamiliar where I felt vulnerable to him.

"One o'clock on Saturday, at Jia Liu."

He flinched.

I finished, "and if you're late, I'll leave."

"Great," Adam said, a twinkle in his eyes.

I turned and walked away from him but he called, "Hey, Carrie, you know Julian set you up on that show, right? Ethan's an actor, he –"

"Karl relayed your message," I interrupted, knowing he'd intended it all along.

"No, you don't understand," Adam continued, "Julian manipulated you into believing you were in love."

"He did a better job of it than you did," I said.

"No, see – you don't love –"

"What?" I asked. I allowed the annoyance in my voice to bubble over as I reached out for the doorbell.

"I'll explain later. See you Saturday," he yelled while he backed down the walkway, watching my hand reaching for the bell. He turned as he came to the sidewalk, and jogged to his car down the street. How long had he been waiting – scouting Andrea's house before I showed up? He did always have a plan. He planned everything, every tiny detail. His unashamed disregard for my right to veer off his plan was almost impressive – almost.

I rang the doorbell.

"Oh, there you are, we almost sent out a search party." Andrea looked like she ran a marathon with Brea in her arms.

"Hello baby girl."

I took Brea and gave her kisses.

Andrea grunted some kind of appreciated statement and then ran back to the kitchen. I closed the door and locked it. Then I breathed in the sweet baby smell that always permeated from Brea while I walked through the house playing with her. I knew I should say something about Adam's ambush, but I couldn't. It humiliated me to think I'd just been manhandled. So, I stayed quiet.

CHAPTER NINETEEN

I stepped down into Andrea's back yard from a back door. It was all one level with a brick terrace next to the house. The wall of her fenced-in pool supported a climbing silver lace vine. The little grass left in the yard was greenish yellow parched from the long, hot summer. A huge climbing tree shaded the whole back of the house and terrace. Andrea often complained of the leaves in the pool, but her quaint yard made for comfortable outdoor entertaining.

Addie stood near the terrace table talking to Mom and Tess. Charles stood behind her with an arm hanging lazily around her waist. Phil flipped burgers at the grill, but turned slightly to listen to the conversation.

"Oh, Carrie, finally," Addie said looking at me expressively, like she waited forever, "Now that everyone's here Charles has an announcement to make."

"What?" I said. My jaw dropped. I set Brea down for fear I'd drop her.

Charles stepped to the front of the group. He coughed a little, and then he announced: "I have asked Miss Adeline Carnegie to marry me. She has accepted."

"What?" I put my hand on my forehead to stop the beads of perspiration that instantly formed at Charles' announcement. What? Hadn't Addie promised she wouldn't try to solve our money problems by marriage?

"You're all invited to our engagement party two weeks from Saturday," Addie said.

"Mom's sending out invitations as we speak." Charles' face grew red as Addie's shining face dimmed.

159

"Charles's mom is very excited," Addie said, then cleared her throat of the distaste this idea caused. She pulled a ring box out of her purse while saying, "I didn't want anybody to see it until it was announced."

"Wow, is that a pink diamond?" Tess exclaimed. Addie held her ring out, and the large light pink emerald-cut diamond framed by tiny clusters of clear white diamonds sparkled. Addie put it on her finger.

"You sure that's not going to throw you off balance," I asked.

"I'll do some core exercises," Addie snapped at me, and then turned to Andrea.

"It's been in Charles' family for over a hundred years. It's considered internally flawless. They said I could have it reset, but I don't know. I kinda like what his Grandma did with it."

"This is really quick, isn't it?" I asked looking from Mom to Charles while Addie told Andrea the cut and karats of her ring.

"Yes, but Mom's just –"

"Not the engagement party, the engagement," I snapped.

"Oh...." Charles looked to Mom to answer.

"It'll be fine," she said.

She smiled at my panic. She dismissed me. I saw no help coming from Mom in convincing Addie she had to ... didn't she understand? Charles wanted something. He would use her.

"We've spent every day together for two months now. In society dating that's like two years," Addie said. She leaned around Tess to look at me like I was being ridiculous.

"I'm not sure real-life experiences convert into a two-month timetable," I said.

She ignored me.

I didn't say anything further. If I became combative with Addie, I'd have a fight on my hands. I would bide my time. I would... not take over. Not like Adam took over my life, no, I'd...

Addie started telling how Charles took her up to Niagara Falls in a helicopter to ask her.

"When did you guys start talking about marriage?" I asked quietly aside to Charles cutting into Addie's remarks to the rest of the group.

"We were joking around on Monday. I asked Addie if I could see the rumored Hawthorne collection your Grandma supposedly has. Addie said it's in the vault – you guys have a vault?"

I appraised him. "Yep," I said.

"Well, Addie said I'd have to marry her and use our firstborn as collateral to get in there... you know, to see the Hawthorne's. I've never been hit with an idea so completely. I've never felt such a strong overwhelming acceptance of anything in my life."

"You must really want to see that Hawthorne collection."

He answered, but I didn't hear. Why did we tell Addie about the money being gone? She'd gone fishing and caught a big one.

I'd fix it. I had to fix this.

"Okay, these burgers aren't going to eat themselves," Phil called from the grill.

Everyone headed toward the table, congratulating Addie. I got behind the cluster at the grill. Everyone gushed over Addie's ring while she explained her plans for an autumn marriage.

"You guys are waiting for a year, or two years?" I asked.

"Nope, this autumn," Addie said.

161

I laughed. She glared at me.

"How are you going to have the wedding of the century, plus get your Dad elected, this autumn?"

Addie shrugged and moved unconcerned toward the grill to get a hamburger. Charles, more concerned by my lack of enthusiasm said:

"We're going to have a quiet ceremony, before the elections. Dad thinks it will be good publicity."

"Yeah I bet ... my dad's friends ... My Uncle Brock will be family ... I'm sure that's an impressive strategy –"

"It's not just about the election. We want to do Europe for at least a month as a honeymoon. After January that won't be possible."

"Why?" I asked.

"Oh, I thought Addie told you. Whether my Dad wins the election or not, I'm going to become the president of United Skills."

"He's stepping down, no matter what?"

"Yeah, he's confident about winning the seat, but if he doesn't, he's still going to pursue some of his measures by lobbying."

"Couldn't he pay someone for that?"

"All I know is there'll be a lot of long work weeks for me in January, and we want to be prepared as a married couple to meet them."

"You're kidding, right?" I said, all pretenses thrown out. Addie ignored me and talked wedding details to Tess and Andrea. Phil slid a hamburger on my bun. I turned and walked to the table. Sitting down hard, I forced all the air out of the chair's vinyl cushion.

Charles walked over and sat next to me at the end of the table and tried to quiet my qualms.

"I'm almost thirty-one. We need a few years just us. I don't want to be a grandpa dad. I want to be married."

"Well, Addie's only twenty-one, she needs to live life."

"Like she's living now?"

"She's finishing school."

"And taking care of your mom."

"So am I."

"No, you're paying for your mom's care, she is caring for her."

"She's not an invalid," I whispered glancing over my shoulder to be sure Mom couldn't hear us.

"No, but she shouldn't live alone, either."

"You think I should be doing more?"

"This isn't about you. I'm saying, I'll move in and help Addie with your Mom. Then Addie won't get lonely while I'm working long hours to get established. We'll all take good care of each other."

"Really?" I asked.

"Addie and your Mom will just switch over to my company's medical insurance as soon as we're married. You can quit here in a few months and everything will be fine," Charles said. He tried to sound casual about it all.

"This isn't an opportunity for you. You don't get to swoop in, save the day, and think I'll let you take over my family because I'm going through some stuff. I'll work my job forever before I let you do that," I hissed.

"I'm marrying the woman I love. This has nothing to do with you," Charles said twitching, "But if it benefits you, why can't you accept it?"

"Listen to me," I said quietly so Addie didn't hear me verbally poking my forefinger on Charles's broad chest, "you do not jump into marriage. You have to know what you're

163

doing. Marriage is a serious thing. Give it another year, please! I can work at Kimbers & Stophers for another year. She needs to finish school."

I didn't want my freedom anymore, not like this.

"That's Addie's decision. You'll need to talk to her about it," he said leaning back.

My gaze followed his to Addie, who gushed to Tess and Andrea in her newly engaged haze. She wouldn't listen to reason.

"Fine! Marry Addie. I'll handle supporting Mom." I folded my arms across my chest stubbornly.

"Of course, you can. What you've done so far is amazing. But you don't have to. That's the whole point. It doesn't hurt to ask the people you know you can trust for help," Charles said.

"I don't trust you. I don't even know you, and neither does Addie."

"That's fair, we'll have to spend some time together."

"Getting our picture taken, no doubt."

"Look I can't help that... my dad, he's... so ambitious. I don't mean to use you guys –"

Charles wouldn't look at me as he said this. There was something going on with him. What was his angle? I had to figure out what he was hiding. I had to find his real interest in Addie, and fast. I interrupted whatever he was saying that completely contradicted his body language, and said:

"Let's spend time together and get to know each other." Charles looked at me doubtfully. I couldn't waste a whole Saturday with Adam when I needed to smoke Charles out.

"What's up?" Charles asked. I paused waiting until Andrea was loudly telling Addie her own engagement story. I didn't want Andrea to know about my meeting with Adam until after it ended, or we'd have a whole other kind of barbecue on our hands.

"Adam cornered me outside the house earlier. He'll never leave me alone. He knows everything about me. He'll just keep popping up if I don't set him straight. I'm meeting him at one on Saturday."

"Do you want me to sic my lawyer on him?" Charles asked.

"No, but you and Addie can come with me."

"I will. Here, let me ask Addie." Charles made to yell for Addie.

"No, not tonight, I don't want Andrea to know."

"Andrea? She's perfect for something like this. I've thought about trying to steal her. Put her as the head of marketing. She's an amazing business woman."

"She'd... I don't need Andrea to take over. I need to do this," I said.

"Sure, I get that," Charles agreed.

"Oh, also while he was in Hartford, Adam got someone to back this business venture he has going on. Do you have any ideas who it was?" I asked.

"It must've been Matthew Wilson. Adam hovered around him all the time," Charles answered.

"That's right. Mr. Wilson thought we were dating," I remembered. "They met at the hospital after Mom's accident?"

"Yeah, and then he brought Adam to the club last week. He introduced him to everyone," Charles answered, still glancing over at Addie. No doubt he wished to be next to her snuggling, instead of stuck here with her spinster sister.

"He's been trying to help me, actually."

"What?" Charles asked, remembering he was supposed to be talking to me.

"Mr. Wilson – I think he's trying to help me... with all this."

"That makes sense," Charles said. He gave a short little laugh.

I flinched. Charles clarified, "In other words, Adam has nothing without you?"

"I bet he doesn't. He must have been trying to get me fired. You know, so I'd have nothing without him."

"He has no right to mess with your life like that," Charles said quietly. I nodded, lifting my eyebrows suspiciously. Charles looked serious – and almost angry.

Maybe a man could be born to affluence and be worth my time. Maybe men were just men – defined by the choices they made, not the situation they were born into.

I sat quietly and listened to Addie making wedding plans while the evening cooled down. After fifteen minutes of Addie's modest wedding plans, I whispered to Charles, "So much for your quiet ceremony."

Charles nodded as Andrea called, "We only have five minutes until *The Whole Package* starts."

We headed for the door.

CHAPTER TWENTY

"No matter how sick it gets, we watch the whole thing," I said, sitting next to Tess on the floor.

"I don't think I could be in as much danger as you," Tess responded pulling her legs to her chest insecurely. I shrugged uncomfortably. Then I remembered what kind of a week Tess must have had.

"Oh, I'm such a jerk. How did your talk with your dad go?" I questioned, realizing I needed to stop being so self-involved.

"I couldn't do it," Tess whispered.

"By Sunday?" I asked.

"Ahh, well ... Saturday's their wedding anniversary."

"Next Monday in the A.M. ... unless you're going to be a financial planner forever? I know a few hotel developers. Could you imagine starting a restaurant, making your own menu and everything?"

"Okay. Monday in the A.M.," Tess nodded as the television started playing the show. I flinched only a little as the theme music began to waft through the living room. Poor Tess looked down sadly when it showed her face crossed out. This time, only Sandra and Veronica's faces remained.

The show dragged through the first part.

"It's not all that interesting without you and Tess. The two of you really were the most interesting characters," Charles said.

"Um hum," I said.

After the first commercial break, Ethan walked up to a good-sized house with a long porch and flowering roses wilting out front. Ethan took the stairs to the front door a little apprehensively, and then smiled into the camera. My heart lurched toward him. As Veronica opened the door and invited him into her house, my heart plummeted, and hatred burned through me. I hated Veronica.

"That's not Elizabeth, New Jersey," Andrea said.

"No. Her parents live in East Brunswick. It's central New Jersey," I said. Ethan had been in a house forty-five minutes away from where I currently sat. I stopped myself. He'd been with Veronica – he'd been there for Veronica.

He put his arms around me first, though. He kissed my mouth first, his minty toothpaste ... Maybe at the reunion show, I'd just walk up to him and ... reclaim him? Could a person claim another person? Isn't that what Adam did to me?

Ethan made his own choice, even if wasn't me.

Jerk! Why didn't he pick me?

For a few minutes, Veronica's family sat in a large front room grilling Ethan, but Ethan looked comfortable. He asked a lot of questions about Veronica as if he'd been given a list. Her charity work, how sweet she was growing up, all the ways she helped the Hungarian community in New Brunswick. After Veronica showed herself thoroughly embarrassed, her dad, the total gentleman Veronica claimed him to be, kindly shifted the focus to ask about Ethan.

"Do you do any research yourself?" Veronica's dad asked after Ethan explained his interest moving that direction.

"No, I really don't have the resources," Ethan answered. "It takes a teaching hospital in most cases. I'd probably have to go back to school."

"Did you enjoy California?" Veronica's mom asked out of nowhere, and I calculated other questions were edited out.

"Some of the time," Ethan answered.

"What was your favorite part?" Veronica's brother asked.

"California's so pretty. I listened to the ocean all night. I took these long runs every morning and had the most beautiful view while I ran. Being around your sister is always so comfortable. I tried to get her to run with me a few times, but she prefers swimming."

I laughed. Not a real laugh, but a frantic, odd sort of laugh. As it moved into a segment showing Ethan playing mud football with the family and some friends, Addie asked, "What's the matter?"

"When you said, you were out schmoozing Ethan every morning while you were running, you were serious?" Tess asked.

"Hey, I never lied," I defended, seeing the hurt in Tess's eyes.

"No, you just joked around so much no one could tell when you were serious." Tess's face shifted from hurt to half-impressed and half-annoyed.

"Sorry, Tess."

"That's okay Caroline. He did say he had a good view and you're a cutie."

"I doubt he meant it like that. Besides he's inviting Veronica now. Is he trying to say he wants her to be his running partner?" I asked.

"Oh, that picture you painted for him. It was of the cliffs by us," Tess realized.

"Yeah, we ran to that lighthouse every morning."

"It's got to be significant; he mentioned it," Andrea said.

"I don't know," I said.

"He said it was his favorite part of California," Charles said, "And Veronica never ran with him."

"I don't know," I answered, disliking Charles even more for talking.

Much to my satisfaction, every time Ethan caught the football Veronica's brothers pummeled him into the mud. Then it went to commercial. The show came back from commercial with Ethan and Veronica helping out at a food pantry. Her grandmother started it to help immigrants fifty years earlier. Veronica's extremely large extended family helped, working hard. Watching her shy, unforced altruism, I forced myself to admit, Veronica had always been *The Whole Package.*

"Her brothers are hot," Tess said.

"She said they're goof-offs, but they're working pretty hard," I said.

"They all seem to really appreciate the opportunity to give back," Phil said.

"Yeah, she really loved her grandma," I said. I couldn't find any fault with the family or their service, and it bugged me.

At the end of the segment, Ethan drove Veronica home and kissed her. It was a soft sweet kiss. It looked tender and affectionate at first and grew into something more before it ended. My heart burrowed down to a dark place. I hated them both. Of course, Ethan loved Veronica.

After another commercial, it showed Ethan going to Sandra's house. Sandra's numerous family members were some of the best-looking people I'd ever seen. They were all beautiful and elfin just like Sandra. Her father pelted questions at Ethan, calling him "son" in a strong southern drawl.

"Wasn't Ethan just supposed to judge who is *The Whole Package?*" I asked.

170

"Yeah, this guy has him engaged to her," Tess said bitterly. It rankled her pride that she'd been booted off before Sandra. It almost became comical when Sandra's dad asked:

"What do y'all have planned for your practice whenever you get off the show, Son? Are you fixing to stay in Boston or are y'all willing to move down here to Georgia?"

"I'm really lucky to have an established clientele in Boston. I'd be a fool to move," Ethan replied with a concentrated look, trying to get the wording just right. "There was a time I thought of moving my office, within Boston, of course. Before everything got put on hold, I had a tour of some buildings lined up. I'm hoping that a friend of mine will still give me a tour after I get off the show. You know location is everything."

"Huh?" Her father looked confused.

"Oh, well a man does have to consider those things," Sandra's mom broke in. Unlike her husband, she looked just fine with Ethan taking her oldest daughter off to Boston. Ethan tried to ask what kind of child Sandra was when Sandra's father insisted, "Well, I could get y'all set up down here real quick. I have an extra office in my building, and I could go part time, and recruit while you took over my patients –"

"You've got to be kidding me," I exclaimed. I admitted to my bitter heart that the tour reference had to be more than a coincidence.

"What?" Mom asked.

"Wait. I want to hear what else he has to say," I said still trying to decide if it meant anything. I didn't want to admit it might after Ethan kissed Veronica.

171

Ethan went back and forth with Sandra's father. Finally, in a blunt uncomfortable declaration, he said, "I won't leave Boston. It's so close ... or ... it's my home now."

Then like weeds that must be gotten through, the commercials came.

"What's the big deal about him changing offices?" Mom asked.

"Okay, we had this whole day planned out. He asked me to take him for a tour of Dad's buildings."

"You were going to take him back to Dad's buildings?" Mom asked. She seemed startled and even slightly frustrated.

"I ... he wanted to see them. Plus, once I asked him if he would ever move office buildings when he told me his rent was high. He said not a chance. The wealthy cliental he served would be outraged. It must have ... he must have meant ... he said his friend was taking him. Did he mean me?" I sounded stupid ... needy ... desperate. Everyone had their opinions. I barely heard Mom's sad voice say:

"You haven't gone to any of them since Dad died."

That's not the conversation I wanted to have. Did I need an intervention for *The Whole Package*, perhaps? Or my complete inability to concentrate – you bet. Maybe even a narcotic to get Ethan off my mind – bring it on. But her insisting I think about my Dad's death over ten years earlier felt so random.

"I just don't think he'd move his office," I clarified, trying to drop it.

"Right, I remember him saying his clientele were obnoxious rich kids. He was doing really well," Tess said, nudging me with her elbow at the words "obnoxious rich kids."

"I guess you would be trying to plug him on how much he's pulling in – gold digger," I rebutted nudging her back.

Phil interrupted Tess. "He said something about hoping she was still willing,"

"This is really uncanny, especially after the whole running comment," Addie said, kicking me in the arm from the couch, "Right?"

"He's still there, kissing Veronica," I snapped.

Everyone wanted to say something, I didn't want to hear. I shushed them when the show came back on. Everyone went quiet so we could listen.

The Eating Disorder Clinic Sandra worked in felt more like a nuisance to her. She and Ethan walked around talking to young women. Ethan quickly proved more interested in helping them than Sandra did.

It must not have lasted long at the clinic because Sandra took Ethan to a park by her house. The one kiss he gave Veronica frustrated me more than the make-out session he had with Sandra. Ethan had nothing to say to Sandra – so he kissed her. During their making out everyone watched me with concern but I had my head cocked and looked slightly amused saying:

"He doesn't look like he's enjoying that."

"Look how his hands are on her arms keeping her body away from his," Phil said.

"Poor Sandra, she's trying to pull him in," I said, "and poor Dr. Corbon. This must be so frustrating to watch."

"Ouch, he just pulled away and walked to his car. He hardly even said goodbye," Phil said. The TV blared commercials for the final episode of *The Whole Package* in a week. A voice-over said, "Don't miss next week for the finale. Ethan will take each woman on a short tour of Doctors

Without Borders in the beautiful Dominican Republic. Then Ethan will determine who *The Whole Package* is, who will win the one million dollars."

After it ended the group wanted to analyze the details of the show over dessert. I got irritable. They compassionately shifted. We spent the evening talking about Addie, and what she had planned. This did nothing to improve my mood. Every once in a while, someone piped up about how the tour reference couldn't be just a coincidence. I tried not to glare at them.

I couldn't wait for the day I would be in the same room with Ethan again. It would be such a relief just to know the truth of how he felt.

CHAPTER TWENTY-ONE

Friday flew by in a blur of meetings. I ended up going to lunch twice for guest appearances.

Out of obligation, I told Karl about my meeting with Adam. I waited until after Andrea left for the day. I found Karl at his desk in his large office. I assured him I would be short and curt with Adam. I explained how he wouldn't leave me alone until I did. I finished with, "I didn't want you to hear about this and think I was pitching to both teams. I don't want to lose my job over this."

"I appreciate that. Look, over the last five years, rumors about Adam ..." Karl stopped. He looked down. "Just don't be alone with him. Take someone with you. I'd be happy to be that someone."

"I'm sure ... No, my sister and her fiancé are going to be there. Addie's pretty scrappy."

"Can I meet you for dinner later and you can tell me all about it?"

"Dinner," I asked. "Just the two of us?"

"No," Karl amended, his naturally red face deepening in color. He looked thoughtful for a moment then continued trying to read me, "Truthfully, Carrie, I'd love to take you to dinner just the two of us. I know you don't think of me like that, though. I'll force Andrea to come and we can have a working dinner. We have Vantose on Monday."

"Thanks for that; it's good for my self-esteem just now," I said, unable to look him in the eyes. "I'm kind of messed up right now. I don't think I could even give enough of myself to try with you. Sorry."

"That's okay, I'd have to put you on someone else's team if you were in sync with your sanity. I plan on making a lot of money off you," Karl said.

Karl smiled at me, and I grinned back but ducked out as quickly as possible. I didn't need another admirer just now.

The next morning Charles and Addie showed up at eleven and Charles checked his e-mail while Addie did my nails. While she worked, she watched the way her engagement ring sparkled. I couldn't help feeling maybe she'd be happy. She looked so content watching her hands – and missing my nails with the polish.

Charles' Bentley reappeared to take us to the restaurant. Traffic was so bad we ended up getting to the restaurant with only five minutes to spare. My favorite Chinese restaurant in New York looked like any other street-level shop in Midtown. When we walked in, I noticed the red walls covered in golden dragons. The intricately carved wooden creatures lined the back wall. The mismatched tables screamed family-owned.

"Grandpa would've loved this place," Addie said.

"He would've," I agreed.

"Carrie," Jia said in her strong Cantonese accent.

"Hi," I said.

"You party here," she said, pointing.

"Thanks," I said, squeezing her hand.

Adam waited for me at a square table near the window and far from the bar. He'd arrived early enough to choose the table. To my astonishment, Mr. Wilson sat with him. Mr. Wilson, bred a gentleman since birth, stood as we approached. Doing a confused double take, Adam put down his pot sticker and stood as well. Adam thought I would come alone. But if he thought he was isolating me in a controlled situation with Mr. Wilson, he had another think coming.

Mr. Wilson looked like he had when I was little, aside from his trim body thickening from all the triathlons he took up later in life. His cropped chestnut widow's peak showed no grey, his matching eyes, ever penetrating, made him appear sharp as a hawk. Charles shook hands with Mr. Wilson. Then Addie and I both kissed him, his mustache tickling my cheek as it always had.

"What's new with you girls?" Mr. Wilson asked in the fatherly manner he always assumed with us as the waitress pulled another table toward Adam's.

"I'm engaged to Charles," Addie said putting forward her ring.

"Oh, I'm so happy for you," Mr. Wilson said, moving in to kiss her cheek again. He gave me a panicked, how-did-that-happen look over her shoulder and I mouthed, "I know."

"I thought you two only recently started dating?" he asked. He looked from Addie back to me.

"Over six months ago," Addie said.

"That's not very long. Will you have a long engagement then?" Mr. Wilson asked.

"A couple months. October," she said.

"Of this year?" he asked.

"Yes," she said, blushing a little at his assessment.

"Well, congratulations are in order," he said.

"Thanks," Addie cooed. "You'll act in my father's place, won't you?"

Mr. Wilson stopped for a moment. He hugged her again. He looked at me in a way that made me feel supported in my concern when he said, "Of course. I'll do whatever your father would have, sweet Adeline."

I nodded. Mr. Wilson would help me push the wedding back. At least until after the election to be sure Charles still wanted to marry her. I was glad Mr. Wilson came. I needed his help. I didn't even mind admitting this to myself. Clearly Adam underestimated my relationship to the man. He was not merely my father's old business associate. Mr. Wilson moved behind the table next to the wall, and Charles scooted in beside him. I sat down between Addie and Adam.

"Carrie, now that we are all settled, I want to explain what Mr. Wilson and I have planned for our future," Adam said.

"Our future?"

"Yes," Adam continued as if I should understand why he linked us in such a way. Adam glanced sideways across the white table top at Mr. Wilson's pleased countenance. I wanted to laugh a little. Adam brought Mr. Wilson thinking I would agree to do whatever he proposed. Truthfully, it did take a minute to swallow. Mr. Wilson would learn what a mess I'd made of my family's predicament, but Adam had no idea the man's personal loyalty to us.

"You see," he continued, "we'll start a company. I know it's hard for you to leave your ties at Kimber & Stophers, but it's for the best." Adam's eyes became compassionate at the task before me.

"Is that why you sent me on the show, to disconnect me from Kimber and Stophers?" I asked.

"I'm sure it didn't hurt," Adam said glancing at Mr. Wilson, who found Adam's business plans less pressing than Addie's sudden engagement. He disregarded our conversation and spoke aside to Addie and Charles, pushing for more information on their wedding plans.

"Why a reality show?" I asked Adam. Adam glanced at Mr. Wilson to be sure he couldn't hear us. Then he said quieter.

"Do you really believe you just happened to stumble upon the sister of the only employee who hasn't signed his annual contract at LEDs?"

"You ... you ..." I stuttered.

"Yes. I set that up."

"You fast tracked her application, too?" I questioned, confused.

"I... I've known James for a while. As a favor to him I actually called my friend who works for Julian. He got her accepted onto the show over two years ago ...." Adam glanced at Mr. Wilson to be sure he still wasn't listening to us.

"You thought I would figure out in twenty-four hours they were related?"

"Well, James did write that article about your dad. I thought you may recognize Alexis Hall."

"I didn't read it," I admitted.

"Well, James is fanatical about your dad ... Alexis only had to hear your name," he said.

"Still. Twenty-four hours?" I asked.

"Alexis was supposed to make it on the show for at least a week, but ... you encouraged Veronica onto the show in her place. I watched you do it."

"Oh, huh! That makes sense. Alexis really thought she had it."

"Still you made the connection in less than twenty-four hours ... you're amazing with people."

"Wait, all this happened two years ago? But we met over three years ago – you asked to meet me three years ago. You didn't recruit me to use my dad to recruit James. You went looking for me before James even published his paper. Why?"

Adam stared at me, unsure what to say. He shifted:

"The real question is after all the work I put into this, how could you choose Andrea to work with Vantose? She's not capable of –"

"What?" I asked. I felt whiplashed at his sudden change in subject, and the frustration that came with it.

"Why didn't you tell me you met her?" Adam bored his eyes into mine and anger flickered there.

I scooted away from him, breaking the connection.

"I had an opportunity to make a name for myself. You would have kept it to yourself. Why would you think I shouldn't?"

"That's a discussion for another time," Adam said glancing at Mr. Wilson again. Anger twitched his clenched jaw, despite trying to contain it.

"No," I said. But I felt my head nodding yes. "No," I said more firmly, forcing my body not to quake. Mr. Wilson heard the tone of my voice and broke away from his conversation with Addie. Adam noticed him watching us. Using his conveniently compassionate voice, he said:

"Look Carrie, the next couple weeks will be hard. Corporate takeovers are always stressful, but it's like ripping off a band-aid. The first step is for you to quit."

This baffled me, but Mr. Wilson seemed to understand. Shifting his concern from Addie to me, Mr. Wilson nodded in agreement to what Adam had said.

"I don't –"

"Anyway, let's discuss the details of this merger. For so many reasons James Hall is our candidate. The contract he signed binding him to you will be moved to our company. If you'd told me about him in the first place it would be ...."

Adam stopped his lecture. He glanced at Mr. Wilson.

"That couldn't be helped; you were just bowing down to Karl. Anyway, the best course of action at this point will be for you to quit Monday morning. Mr. Wilson and I will take care of everything else."

"What are you talking about?" I asked.

"Do you think you can quit?" Mr. Wilson asked.

"Let's not worry about that here," Adam said.

"This is a safe place," Mr. Wilson said.

"That may be a conversation for later," Adam said.

"There is no later. I don't know what you're talking about. Why would I quit?" I asked.

Adam leaned over to Mr. Wilson. "I think she's in denial," he said in a low voice. "I thought this might happen."

"What?"

"Your boss, he's been... he's been harassing you," Mr. Wilson said, looking angry.

"What?" I asked.

"It's hard to ask your boss to back off. You'll be vindicated when you quit," Adam said, "Anyway moving –"

"Vindicated?" I said.

"Adam told me your boss has been making inappropriate advances toward you," Mr. Wilson said. He stared at me, concerned.

"No, he offered to put me on someone else's team so we could date. I told him I'm not interested and he backed off," I said.

"Oh, good for you. I didn't think you'd put up with that kind of shenanigan," Mr. Wilson said.

"Karl isn't the sort to take no," said Adam.

"Really? Coming from you?"

"You know," Mr. Wilson cut in, "with Charles in the family we may have to take a much closer look at things, Carrie."

Seeing me safe, he already shifted topics, looking at Addie.

Adam flinched a little but smiled politely at Mr. Wilson. I smiled genuinely at Mr. Wilson. I could see the picture Adam had painted for him. But now it was time to scrape that canvas clean.

"Mr. Wilson," I said, "I'm not sure what's going on, but I'm in no way affiliated with Adam's plans. He's my ex-co-worker. He is now branching away from the company we both worked for. That's my whole relationship with him. I'm sorry to disappoint you, but I have no intention of breaking with Kimber & Stophers."

"Carrie, let's talk outside," Adam said.

"No," I refused. Overwhelming annoyance bubbled inside me, "I'm done with you. You have to see this situation for what it is, and not from your warped perspective."

"Let me explain what's going on. You're confused," Adam said, his flustered eyes glancing from me to Mr. Wilson. When we met with clients, I spoke only when spoken too. Of course, he thought I'd keep my mouth shut. Well, not this time.

"What don't I understand?" I whispered loudly, failing to calm myself, "You recruiting me for some random business startup I don't even want? Perhaps, your attempts at charming me by sending me on a reality show where I had to make another man fall in love with me to win a million dollars? Actually, you're right. I'm not sure I fully understand the logic behind that strategy. There are a million different ways I could have met Alexis."

Adam stared at me. He looked confused. Adam thought I'd be subjected to societal niceties with Mr. Wilson around. Mr. Wilson or not, I was going to finish this.

"You used me," I replied in a harsh whisper, moving the flimsy table and spilling the soy sauce. "For years, you've been using me. Plus, you broke into my computer to win a bet."

"What? No... Carrie, no. That's not..." Adam said. He looked anywhere but at me, while his head nodded yes, like his body admitted I figured him out, even if his mouth never would.

"Carrie, I'd never do that! Karl has been lying to you about me. You know he's just as in love with you as I am!"

I stuttered. Adam looked so proud of himself. There was no room left in that look to confirm any actual fondness for me. I'd been loved before. I'd been near worshiped before. This was not that. Perhaps emotionally unavailable did describe Adam, because he really did think I was supposed to be playing my role in his fantasy.

I am a human being with a will of my own. Now I will assert it.

"You only love yourself. You've been planning for you. You may actually feel justified climbing over the back of anyone who gets down and crouches for your manipulating feet to stomp on, but I'm done crouching."

"Carrie, we are the same. We both want to build something," Adam said. "This isn't just about a business. It isn't just about me and you. This is about money, about power. Maybe even the White House. You have the name, and soon we'll have the money. We'll be inspirational to people."

I could imagine Adam giving long, impassioned speeches. He certainly had the character for politics or a used car salesman. Either path he chose, it wouldn't include me.

A waiter came to the table. I ordered dim sum. Everyone at the table stared at Adam when they weren't ordering.

The people next to us already noticed our conversation more interesting than theirs. Mr. Wilson pushed the conversation: "Carrie, you two really aren't dating?"

"No sir." I squeaked the answer through my lodged-up throat.

"Yes, we are," Adam insisted, looking sternly at me as if I was going to crumble under his glare.

"Are you suffering from a mental breakdown?" I replied, this time not even trying to keep my voice down. "What could possibly have given you the impression we're dating?"

"I practically lived at your Mom's house with you," Adam said. He looked around, embarrassed.

"No, you made yourself at home in a hotel by Mom's house. Besides, who asked you to do that?" I snapped back.

"Carrie, you have to see we're best together. You think that fool James… or no – do you think Ethan had any idea how valuable you are?"

"Valuable? Like a car valuable or finding-just-the-right-shoes-to-go-with-your-outfit valuable?"

Adam looked confused. I continued, even more high pitched, "I'm not something you can own and control. What did you expect to happen? Did you really think I'd give up my life to you and your insane ambitions?"

Adam stopped talking. He looked hurt. Then came the sigh. Adam had two sighs. First was his impatient sigh – the sigh that always hurried me up when I moved too slowly. The second sigh I knew even better. It was Adam's most effective tool. The sigh that meant I'd hurt Adam's tender little feelings. He finally said in his most condescending voice:

"I thought you'd be guided by me like you were when I saved you from losing your family home."

"I did that, not you. You didn't do my job for me," I said.

"Carrie, I need you to be reasonable."

"Oh, there's nothing reasonable about this. You seriously thought I was going to roll over, quit my job and what? Finish the picture for me. I'm not sure if I was supposed to be your business partner or your wife?"

"You'd be both," Adam said. He tried to make his voice sound loving, with an affection I couldn't believe him even capable of. He reached for my hand. I pulled away with a shudder. Adam's face contorted, and he looked like a wild animal ready to strike as he said:

"You flirt with me all the time!"

Astounded, I answered, "Nope. I didn't even respond to your flirting."

"Only because you've been mourning, but Gordon's been dead for more than three years. You need to move on," Adam said.

"I did. For Ethan, not you," I said.

Adam looked at me completely perplexed.

"You're sick," Addie sneered.

"I will see my goals achieved, you pretentious –"

"You'd better be very careful how you finish that sentence," Charles cut in, leaning forward.

Adam's anger flowed more impressive and boisterous than mine. He turned his whole frame toward me and bellowed, "I did so much for you. I kept you from losing everything. I got you a job. Nobody else even tried to help you, I did that. You owe me!"

185

"You used me –"

"I'll be so successful, and if you don't get on board, you'll be sorry."

"I'm already sorry I didn't see you sooner for what you are," I answered, quieting down.

Adam, seeing me subdued by his anger, calmed. He finished much more quietly, arguing his point again. I listened to him, discovering I was in the compromising position of a Mr. Gibson: I tried to reason with one who either can't or won't see anything but their own point.

I let go of my guilt. I stopped caring what Adam thought. It became clear he had no more regard for me than he would his car – yes, he took care of it, but only so it made him look good.

I felt like a coward for running away and not confronting Julian on *The Whole Package*, but I realized it wouldn't have mattered. He wouldn't have listened, he would have pushed until I left or he got what he wanted. I'd been so beat down. I needed Andrea and her support at that time. Was it so wrong to have a friend at time like that?

"Carrie, you still have a part in your father's blueprints being litigated. We will build his final three buildings together," Adam promised.

"I can't even get at those," Mr. Wilson said, proving he wanted to help, but couldn't see how.

"Well there's Shades," Adam said, "After our business takes off, we'll fight to get it back. Your family still has a claim on it. The aeronautical technology they've got at Shades is an untapped market."

Charles flinched, and it caught my attention. Mr. Wilson also watched Charles as his cheeks fired up. What had Adam

186

said? Charles no longer looked angry. Now he looked... was that embarrassed or ashamed?

What did Adam say to make Charles' eyes dart about like that? The longer Adam ranted, the more I did not trust Charles. Mr. Wilson watched Charles looking around the room watching the people who watched us. Our eyes connected. Charles was not what he seemed. Why did these sorts of people follow us around like we were their personal step-stools?

Adam concentrated on what he said. He didn't notice he lost his intended audience and performed only for the restaurant. He must have thought my silence indicated a conversion to his cause. Putting a hand on my arm he said:

"You'll find it a little uncomfortable turning your back on Andrea. We'll need the Vantose account. It'll set us up for at least a year."

"You think I'm going to – "

"No, no, we don't have to enter into a more intimate relationship until you're comfortable with it."

Mr. Wilson made a move like he was going to backhand Adam, but he was pinned behind the table.

"Let me put it simply for you!" I pulled my arm away angrily. "Stay away from me and my family. I don't want you anywhere near us ever again."

With a guilt-wrenching voice, he purred, "Carrie, after all I did for you –"

"No," I cut in, nearly screeching. I slammed my hand on the table and all the dinnerware jumped. A man walking past looked up startled so I lowered my voice, "No, I'm tired of feeling guilty. I'm tired of being walked on. I don't want you anywhere near me. Not now – not ever!"

Adam stood up and in one movement pulled me up. His anger came on strong and fast and real this time. My chair fell over backward and my arm bruised under Adam's strong grasp. Frightened, I pulled uselessly as Adam started dragging me.

"We'll talk outside," he said.

Charles made a move to interfere. Mr. Wilson pushed the table out of his way and in one step grabbed Adam by the collar of his cuff-linked-hundred-percent-cotton shirt. Mr. Wilson pulled Adam so hard that he let go of me and I fell backward over my chair. He pulled Adam close to his face. In the most intimidating voice thus articulated for the restaurant's customers listening pleasure, he said:

"You do not grab a lady like that. You don't talk to a lady like that. You will never talk to Carrie again."

Adam said something strangled while I wrestled with my chair to stand up. Mr. Wilson continued:

"You stay away from these girls, or I will break your nose. Then I will smack you with a restraining order. It will be publicized just enough that anytime anyone Googles you it will be the first thing to come up. That will give you an embarrassing criminal record for your political opponents to rub in your face. Do you understand?"

Adam stood still, unable to look at Mr. Wilson because his shirt collar stretched so tight. Mr. Wilson shook him and boomed, "DO YOU UNDERSTAND?" His voice echoed in the silent restaurant.

"Yes," Adam said in a constricted voice.

A few of the waiters came over and Mr. Wilson shoved Adam back into them.

"You can forget about me giving you any money," Mr. Wilson bellowed.

188

Adam tumbled backward, freeing himself from the extremely thin Asian men trying to subdue him. He called me a boorish name in a strong accent that was somewhere between the West Virginia twang and a New York curl. Then he was pulled out of the dining area. I'd never heard the name he called me. I only understood it was offensive by the way the other patrons reacted to it. I'm pretty sure it had something to do with a high-priced hooker. I couldn't feel offended when he so totally missed his mark. Spastic spinster or prudish snob may have made me at least evaluate myself. If I had my wit about me, I would have asked him for some intelligible curse so I could feel insulted.

All that came out instead was a slight whimper and an amazed nod of the head. Adam finished fighting the waiters and the bar tender who came to help get him out the door. Before he exited, he bellowed:

"Just because I wasn't born a Carnegie doesn't mean you get 'ta treat me like this.'"

"Whomever you were born to – they screwed up, freak show," Addie snapped because I was still in shock.

Adam angrily started shaking the waiters off him again. Mr. Wilson took a protective stance between Adam and me in case he re-launched himself in my direction. Adam stomped out the door. Mr. Wilson breathed hard and sweat poured off his face. He stood still for a few moments to regain his composure.

Then Mr. Wilson turned to me and picked up my chair that fell over. He put his arm around my shaky shoulders and asked if I were okay. Despite the throb in my leg, I quietly responded:

"My pride is mortified. Otherwise I'm fine."

189

My spastic spinster comment would have to be later, for Andrea's benefit.

Mr. Wilson pressed a kiss on my cheek in a smashed, discomfited way. Then he situated my chair to indicate I should sit in it.

"You've not embarrassed yourself," he said as I sat down. "I'm afraid Adam made fools of us all."

Mr. Wilson turned and apologized to the restaurant. He insisted Jia allow him to pay for the rest of the patrons' meals. Aside from one man who grabbed the drinks' list excitedly, everyone else appeared startled.

The restaurant as a whole went back to eating in hushed uncomfortable whispers. I heard my name a few times, indicating that yes, I had been recognized.

I quietly picked at my food that arrived. A few people, whom I didn't know, walked up to me and asked me by name if I were okay.

"Oh dearest," a woman said, hugging me from behind, "that man just didn't understand the love you share with Ethan."

"Ah kay," I said. I felt my neck crawl.

"Can you sign this for me?" She handed me a napkin.

Mr. Wilson handed me his heavy ball point pen.

"Don't worry Carrie, the reunion show is around the corner."

I handed her the napkin back and she said:

"Enjoy your meal."

"Thanks," I said as politely as I could muster.

CHAPTER TWENTY-TWO

After a while murmurs in the restaurant grew. I heard one woman telling a story about when she lived through her own public accosting. Once the room settled, I said quietly to Mr. Wilson:

"I'm so sorry. I should never have let him into my life. He's like a mole; he burrows his way in and starts taking over."

"How can you help it? You've been left to figure out so much on your own," Mr. Wilson said, having calmed down himself.

My face fell.

"I miss him, too," Mr. Wilson said with a sad smile.

I nodded, but felt nothing. I'd become a hollow shell where my father was concerned. Nothing twisted inside of me at the mention of his name. It scared me—the weight of nothing was heavy. Nothing wasn't empty exactly, it was just something pushed down far enough to become nothing. I filled that something with heavy lead so it couldn't come up again. But it was back-breaking, and so full of void it took all my effort to simply exist.

"Your father was so proud of you girls. Having you is like having a piece of him."

Neither Addie nor I could say anything. Mr. Wilson turned toward Addie: "I was anxious to help Adam because I haven't taken care of you girls like I should've. I knew your grandma took everything your mom had. I assure you this won't happen again. I will be more involved."

"Together we'll get it under control," I said glancing at Charles.

"You were always Arthur's girl, Carrie. You always did what needed to be done. Just like him."

I shrugged. That old feeling of not doing enough crept over me. Adam's assurance of my incompetence only a quarter of an hour earlier didn't help.

"Wait. Grandma took Mom's money?" Addie entered the conversation after connecting the dots for the first time.

"It was a combination of things, but your Grandma, well, she had expensive tastes," Mr. Wilson said.

"Which means you guys should have some really valuable stuff somewhere," Charles said. He didn't look at us, but at the waiter coming to fill our drinks. He ticked his fingers on the table like he'd just shown us his tell in poker.

"We could go on a treasure hunt," I said baiting him.

"Don't you guys maintain a series of safety deposit boxes? Addie said you did."

Charles tipped his hand. Whatever he wanted waited in grandma's vault.

"That's right. Charles wanted to see the first edited edition of Hawthorne's that Grandma bought. Are they still there?" I asked Mr. Wilson.

"I have no idea. Sounds like you'll have to take a trip to the bank." Mr. Wilson looked at me. "I'll do some research, maybe check on some of the rumors I've heard."

I nodded.

"Carrie has her jewelry," Addie said. "Grandma couldn't have sold the Carnegie pieces if she wanted to."

Addie didn't notice Charles a little too interested in grandma's vault, nor did she notice the nonverbal conversation Mr. Wilson and I were having. Out of a morbid need for Charles' façade to fall apart I said:

"I don't know what else will be in there. Grandma said she used everything liquid to keep us going while I finished college."

I waited for Charles to disagree.

"I'm sure there's still some pretty valuable stuff in there," he said nodding at the waiter.

"Poor Mom was too overwhelmed to do it when Grandma first died," said Addie. "But four years is enough time."

"Well, if we can help it, she won't be poor for long. We don't need that stuff, do we?" I asked.

"I don't want it," Addie answered. I suspected she was forcing herself to say so, but good on her. She was more substance than I often gave her credit for. Charles did not get her. Lunch ended shortly after that and I left with Charles and Addie. Mr. Wilson hugged me, and whispered in my ear:

"I'll check your family against his, ask around. His interest has to be in your father's blueprints or your Grandfather's company. Adam's mention of them is where he really started to turn green. You have to find whatever he wants in that vault before Addie ah – don't let him near it."

" 'Kay," I whispered wondering if I had any fight left. This was my baby sister. My dad was dead. I was the only one left to fight. I had to.

CHAPTER TWENTY-THREE

Too exhausted to fight traffic, I caught a cab to my work meeting with Karl and Andrea later that evening. Andrea did not appreciate being left out of Adam's breakdown. It took time, but eventually she agreed I did need to confront him myself. Karl and I were regaled over dinner with Andrea's impressions of Adam as the President of the United States. I only felt a little mean for laughing.

Because I worked so many nights, I asked Karl if I could take Monday afternoon off. He said that after we met with Vantose I didn't need to return to the office. Karl lingered with Andrea and me after we finished working our pitch. He kept by my side, like he wanted to talk to me privately. I couldn't be sure what he wanted. Andrea wouldn't take the hint and leave. Instead, she asked me to split a cab to Penn Station. Karl walked us to the street but his car was waiting for him in traffic, and he was heading in opposite direction. Out of reasons to stay, he left.

"What's going on with Karl?" Andrea asked as we climbed into a cab.

"Huh?"

"Don't pretend with me," she said.

"Fine, he fished a little, but I told him I'm not interested."

"Are you sure?"

"I don't think I am. I guess we can see what happens."

Andrea laughed.

"What?" I asked.

"I'll tell you what'll happen, Carrie. You'll end up dating Karl. He's just as good at getting what he wants as Adam, though obviously more principled."

"You think I should date him?" I asked.

"No, I don't. You should date Ethan, or someone like Ethan. Someone you connect with. Would you even consider dating Karl if he hadn't fished?"

"No, I guess not," I said, "What am I supposed to do? Guys like Ethan don't come around me, and the original is making out with Veronica."

"That's not true."

"It was publicly televised," I said.

"Funny," she said, "I meant, men throw themselves at you. Nice guys included. You don't give any of them a chance."

"Not uh," I said.

"Oh, please. At dinner with Gytech, all those guys were trying to get your attention. You should have seen how Karl gloated when he demanded your attention and you gave it to him."

"Karl did single me out instead of the client we were supposed to be schmoozing, didn't he?"

"Do you know how you and I became friends?" she asked.

"We work together," I said.

"Right, but actual friends?"

"You asked me to join your book club," I said.

"We became friends because I took the enormous effort to get to know you. I did it because it pissed Adam off."

"That's why you befriended me?" I asked.

"It's not why we stayed friends, we stayed friends because it turns out you babysit for free –"

"Hey –"

"And intellectually, you are my equal, which I love, but getting know you was hard and I only did it to piss Adam off," she said.

"I know... thank you for trying with me, even when I didn't try with you at first," I said.

"You're welcome, but not my point. My point is men like Adam and Karl see you as the ultimate chase because you're so closed off. They have to fight to get you. You become a prize instead of a person. You'll always end up with someone pushy and controlling if they're the only ones you let in. In fact, you don't let them in. So they push until you tolerate them. That isn't the same."

"You think?" I asked wondering if this had something to do with the target painted on my forehead.

"Yeah, I do. The only reason you kissed Ethan was because Julian did all the pushing for him. The first few times you shot him down, Ethan may have seen you as a bit of a challenge and pursued the chase. Eventually, he would have given up on you."

"Like the lacrosse player," I said, remembering how much I liked him, but after Gordon saw us together, I blew him off until he went away.

"You only respond to an Adam or even a Karl who force themselves through your shell. Ethan would never have made it without Julian's help."

"I don't know how to be open," I said. I knew Andrea had a point I could no longer ignore.

"You do too. It's just freaky."

"I can't handle losing people," I said, putting my hands out when the cabbie braked to hard in front of the train station.

"Loss is always a possibility. Do you regret loving your dad?"

"No but – "

"Your grandpa?"

"No. Of course not."

"Then love people. You can't know how long they'll be in your life. Love them anyway," Andrea said nodding at me. She paid the cabbie and jumped out of the car after another cabbie honked at us. I gave the man my building address and he drove away while I wondered about all the people to whom I never gave a chance. Maybe I could be a kind, open sort of person. That is, if I could be friends with people who only wanted the best for me, like Andrea.

CHAPTER TWENTY-FOUR

Monday, we went to the business offices of Vantose, the largest construction firm in Manhattan, averaging over nine billion dollars a year in projects. The CEO, Winston Reeves, looked close to retirement. He still feathered his bangs and had a pronounced clef in his chin. Instead of allowing human resources to do their work, he focused entirely on me, recalling all the times he worked with my dad. Though I didn't remember him, he remembered me coming out to the skyscraper a few times while they were building it.

James Hall spoke competently on all the projects Mr. Reeves referred to, and even matched his enthusiasm for my father's work. James' talent and reputation were both considerable and Mr. Reeves quickly took a liking to him, though I couldn't imagine anyone not. In no time contracts were signed, Mr. Reeves making it clear he'd do almost anything for Arthur's kid.

Andrea finagled with Human Resources and easily got James more than I made in a year as a signing bonus for a three-year-contract. I received twenty percent of it. I could breathe easier. Mom's house wasn't going to be auctioned off for taxes.

"Thank-you. Thanks for… remembering him with me," I said feeling at peace as Mr. Reeves walked me out.

"I don't think I've ever witnessed human suffering as raw as yours at his funeral. I'm so sorry he got sick," he said.

Something inside me closed up instantly. What could I say?

"How does anyone recover from such a thing?" James asked, gently. He ushered me out of the conference room.

"I don't think they do," I said. I waved to Mr. Reeves, who nodded back looking very concerned.

I pushed that day deeper down. I worked hard not to remember my father's funeral.

"You okay?" James asked as we walked out of the high-rise toward the street.

"Yeah, it just stings a little at times," I said, then pushing it all down to the place I put things I refused to examine, I finished with, "Anyway I have a question for you."

"Yeah, Carrie."

"Did we meet before I called you?"

"Oh, um I ..." he blushed scarlet "I met you at Gordon Shaw's funeral. His dad was my big brother, you know, in the program?"

"Oh, okay, yeah, James. How, how did I miss that?"

"Any pictures taken would have been when I was ten, and there is a lot of confidentiality so I doubt anyone would have told you my last name. You and I only met once, and you were in a really hard place," he said.

"I know, but I should have known you. Gordon talked about you all the time," I said realizing I thought of Gordon's James as a child.

"Gordon talked about you, too, but we only met the once," James said, looking at me, trying to read me.

All of the sudden everything came into place. Gordon, or his father, got James into the Art Institute of New York. Then there was James's published paper. Everyone in the architecture world had read it, immortalizing my father.

"Did Gordon help you write your Thesis?" I asked.

"A little," he laughed.

"Why didn't he tell me?" I asked.

"He wasn't sure you'd approve. He always said it would be a big surprise for you."

"That was nice of you," I said wondering how I felt about this little deception.

"Making sure Gordon's girlfriend's father was remembered seemed a little price to pay for all the opportunities the Shaw's gave me. Besides, I believe every word I wrote. It was an honor to do your dad justice."

"Thank you," I said looking down, "Did Gordon read it, before he died?"

"Yeah, one of the last times I saw him. He and Adam Pell were the only ones to proofread it before I submitted it. Gordon loved it, Adam wanted me to tone down all the stuff I wrote about your dad, but I didn't want to."

"Right. Adam was your recruiter. Did he know Gordon?"

"Yeah, Gordon introduced us just before I finished my program."

"How did they meet?" I asked.

"No idea. Gordon didn't want Adam and I spending much time together. He introduced me so I'd get my dream job right out of college."

"I got you the job Gordon wanted you to have?" I asked.

"Yes, you did," He grinned. I grinned back. This made me overwhelmingly happy for some reason.

"Why didn't Adam?" I asked.

"When Gordon was around everything stayed positive. Yeah, Gordon wanted me to write about your dad, but it was more like he wanted to lift everyone up. Gordon cared about us and wanted us all to succeed, especially you," James said.

"Yeah, I know," I said. I remembered that Gordon. I'd always had an enormous respect for that part of him. I did love Gordon, perhaps in the only way I was capable of at the time, but I did love him. James was saying: "After Gordon died, Adam changed. He's a control freak; he tried to tell me what to do. Plus, I think he ... Alexis won't talk about that time, but I think he hurt her."

"He's such a jerk" I said, "a friend of our family almost gave him a bloody nose, now I wish he had."

"All I could do was fire him."

"That's something," I said.

"Except I ended up at LEDS, designing neighborhoods out on the shore as my only option. Adam had to negotiate any employment I entered into with Vantose for two years."

"Sounds like him," I said.

"Yeah," he said.

"I took care of you, though, right?" I asked.

"And then some, I can't believe how much Andrea got me," he said.

"More than Adam would've," I said.

I'd recruited James. Something Adam couldn't do. I earned his business and the business of Vantose. Adam connived and controlled until no one wanted to work with him. That's why he needed me. I did not need him to be successful. James's cell phone buzzed for the tenth time breaking the pleasant feeling of camaraderie between us.

"You probably need to take Sophie shopping now."

I grinned at James. He didn't grin back, but locked eyes with me. His intensity startled me. I saw something too heavy for me to examine. Was James just another one of the nice guys I never gave a chance too?

"Here, James, let me get your cab," I said breaking the connection and waving my arm. I reached in and handed the cabbie a twenty. I turned, but found James even closer to me. He took my hand, and leaned in:

"Gordon loved your painting. Watching you paint on the show, I could see what he was talking about. Are you doing what you're passionate about?"

"I'm taking care of my family. That's my... duty. Some of us don't have the luxury of passion," I said, unable to fake anything with him.

He pulled my hand up to his lips. He kissed the joint of my thumb. Then he said: "We are artists before anything else. We can't help it. That is why Gordon loved us both."

He climbed into the taxi. I couldn't even wave. I just stared after him. James could have made me happy if I'd ever even noticed him after Gordon died. Why didn't I read his paper sooner? He was requesting an introduction into my life, and I didn't even notice.

After he left, Andrea and Karl came toward me from the respectful distance they'd assumed while I talked to James.

"I've got to go, too. I have a meeting at the office in an hour," Andrea said. She raised her hand to the next cab driving down the street.

"Oh, can I ride back with you? I've got to get my car," I said.

"Carrie, we should go out and celebrate," Karl said putting his hand in the crook of my arm to pull me back.

"Oh, sorry. Mom's expecting me. I have some pretty pressing family stuff to take care of," I said lifting my arm as if to wave, but it was really so he'd let go. I could never connect to Karl the way I did with James, let alone Ethan. So I slid into the cab before Andrea.

"Bye Karl," I heard her say, but she looked hard at me while she gave the cabbie our address. I thought Karl said

202

something about his car not being here yet and sharing our cab back to the office, but the cabbie didn't stand still long enough for him to make up his mind.

CHAPTER TWENTY-FIVE

A few hours later I met Mom and Addie in downtown Hartford at the parking lot of our bank. I wore a gray suit and carried a briefcase contrasting with Addie's white summery dress, and Mom's silk blouse and taupe trousers. I looked like their attorney.

After finagling with the bank manager, I led as he took us into the vault. Together, we opened drawer after drawer while Mom started to catalogue everything in them. The longer we worked, the madder I grew. We weren't poor. We didn't have ready money, but with all grandmother's collections, we weren't poor.

After a few hours of itemizing everything in the vault, I found well-hidden stock certificates proving we still owned most of Grandpa's company, Shades. What Charles wanted with the obscure little company I couldn't say, but he worked in aeronautical engineering. It's the only thing I found that made any sense.

When we left the dimly lit room, Mom wore a thin gold chain bearing a square ruby. She told us how she played with it as a child when her paternal grandmother wore it. Addie took the tiara my mother wore on her wedding day, with matching earrings and necklace in her purse – she was getting married, after all. I took the stocks.

Once we were in my car, we started to discuss what happened next.

"Mom, these stocks have to be worth money. If we sell them, we won't have to sell the house."

Mom nodded, but didn't look convinced.

"I bet Charles will help us. He builds airplanes, and Shades builds airplane windows," Addie said.

"Among many other things, but stocks are Mr. Wilson business, so we really ought to call him," I snapped. Addie looked offended so I said, "Poor man – he wanted to help us so badly. Besides, it is his line of work."

Mom and Addie grew very quiet as I dialed Mr. Wilson's cell. After the necessary opening pleasantries, I asked:

"Hey, we've been to the vault. I need some help after all. Are you still willing?" Mr. Wilson agreed. When I hung up I said:

"He wants us to meet him at his Lake home."

"Seriously, he can't just meet us at his office down the block," Addie complained.

"Nope," I said.

"It's not even a lake, it's a pond," Addie said.

"When you have your own body of water, dear, you can name it what you like," Mom said with a tremor. Her hasty defense of Mr. Wilson bothered me. She glanced away and scratched at the door where Addie had spilled the last time she rode shotgun.

We drove in silence for a half hour. I pulled onto the Wilson's private road, driving around the pond. Then we drove up a gradual hill through the wooded area. The woods opened up to the three-story white farmhouse style vacation house the Wilsons used when they weren't down on the Gold Coast. The clock in my dash glowed six o'clock and I remembered Mrs. Wilson and her punctual meal times.

"It's dinner time. Do you think we're interrupting?" I asked.

"Not likely. Mr. and Mrs. Wilson haven't lived together for over a year," Addie said.

"What?" I asked.

"Addie," Mom said blushing again.

"Come on Mom. Mrs. Wilson once told me not to chew gum because it made me unladylike. She moved her boyfriend into her husband's family estate, what does that make her?" Addie asked.

"How did she of all people let go of the pretense?" I asked.

"Those who hold most tightly to society's decorum burn out the fastest. But then if you never stop and take the time to develop opinions of your own, anyone can skew your perspective with only one piercing blow," Mom said. She looked pointedly at me for some reason.

"She's warped, though," Addie took the opportunity to say. "They separated over a year ago, but she still refuses to sign the divorce papers."

"Pre-nup?" I asked.

"She'll lose everything," Addie said, glancing at Mom.

"Please my loves, don't repeat those stories," Mom said. "I did not raise gossiping girls." Her eyes set sternly in my direction.

"Who would I tell?" I asked. Addie rolled her eyes at me as we climbed out of the car.

Addie rang the bell. I examined Mom smoothing out her hair. Her action irritated me. The maid opened the door and Mr. Wilson, still looking ageless, greeted us warmly from behind her. His white shirt opened at the neck. Only his gray slacks, though fashionable, hiked to a little too high, betrayed him as belonging to an older generation.

Mr. Wilson turned his whole attention to Mom with a stiff, but genuine friendliness. "Hello Irene, how are you?"

Mom blushed, but said calmly, "I'm fine thanks, Matthew. How are you?"

"Fine," Mr. Wilson's piercing eyes took in Mom's casted arm with a concerned look like he didn't believe her. His level of concern could only be rivaled by the concerned way that she looked at him in his huge empty house.

"Anyway," I interrupted, annoyed. What was this?

"Carrie, what's going on? You said you needed my help?" Mr. Wilson asked refocusing on me. I yanked the stocks out and, handed them to Mr. Wilson. I didn't even try to stop the negatives of my parent's wedding fluttering to the floor.

"Oh oops, Mom those were for you. You said you wanted to talk more about dad. Let's get some pictures developed," I said bending down to pick them up. I handed them to my mother.

"Those are stocks, right?" I asked Mr. Wilson pointedly after he examined the papers.

Leading us through the house Mr. Wilson whistled.

"These must be your Grandpa's," Mr. Wilson commented, nodding at me like I'd done good work.

Trying to figure out why he looked at Mom all weird, I forgot Charles.

"Here let's go sit down," Mr. Wilson said. I cringed at the entryway of a white room with dark cherry wood trim. Huge windows looked out over the picturesque pond. Visions of Mrs. Wilson scooting me out of this sitting room as a child halted my wandering foot.

"Here sit down. Maria, can you get us some lemonade? Irene would you like a drink?" Mr. Wilson said, not realizing both Addie and I had surpassed the age of twenty-one.

"No thank you," she said.

"It makes her MS symptoms worse," I said. Everyone looked at me awkwardly. Why did I mention that? We didn't talk about Mom's illness.

"I'm sorry to hear that, Irene," Mr. Wilson said.

"Thanks, Matt," she nodded back. Then to my horror, he started asking her specifically about her MS symptoms, and she openly answered every question.

I sat carefully on the white loveseat next to Addie. I wondered if I should have taken off my shoes. I spied a wood tray with inlaid gold butterflies that held candy. Carly, Mr. Wilson's daughter, always tricked us into sneaking into the room to steal the only treats they ever had lying around. For old time's sake, I picked one up and unwrapped what I soon found to be a stale Belgium chocolate in gold paper. I remembered them being fresher. Finally, Mr. Wilson stopped chatting with Mom and examined the stocks.

"You're not getting residuals off these?" he finally asked, but knew the answer.

"No," I said. I was so startled by the question that I almost spewed the thick, juicy chocolate all over the white rug.

"You should be," Mr. Wilson said, looking unnerved. "Your Grandpa died so suddenly, we didn't know exactly what he'd done. Your grandma wouldn't let me help much at the time. She didn't want me to see what she'd done with your dad's wealth. I assumed your grandpa already sold these in his life, considering how badly they needed your mom's money. I didn't see anything regarding his business after your Grandma died."

I had to swallow three times to get the mouthful of chocolate down.

"Can we sell them?" I asked tapping my foot, overwhelmed at the sudden freedom they promised. No grandma, no sick mother to support, I could be my own person. I could find my passion.

"You can cash them into the company, or you could sell them to pretty much anyone. It isn't a publicly traded company. There are a lot of large companies that would love to acquire... In fact," – here Mr. Wilson paused and looked at me, tentatively nodding a little at Addie.

"What?" I asked.

"Does Charles know you have these?" he asked me.

"No, we came here first. Why?" Addie answered looking from me to Mr. Wilson suspiciously. Mr. Wilson made his next statement with the delicacy of the diplomat who drew the short straw.

"Addie, I know this sounds paranoid because we've been through a lot in the last few days. But, just humor me. Charles hasn't asked to look through any of your paperwork, or take a look inside the vault, has he?" Mr. Wilson asked, knowing he had.

"No," Addie laughed. "You're paranoid."

"Actually, that's not true," I cut in. "He's been joking around, asking Addie to see the Hawthorne collection – which would obviously be in the vault."

"Why do you ask?" Mom asked, catching on something was wrong.

"Charles would do well if he could get himself on the board of Shades," Mr. Wilson said. Comprehension dawned on my mother's face. She eyed Addie nodding apprehensively like she understood the problem.

"Why?" I asked, refusing to tiptoe around the matter.

"Yeah, what would United Skills, a multibillion-dollar corporation, want with a dinky little company like Shades?" Addie asked, laughing defensively.

"Back in the 70's, your grandfather's partner, a man named Ellis, had an idea for a shading technology. He used stretched acrylic that would block the UV rays in airplanes. Pilots have benefited the most," Mom explained.

"That can't be worth much to Charles," I said.

"From what I understand Shades still owns all their chemical formulas. They're always in the lead developing stretched acrylic," Mr. Wilson said.

"Really?" I asked.

"They're even finding ways to use it in solar panels. If they can make it work, it would cut back on fuel costs for airlines – it's a whole new playing field."

"Is it really worth that much?" Mom asked.

"Domestic airlines combined spend over two billion dollars on jet fuel a month," Mr. Wilson said.

"That's a lot," Addie said quietly.

"It would pump up every airline's bottom line to cut down on that cost. If United Skills had that technology, they'd be building planes for every airline, not to mention government contracts. They could name their own price. Parker Goodrich owns what? Twenty percent in United Skills?"

"Over forty, at least that's what Charles said," I answered.

"No, Carrie. Parker Goodrich has been shifting his stocks over to Charles," Mr. Wilson said. He looked at me – willing me to understand.

"Oh crap," was all I could think. I said nothing.

"United Skills tried to buy Shades ten years ago. Ellis would never sell his science. I'm sure Parker Goodrich was disappointed when the sale didn't go through. With Shades technology his shares would split, and he would make a lot of money. Ellis the younger is sitting on an undiscovered gold mine."

"He hasn't done anything with it?" I asked.

"They are scientifically minded. Not one of them has a head for business," Mr. Wilson said.

"Didn't Charles say something about needing to bring United Skills up to date?" I asked thinking hard back to the evening I played a board game with Charles.

"You know this would be quite the feather in his cap if Charles could get a stronghold in Shades. He'd easily take Parker's place as president of the company. Parker must know you have these stocks." Mr. Wilson clarified, "Irene I could have sworn your dad sold out when your brother quit law school. I always figured your mom's claim at being cheated was to cover up her squandering the fortune he got."

"Unless she didn't know," I answered. Mr. Wilson looked at me.

"Why do you say that?"

"I found them in the negatives of my parent's wedding photos."

"So?" he asked.

"After Dad died, we weren't allowed to have pictures of him around. Grandma said they depressed her."

Then speaking to Mom, I said sounding a little too accusatory, "Grandpa knew Grandma was sinking them. He may have hidden the stocks as a last-ditch effort to save us. He would've thought the negatives of your wedding photos were something you'd value and Grandma wouldn't. The way they were shoved in there –even if she found the envelope she wouldn't have looked closely. Not after noticing the pictures were of Dad. You on the other hand – first chance you got after Grandma died, you should've gone looking for them. They weren't in the drawer filled with the rest of the negatives."

Mom looked at the floor, not answering. Had she really accused me of disregarding my father's memory? Not a day went by I didn't remember him, and then force myself to forget. Apparently, he had escaped her memory long enough for her to start some sort of flirtation with Mr. Wilson—a married man.

"He must have found some way to secure the residuals, though," Mr. Wilson considered. "There may be something illegal happening." This last part was more him talking aloud to himself, but he looked at Mom like he would do whatever it took to protect her.

"Illegal?" I asked, the word hitting my chest like a gale force wind. How would I protect my mother from prison?

Mr. Wilson started at my tone and looked over at me.

"Don't worry little one, I'll take care of this. Your grandpa must've known he was dying and hid them for you. He wouldn't have put your mother in harm's way."

"No, he wouldn't have," I said, breathing again.

"Carrie, he might've set it up like this so you could take his place within the company. You were only seventeen, but you've always been so smart."

"He never tried to steer me toward business. In fact, he never tried to steer me at all, except he always wanted me to be a lady. I would never have thought about an MBA if not for Adam."

My grandpa knew. He knew his company could make money – lots of it. He knew I was smart enough to succeed where my uncle failed. He never said a word. His ambition never clouded him to ruin my happiness. That was love.

"Carrie, I could help you. You could potentially do very well for yourself acting as CFO of shades," Mr. Wilson said, looking to me. I considered.

Truthfully, I wanted to carry on Grandfather's legacy. I wanted his company to succeed just as he had wanted it to. Huge amounts of wealth slipped through my fingers, but no matter how good the opportunity, I couldn't force myself to take it. No matter how much I loved another person, I still couldn't live in their cage.

I saw my grandfather's face, his bald head surrounded by white hair, his eyes – my mother's eyes, my own reddish-brown eyes – told me to stand up, to be a lady. Finally, I said:

"I want to be an art teacher."

"Really," Mom said, smiling at me.

"Yeah, Grandpa wanted me to be a lady – to choose for myself. That's my legacy from him. I will live my own life," I said blushing.

"Well then, you're doing the right thing selling them," Mr. Wilson said to Mom.

"Thanks, Matt," she said in a tone of relief that I'd been unable to evoke throughout all my comforting assurances at the vault. There was something between the two going unsaid. How dare my dad leave me to deal with this?

"Let's just turn them into the company. One of the partner's sons runs it now, right? I'm sure Charles won't care. He has nothing to do with Mom becoming financially stable," I said bluntly bringing up the point the rest were willing to forget.

"If Charles' company swallowed shades, it would all stay in the family after he married, Addie. Like I said, Ellis's son would never sell, but he doesn't understand what he's sitting on either." Mr. Wilson said.

213

"So United Skills can't just buy Shades," I asked just to be sure I understood.

"No, Ellis won't sell. Plus, knowing your grandfather, there's probably some first rights of refusal for the Ellis family if you wanted to sell. Only a member of your family could lay claim to Shades without Ellis giving his go ahead, which he never will."

That's why Charles involved Addie!

Technically he'd be a member of the family in a few short months, and that would give him legal claim to the company without any shadow of a doubt in any courtroom. If Charles married Addie, he inherited Shades, because he couldn't buy it.

"Charles isn't going to be upset when we sell the stocks back to Ellis is he?" I asked.

"I suppose it'll be the first real test of our relationship," Addie said, shrugging as if it were nothing.

"Yes," Mr. Wilson returned less optimistically. "It would add substantially to his fortune if he could accomplish the merger and force your Grandfather's company to go public with their stock."

"Substantially?" Addie asked.

"He would join his father on the Forbes 400 list," Mr. Wilson said.

"That substantial?" Addie asked.

"Addie!" I admonished.

"Why can't we sell them to him?" Addie turned to Mom, knowing she was the weak link.

Mom stammered a little. Seeing her crumble, I interrupted: "Addie, you've only been seriously dating him for a couple months. He's already talking marriage. He's so much older than you. I know this could all be coincidence, but if he knew about the stocks –"

"What?" Addie asked turning on me with barely any breath behind it. Her eyes incensed that I'd even suggest such a thing.

"It does seem a little convenient...." Mr. Wilson, who could boldly face anyone in the financial world straight on, looked at the floor instead of looking Addie in the eyes when she turned on him.

"You think he's marrying me to get his hands on those pieces of paper?" Addie asked looking from Mr. Wilson to me, waiting for someone to be brave enough to answer.

"We don't know anything of the sort," Mom said. "We'll just sell them back to the company."

"Then we'll see, won't we," I added with venom dripping from each word. Everyone stared at me. Tears pooled in Addie's eyes.

Maybe I didn't want to be a cruel person. "I didn't mean that Addie," I said, "I'm sure Charles won't even flinch."

I said this last kindly, but with no conviction; I couldn't believe it. Addie nodded and everyone went quiet.

"Mr. Wilson, what do we have to do to sell 'em?" I asked, pushing forward. The best dose of reality for Addie would be Charles leaving after he found we were no longer in possession of the stocks.

"If you're certain you don't want to go into the aerospace business, Carrie... you really should research it. Ellis's son doesn't comprehend his business opportunities. He's a chemist."

"I'm going to be a teacher," I said not even wavering this time. How many times would the red eyed dragon spin me before I could get off the ride?

215

"I'll go get my briefcase," Mr. Wilson shrugged, incapable of understanding such a stance. "Your mom will need to sign some paperwork and then I'll do the rest. I'm sure I can at least take care of this for you."

He looked at her with regret of some sort. Mom shook her head slightly but intently in disagreement. Addie didn't notice them. She was still thinking about her own problems.

"Do you think Charles will be disappointed in me for not giving them to him?" Addie asked.

"It isn't your choice, Honey," Mom said. "They were part of grandma's estate, which makes them my stocks. We don't even know if he wants them. Ten years is a long time. His company's probably going in a different direction now."

I rolled my eyes. A thirty-one-year-old engages himself to a twenty-one-year-old after two months of seriously dating, and somehow this isn't involved. I fought every hateful impulse to tell Addie to move on. She'd found a lemon of a man. It all added up too perfectly to be a coincidence.

How could I have left Addie so unprotected?

Mr. Wilson left and returned to a silent room. After Mom signed the papers, Mr. Wilson put a consoling hand on her shoulder. She looked up at him with some measure of affection I hadn't seen since my father died.

Seriously – we were in the room? Mom held the photos of her dead husband in her hand – Mr. Wilson had a wife. Seriously? Mr. Wilson ended the visit by carefully picking up the stocks and placing them in a safe in his office.

As he walked us out to my car, he said he would work on it first thing in the morning. We were all at our respective doors when Mr. Wilson said forcefully: "Until your mom has a payout in her account, none of you can say anything. It's a tricky business when you're holding such a hot commodity as these stocks. Addie, can you do that?"

"I guess," she answered.

"It isn't your secret – it's your mom's. I'd have you sign a confidentiality agreement, but I'm sure we can have confidence in you keeping your word," Mr. Wilson said.

"Okay," Addie said.

"Addie," I said, wondering if she would strike me down if I asked Mr. Wilson for the agreement, "I think it's best if we pretend we don't know he wanted the stocks at one time. Then we'll see how important they are to him by how he reacts when it becomes known that they're being cashed in."

"Why don't we just say we found them? Addie asked. "That way if he really wants them, we can sell them to him."

My face dropped. Mom looked to Mr. Wilson for guidance, but at the same time Mr. Wilson shot me a quick "no." Through a shake of his head, he placed the bulk of Addie's protection on my shoulders, not on Mom's. Mom reared back and her face tightened. Mr. Wilson instantly realized his mistake. Mr. Wilson tried to look sorry, but Mom looked away from him indignantly and climbed into her seat.

"Uh, his company will be given equal consideration if the mother company does not choose to reclaim her offspring," Mr. Wilson said not really talking to Addie, but leaning down to see what happened to Mom.

"I guess we'll have to see how this plays out," I said tartly, unsure what I was referring to. I slammed my car door in frustration.

Distracted, I drove Addie and Mom home. I ran a stop sign and almost hit another car. Fortunately, the other driver was more alert than I, and swerved.

217

"You took my car keys?" Mom said. "Perhaps we should have taken a cab home as well."

I was too startled to appreciate Mom's wit. When we pulled into the back drive I saw Charles leaning against his car by the house talking on his cell phone. He waved to us.

"What was I worried about? Charles doesn't have a deceptive bone in his body," Addie said.

Mom nodded, but I saw the same panic show in her eyes that pumped in my chest. Charles knew we'd been to the vault. Didn't very young vice presidents have to be at work still? How long had he been waiting for us to return? Addie hadn't called him. He didn't know what we knew. I needed to talk to him before Addie spilled it. Despite Mr. Wilson's caution, Addie would spill it. She couldn't keep anything a secret.

CHAPTER TWENTY-SIX

I slowed the car and parked near the detached garage across the flagstone driveway, a few hundred feet from Charles.

"Addie, don't say anything to Charles about the stock, okay?" I reminded as I pulled a U-turn so my car faced the back gate.

"I don't know why not; we're not selling them to him. It isn't going to affect him," Addie said, sulking.

"Well," I said giving her a side glance, "Maybe if I can talk to him, you know, find out the story behind the takeover, we can see if we want to keep it in the family after you guys get married."

Mom looked at me hard. She'd seen me play this game with Addie. I put the car in park and turned to the back seat. I smiled at Addie.

"Just don't say anything, okay?" I said.

"Fine," Addie said. "But I don't like having secrets from him."

"Don't you wish Charles felt the same?" I asked, annoyed at Addie's childlike faith in him.

"Sweet Adeline," Mom cut in, scowling at me, "It isn't your secret. It's mine."

"Whatever. Carrie's just bitter," Addie said matter-of-factly. Like she understood I was going to probe Charles, and then I would see – Charles loved her. She had complete faith in Charles. I hated him for doing this to her. Addie jumped out of the car and ran over to Charles.

Mom and I sat in the car and stared at each other. I broke the silence by saying, "This sucks."

"You will be kinder to your sister about this. You've said some cruel things since you left that show. It isn't like you to be cruel, no matter how you've been hurt," Mom said.

"Yep, like always – take her side," I snarled.

"Stop being such a child!"

"Excuse me?" I said.

"Don't pretend you want me to mother you. You don't even remember I exist unless I'm in trouble. Even back when your father died ... I would have smothered you with affection if you let me. You pushed me out. You still push me away. And then you act like I'm the one who deserted you?"

"I...I didn't – "

"Maybe I should have pushed harder, like Andrea, to get back in. It isn't my way," she snapped.

"Sorry mom, I'm sorry. I...."

"I love you, Carrie. I would take your side if you'd let me. Let me help you mourn – I'll help you. Just open up to me – tell me what you feel about Ethan."

I stopped.

"I'm ... I'm fine."

"Okay, let's talk about your dad's funeral – let's talk about what Grandma said to you."

"I can't," I snapped, needing her to stop.

"You think you'll win any prizes blocking everyone out and doing it all on your own?"

"I ... I just wanted to...."

"You wanted to take your dad's place. You didn't. Nobody could," Mom said. I wondered if she saw the way I glared at her when she blushed for Mr. Wilson.

"I'm sorry Mom," I said again.

"We'll talk about this later," Mom promised when Charles gestured toward us, but Addie pulled him back to her.

"Poor Addie. I think she's going to get her heart broken," I answered.

"I don't want to think Charles bad, but I've lived among these people too long. A father would sacrifice his firstborn if it substantially enhanced his portfolio."

"Charles probably went home after Addie asked him out, bragging that a Carnegie hit on him. He and his father must have hatched a plan."

"Only one way to find out," Mom said.

"I'm on it," I said reaching for my door.

"I guess at a certain point you did become the head of the household, didn't you?" Mom said bitterly.

"Come on, Mom."

"You act like you have every right to make decisions for us because you are earning the money, but you don't."

"I know," I said, but I couldn't dispute her claim. Why did I place so much importance on my role in the family? Did my earning money really enslave Mom and Addie to my decisions?

"You never asked me what I wanted to do about Addie and the stocks. You never asked if I wanted to hire someone to run Shades, or somehow keep my shares in my father's company," she said sniffling.

"I'm sorry Mom," I said. I hadn't consulted with Mom about what to do. They were her stocks, and she was Addie's mom. Why did I charge forward, so caught up in the problem, instead of asking Mom what she wanted?

"You're the head of our family," I said more humbly, "You take care that we're healthy and all that – all the important things. . . .. Do you not want to sell the stocks?"

221

"I think we have to. I think it is the only way to keep Addie safe, but I wish you'd at least thought to consult me."

"I'm sorry Mom. Can I... or I mean should I, talk to Charles?"

"Carrie, you're not letting your chances for love in the future ride on Charles's integrity, are you?" Mom said, scrutinizing me.

"No, Mom," I said, staring at Addie hand-in-hand with Charles, standing near the house.

"Carrie, maybe I should talk to him," Mom said. "Not that I pretend to understand as well as you; it's just that you're cynical about relationships right now."

"Mom, I love Addie. If there's any way that her relationship could still work out, I'll find it. I promise."

"Well, your promises are good. I know I can trust that," Mom acknowledged. She always put the weight of her trust on me, knowing it would go further than any other form of coercion. The effect took place in my eyes instantly as they dropped and I yielded.

"You do guide me, Mom," I said, "It's just in a quieter way than Adam and Julian. Andrea says I don't recognize guidance unless it's a strong hand shoving me."

"That's true," she said.

"I do prefer your gentle hand, Mom. I thought about everything you said about Adam. I really did and it helped me see him in a new light. I appreciate you even if I don't acknowledge it most of the time."

"Thank you for that, Carrie," she said.

"So, I'll fix this?" I asked.

Mom nodded and I pulled a little too hard on the door handle climbing out of the car. Addie showed Charles the tiara. He looked at me coming toward them, distracted.

"Hey! I was hoping you guys would've brought something I could mooch for dinner, but I see I'm on my own," Charles called, but his phone chimed, and he pulled it out and started typing something in it.

"Addie and I'll go get some Chinese; poor Carrie's been asking for it for a while now. She kind of needs it sometimes," Mom called, sticking her head out of the car.

I stopped in surprise and turned back to Mom. She smiled at me. Only then did it occur to me my mother knew me better than I knew myself. When I had been content to ignore my life, she watched like a hawk.

"I love you Mom," I said.

"I love you too, sweetheart," she said, and of all things, she was tearing up again.

I ducked my head and walked quickly along the flagstone, my clicking heals warning Addie of my approach.

Addie started toward me while Charles examined his phone intently like something was wrong. I tossed Addie the car keys from ten feet away. She picked them up and glared, but moved to get into the car with Mom. She passed close to me whispering, "Please remember I love him."

"Addie, you may want to take off the tiara," I said back to her.

Addie took my place in the car and rode off with Mom. I could see them arguing through the rear window as they drove away. I sidled up to Charles like the proverbial snake ready to entrap my victim.

CHAPTER TWENTY-SEVEN

"How's business?" I asked.

"Busy. Today I had a manager quit so now we're going to have to go through the hiring process. If you have anyone available, I'd love to interview them," Charles said still staring down at his phone, distracted.

"I'll look into it, but I'm not sure how mixing business and family would work out," I said bluntly, then asked. "Must've been hard when they made you a Vice President right out of college. Have you had a lot of turnover?"

"I was a floor manager for two years. I've been VP for three. I have had some turnover, but putting my own people in place can be better," Charles said. "Sorry, just a sec."

He e-mailed someone on his phone. With his thumbs blurring, he didn't even look at me. Then he stopped in the middle of a key stroke. My piercing stare must have caught his attention because he looked up at me with scrutiny. I did not flinch. He looked around. He realized in his distraction he'd been left alone with me.

Addie, his defense, was gone. My mother – the nice one – gone. I saw the fear register behind his eyes.

"What's…?" Charles looked away from my penetrating eyes, out into the wooded area around the house. Finally, he said:

"You found the stocks?"

"Yes," I said.

"Who told you about my father's attempt at buying Shades?" Charles asked.

"Mr. Wilson," I said.

"Well, this should be nice and complicated," Charles said. He looked away, bouncing a little.

"You won't get them," I finally said after a long pause to see how Charles would react.

Charles nodded. He went back to writing his e-mail. He didn't look comfortable, though. I hoped he was remembering my confrontation with Adam. How I stood up for myself. I had more fight for my little sister than myself.

It was a quiet evening, stifling hot and bright, though it was nearing six-thirty. I stared at Charles without flinching. Sweat poured down his face as he finished his e-mail. My suit stuck to my body. Why didn't I leave my jacket in the car?

"Can we go in the kitchen – out of the heat to talk?" Charles asked finally.

"Actually, I just sent my keys with Addie," I said. "I'm sure the house is locked. Mom and Addie are here alone most of the time. Could you imagine coming home to a thief – but I suppose there are worse things that could sneak into your house while you're away."

"Carrie," Charles groaned, turning to me, "It's not like that... I knew you guys would discover the stocks."

"Then you should be prepared to give me an explanation. You're dating – no, no. Ready to marry my little sister to get your hands on my grandfather's company?" I accused.

"No," Charles said, "Ur... it's more complicated than that."

"Sift through it," I said coolly. The nicest thing I could do for my sister was to chase him off before she came home.

"I didn't know Addie could be connected – "

"You weren't even interested in her at first," I pointed out. "She asked you out, and you said no."

Charles nodded. I saw the wheels turning in his head as he said, "I'll start from the beginning, then."

"Yep," I said.

"After the fundraiser where I met Addie, I told my family that Addie asked me out. My dad told me I should get to know her. I figured it had to do with the election, so I did. I didn't even know about the obscure little company at first – I swear."

I nodded my head in disbelief.

"My dad led me in gradually," Charles continued. "I thought he wanted to be related to the last name of Carnegie. After we started dating, your Uncle Brock invited us out to Fisher's Island for a round of golf with a U.S. senator, a law clerk for a Supreme Court judge, and –"

"I know his pull," I said.

"He's thrown his considerable weight behind my father's candidacy. Do you know what it means to –"

"In other words, you're climbing. Using my sister as your footstool," I said.

"I know... and I've always hated those people."

"Yeah, me too," I glared, wondering for a moment where all this anger was coming from. I was seething at Charles. I had to calm down. I had to be rational. This wasn't Ethan, and it wasn't Adam, it was Charles and he deserved his own chance. It would only be one.

Charles was saying, "...Carrie, I can't honestly say that wasn't the reason I went out with Addie off and on for the first few months. I never really got to know her. My dad sold tickets to his fundraisers because people knew she was going to be there, they loved seeing us together. People loved your dad. They loved your Grandma Carnegie."

"How could you let him do that?"

"She wanted to come. I didn't force her."

226

"But you used her," I said.

"She used me too. She wanted to get out. I took her where ever she wanted to go, and her tastes are expensive. I just figured we were using each other."

I didn't say anything.

"Anyway, my father was being stubborn about letting me make any changes at United Skills. After I started dating Addie, he came around on a few things I'd been suggesting. I didn't know why—I didn't even correlate it with us dating at first."

"And after you found out about the stocks, that's when you started dating her seriously?" I said nodding.

"No," Charles' voice grew tense. He said, almost offended with me, "When I saw how funny you were on *The Whole Package* .... Addie and I'd been so formal with each other. I started making her laugh."

"Yeah, she said you were a stick in the mud. I didn't realize I was leaving –"

"When you were so funny, I started testing my jokes on Addie. She laughed –"

"Moving on to the stocks," I interrupted, sickened, utterly unconvinced.

"My Dad told me about the stocks a few weeks ago – before you got off the show. He told me I could be president of United Skills in January if I got them." Seeing the look on my face he added, "This arrangement had nothing to do with me asking him for the pink diamond. He didn't tell me to ask Addie to marry me or anything."

"That's the only way you can really get at them – to be a family member," I said.

227

"He's not that mercenary. He wouldn't require me to –
he's my dad," Charles said this like he needed more
convincing than I did.

"It's all too interconnected, too confusing. How could you
really know?"

"I fell in love with Addie before I knew about the stocks, I
swear," he said.

"But your dad pushed you to love her, either way."

"Maybe. He's no fool. He'll use whatever advantage
comes his way, but I do love her, I do want her to be my wife."

"What a neat little package: Addie and the stocks. Your
dad must be so proud," I snapped.

"He's transferred enough of United Skills to me that he
expects me to go after the stocks. He'd regain every penny
when the stocks split. I'd establish my foothold in the
company and make a fortune for myself, without my trust
fund."

"Addie and her dowry all coming together in the very
convenient time-frame of October—right before election," I
snapped.

"That's what my dad would like, but like you said, it's not
going happen," Charles answered calmly taking what looked
like his first deep breath in weeks.

Now confused, I asked, "What?"

"Why do you think you guys haven't met my family yet?"
Charles asked, pushing his white sleeves up further.

With just the right amount of malice, I shrugged my
shoulders. Charles said more lightly, "Besides Mom being
fanatical about *The Whole Package*. Seriously Carrie, it's going
to be uncomfortable for you."

I shrugged again with more menace in the action. Charles
quickly said, "I told my Dad I'd establish myself in some other

way. I told him I wouldn't chance my relationship with Addie to get the stocks for United Skills. When he meets you and your mom, he's going to talk you into selling me the stocks after I marry Addie. He's prepared to offer your mom an obscene amount of money for them."

"You're purposely keeping us away from each other?" I asked, squinting at Charles.

"I tried. Two weeks ago, after I asked for the pink diamond, unbeknownst to me, my dad called our club. He had it reserved for a fundraiser. He canceled so we could have the club for an engagement party instead. A day after we were engaged, Mom sent out invitations."

"Yeah, I heard she sent Mom's out too," I said. "How perfect, my dad's brother and all our influential friends show up at an engagement party so Parker Goodrich can go chumming for votes."

"Carrie, my father using your sister for votes is annoying, but that is not really what we're talking about. Can we table that until later?"

"Well, don't I feel managed."

He raised his eyebrows at me.

"Fine, Addie, with the stocks as her dowry," I said.

"At lunch on Saturday, I was being obvious about getting into your vault. I knew you could tell I had an agenda, but you can't meet my parents until this is resolved. I didn't know how to tell you guys about the stocks. I'm not a moron – I see how it looks. I thought about confessing it outright... but it makes me the bloodsucker," Charles said.

"So, you asked to see the Hawthorne's?" I accused despite he'd just confessed.

"I reminded you of your family vault. It didn't make sense – you supporting your family. You have all of these assets –

it's at least ten million in stocks. It's not publicly traded so I can't be sure, but it's significant enough to support your mom. Not to mention, you could make far more at Shades than Kimber & Stophers. You have an MBA, you know how to market. Hire Andrea, and you have your own fortune."

"You should have told us all this."

"I kept hinting about the Hawthorne's, hoping you would discover them on your own."

"That wasn't enough. You should have told me straight out. You should have come to me, asked about the holdings my mother owns that you wished to acquire."

"I didn't realize you didn't –"

"Why did you have to bring Addie into this? You proposed to her!"

"Carrie, I love her,"

"You have a crappy way of showing it, asking her to marry you while you're trying to suck all we have left out of us," I scolded.

"I need to marry her," he said, "I need her to be my wife."

"You could have waited," I said.

"I thought ... I thought if I married Addie, then after we were married I could explain."

"Then why did you tell us to look in the vault?"

"My Dad? The engagement party a week from Saturday?"

"Right," I said.

"Everything just kind of spun out of control," Charles said. He wiped his brow looking to the wooded area around our house like he didn't know what went wrong.

"You don't deserve her," I said, "She was honest with you. After she found out I was supporting the family she told you the first chance she had. It was scary for her, but she did it because it was right. And it turns out the only reason you didn't care is because we have something you want."

"Are you kidding me?" Charles drew up to his height, growing heated, "You don't get to tell me how I feel. You don't get to smear that moment. That was one of the best moments of my life. Addie was so brave. That's when I knew I wanted her as the mother of my children. I didn't care about anything but her. She told me the truth no matter what the consequences."

"And yet you couldn't do the same," I retorted.

"No," Charles said kicking a rock in front of him. He deflated. "I couldn't do the same. I couldn't tell you about the stocks because I was terrified of losing her. You came off the show early, and you were strong. I knew you were going to fight my being with Addie if you knew why I started dating her, so I panicked and asked her to marry me."

"What now?" I asked feeling so twisted around I didn't know what Charles was asking anymore.

"Mr. Wilson will cash the stocks in to the Ellis Family," Charles nodded, calming down. "They'll take 'um too. I don't see that company ever taking off – they're too introverted."

"Seriously? You don't want the stocks? You can't say you don't want the stocks." I said with a disgruntled laugh.

"Of course, I do! I see how easily I could turn the focus of the company. If I had the power of a new line of partially solar powered aircraft behind me, I could do anything I wanted to. The government sinking money into it alone would – "

"It's environmentally responsible," I said egging him on.

"Your grandpa saw it. He recognized what Jerry Ellis did, and he bought in. They have the market on a green energy source if they can figure it out. It isn't just about keeping airplanes from leaving a carbon footprint, it's so much more."

"It would make you so much money," I said tilting my head forward.

"But at what cost?"

"What?" I asked waiting for the twist that would get him the stocks and not lose face. But then Charles said:

"Addie completely trusts me. We had a crummy start to this relationship, but I will prove myself worthy of her. I'll never see the pain of distrust in her eyes. She'll never come home from the club, or some evening out where her friends all implied the only reason I married her was because I wanted those stocks. The price of those stocks is way too high. They'd hang over us our entire married life."

I analyzed him for a minute. I needed Charles to be the bad guy.

"She wants you to have them."

"Eventually, it'd hurt her. I'd never do that to her."

"So?" I asked looking for his angle.

"So, the company will revert back solely to the Ellis family, and I'll marry Addie in two months. I'm getting the better end of the deal."

"You're not going to do anything to get the stocks?" I asked.

"Nope," he said.

"No?"

"No," he repeated, "to really love her, I have to hold onto her and let go of everything else."

What could I say to that? I clenched my jaw certain he was trying to trick me.

"Well my uncle has taken an interest. Just marrying into the name will never keep the playing field level," I said desperately reaching for some other motive – some reason why Charles wasn't legitimately marrying my sister.

Charles shrugged. He didn't care?

"After the marriage, you and Addie can go after a merger or whatever. And she'll have part ownership in my dad's drawings being litigated. So even without the stocks, you're marrying into an advantage."

"Who doesn't want to marry above himself?" said Charles, his tone blanched with sarcasm. "But with all due respect, she isn't exactly marrying into a family of unknown paupers."

"She's still a Carnegie. You know the prestige that comes with that," I said knowing I was defenseless.

"It's funny. My dad said the same thing. At least we'll marry into the name. He said it looking up to you, and you say it looking down at us, either way, I don't care. I just want Addie to be my wife. I love her. We're going to be happy. You can duke it out with my dad—who's more important. I don't care," Charles said.

This stripped me raw, down to the fundamental core of what I held important. I did care too much about my last name. How ridiculous and little I felt next to this man ready to sacrifice so much for my little sister. He'd chosen his path. He must have fought to stay on his path with his dad, over and over again.

Would I ever have my own path to fight for?

"I know I'm not there now, but I promise, Carrie. I promise I will endeavor to deserve her for the rest of my life." Charles said like it was my permission he needed to marry her. Whether it was my right or not I said:

"Okay, I'll ... I can respect that."

"Okay," he said letting out a deep sigh.

We were quiet for a time, each of us processing what passed. Finally, Charles said:

"Could we not mention this conversation to anyone, except your mom and sister?"

"Sure, but why?" I asked, thinking I would like to tell Andrea how Charles may be an addition to the family after all. In a year or two. Seriously, who gets married after months?

"I'm not a coward, but I'd rather my father not know the stocks were found until after they're sold."

"Yeah, I get that," I said, "Mr. Wilson did tell us not to say anything to anyone. We'll keep it at that if your Dad ever asks. I won't even tell Addie and Mom until after we get a check. I never actually told you anyway. We never have to say you figured it out."

"If Addie brings it up, I'll ask her to trust you on this one," Charles said.

"Thanks," I said taken back.

Charles and I talked about his dad and all the pressure he put on him. We were interrupted by Addie and Mom with a brown paper bag full of little white containers. Looking at the excess of food they bought, my face tightened. I wasn't sure if we had enough money in the account to cover the Chinese food and the electric bill.

Mom caught this face as Addie parked the car. I saw her tense, thinking Addie would be heartbroken. Then I remembered my bonus for James would be deposited in the checking account in two days. That would cover the electric bill on Friday. Without meaning to, as Mom climbed out of the car, I smiled at her in such a way that all the stress in her face disappeared.

"Come on, Ma, I've got to drive back to the city. Let's get eating," I called. I felt content. I never felt the jovial high I achieved in past days, before *The Whole Package*, but I was relieved.

Addie looked confused but noticed I didn't interfere when she went to hug Charles. He wrapped his arms around her with such devotion I knew he loved her. I had no doubt he would continue to sacrifice the rest of his life for her love. Love meant sacrifice. I learned this from a trust fund kid, of all people.

I never fully explained my conversation with Charles to either Addie or Mom. The first because Addie loyally wanted Charles to have the stocks no matter what the cost. Plus, why bother admitting to Addie that Charles had been nudged into dating her?

I didn't tell Mom because she had been right – some part of me gauged my faith in love on Charles's integrity. Fortunately, Charles was good – flawed, even at fault in places, but overall a good man. If it could still work out for Addie and Charles, did Ethan and I have a chance?

If Julian had been producing my run-in with Charles, would he have ended up the hero or the villain? Instead, he turned out to be good old flawed Charles, a human like the rest of us.

CHAPTER TWENTY-EIGHT

The week of the final episode of *The Whole Package* played out much like the week before. I stayed busy doing everything in my power not to focus on what Ethan may or may not be doing.

Adam wrote me an email apologizing and assuring me that when we both calmed down we'd figure things out. I printed it out, and filed it in new folder I labeled "Restraining Order." As I did this I subconsciously fiddled with my car keys, now adorned with pepper spray. Mr. Wilson bought it for me and had it delivered to my apartment with a registered letter stating the account number and instructions on how to access a very healthy savings account accruing residuals from the stocks. He explained the IRS actually owed us almost a million dollars, so they weren't too fussed about reconciling the account. His tax attorney would clear it up for us.

Andrea asked me if I wanted to come over to watch the final episode the morning it aired. I declined.

"What if there are more messages to you?" she asked.

"You look for them, and let me know," I said, "Ethan is going to be with other women. I don't want to see that. Julian's somewhere trying to skew the end of the show so we see what he wants us to see. I'm done with his perspective. It turns out I prefer my own. It may be wrong, but at least it's mine."

"Good for you," she answered, "Plus, that means you can take care of all this Vantose paperwork." She handed me a thick folder. I stayed late to finish it all and didn't make it home until prime-time television ended.

I finally broke down about midnight and learned from the website that Ethan chose Veronica as *The Whole Package*. An invisible hand reached out and gut punched me. I didn't sleep, because the happy couple imprinted behind my eyelids started kissing every time I tried to close my eyes. Friday morning, I went into work early, but by mid-day aggressive paparazzi were hassling the building's security. Karl sent me home. I didn't even bother with my apartment and drove to Mom's.

On the drive, Julian called my cell phone and asked if we could move up our meeting to that evening. I'd totally forgotten about it. I assured him I wouldn't be back in New York until Monday. With some measure of relief, I pulled into the seemingly peaceful estate in Farmington Valley.

"Did you see it?" Mom asked when I walked through the kitchen door.

"See what?" I asked, looking at Addie.

"On the mid-morning show, Ethan was asked if for some reason, it didn't work out with Veronica, if he would pursue you again."

"What did he say?" I asked.

"He said 'yes' with every bit of energy in him. Then he realized what he said and looked all apologetic to Veronica. He pulled her up out of her chair and they walked off the stage before the interview finished."

"No way!" I said.

"He's just finished another interview and he's been back-pedaling ever since," Mom said. "He may have gotten in trouble."

"No wonder I'm getting so much attention," I said.

"We should go away for the weekend," Mom decided. I agreed, desperate to be away before the place crawled with reporters.

"We could make Old Orchard Beach by six," Addie said, "Carrie has some unfinished business up there."

"That's true," Mom said.

"Go back to Maine," I whispered. I'd only been once without my dad.

"Is Grandma Carnegie's old friend still up there?" Addie asked.

"Yes, her daughter runs the B&B now," Mom said. "I'll call her. We could stay in the villa we always stayed in with Dad and Grandma Carnegie."

It only took a half hour for us to get our stuff together. I kept my cell phone and laptop handy in the car. I asked Addie to drive so I could work. Every few minutes my cell phone buzzed. I stopped answering after the first few reporters asked me for an exclusive. Instead I stopped working to listen to every message after I let the buzzing go to voice mail. Then Addie would ask:

"Did Ethan call yet?"

"How would Ethan have my phone number?" I asked incredulously. Yet I continued to check.

As we pulled off the freeway toward the ocean, my frustration peaked. Charles called Addie, and Addie had to apologize for not keeping their date. All the simpering and way too many utterances of "I'll miss you." I was ready to strike when she hung up.

"You aren't really going to marry him in two months, are you?" I asked.

"Yep," Addie said.

"Seriously, this is ridiculous. Mom, can't you say anything?" I asked, seething.

"Carrie, I need you to understand something," Mom said, cutting into Addie's venomous reply.

"Oh, not a lecture," I said banging my head against my window pretending to try and break out of the car.

"I'll make this quick," Mom said.

"Fine," I said.

"Power versus control. I know this isn't your favorite, but it's what I know, so I will use the Bible to illustrate," she said.

"The whole Bible? Couldn't you abridge a little?" I pleaded.

"David and Goliath," she said.

"David kills Goliath," I said nodding.

"Yes, with an amazing power and self-assurance. He could do what was required of him. David is able to kill Goliath."

"He controlled Goliath?" I asked.

"No, he controlled himself. He tapped into the confidence and power within himself and God to slay the giant Goliath," Mom said. Her lips pursed like any good Sunday school teacher.

"Okay, so I have to –"

"I'm not finished," Mom said, "Years later the boy has become king. He directs armies. He has a whole land doing his bidding, and yet he cannot cover up one little indiscretion. He lost control of himself and instead feels the need to control everyone around him. The situation quickly slips out of his control, and he ends up getting a good man killed."

"That's control?" I asked.

"Controlling others is like holding the reins too tightly on a horse's neck. Eventually he'll buck."

"Some horses still canter," I said.

"Only the ones who have been thoroughly broken," she said, "To see any of God's magnificent creatures lose their power is maddening, but to see a woman broken, that is infuriating. Is that really what you wish for your sister?" Mom said.

"Of course not," I said. I looked away.

"You need to find the power that is in you, for yourself. What gives you confidence and lights up your eyes? It's time to stop trying to control what you have no right to control."

"What do I do?" I asked.

"Focus on yourself, Carrie. Take back your life so you don't feel the urge to try and control everyone else's," Mom said.

I was silent for a long time.

"I'm just scared for you, Addie. What if –"

"I get hurt, or divorced?" Addie asked.

"Yeah," I said.

"Then those are the consequences of my actions, which I will have to live through. Luckily, I have a big sister who will support me no matter what comes," she said.

"Yes, you do. I'm not above kicking Charles in the shins should you need me to," I said. She smiled at me through the rearview mirror.

I was quiet for a long time. Thinking about boundaries.

CHAPTER TWENTY-NINE

When I finally saw the ocean, it felt like bumping into an old friend I still valued but hadn't parted well with. My new memories of running with Ethan flooded me, and swirled with older memories. We turned down a frontage road. A long pier with a carnival perched on it stretched out into the water. I couldn't count how many times I walked down the pier with my dad. He'd pick me up and pretend to throw me off. Mom and Grandma Carnegie would be upset with him, but I just laughed because I was safe.

We parked in front of a lovely two-story country style home, worthy of Norman Rockwell, stuffed into a little grassy lot along the shoreline. Mom went to sit and gossip with Grandma Carnegie's old friend on the long veranda of the Bed and Breakfast. Addie and I put on our bathing suits and headed for the beach to bask in the late evening sun. Pulling my flip flops through warm sand spilling over my feet felt familiar.

Addie ran ahead and sat in a low blue-and-white striped chair provided by the villa. She shoved her bag onto the chair next to her. I didn't know if she did this because she needed to be alone, or she felt I did. I had no choice but to sit in the chairs behind hers.

I allowed my feet to cozy into the warm sand. They reached the cold wet sand beneath. The falling sun made water in the distance glimmer.

How long did I have to grieve before Addie let me sit by her? She opened a wedding magazine, but set it on her lap like she didn't really see it. Addie stared out at the ocean. I

knew what disturbed her enough so she wiped her face –
certainly not the wedding. She was brave. She remembered
what I could not. It hurt so badly to remember.

The last time we'd been on this beach our father had just
died. Mr. Wilson brought us up here while Mom oversaw our
move into her parent's house. Mr. Wilson compassionately
left us alone. After this trip, our Grandma would never allow
us to do what she deemed moping. The trip was the only
chance either of us had to mourn the loss of our father.

Addie sat in the sand next to my chair that weekend long
ago. She said nothing to me. Time after time she tried to put
her hand in mine. I wouldn't take it. Addie was only eight. I
pushed my eight-year-old sister's tiny hand away, time and
time again, refusing her efforts to commiserate with me.

Instead, I died inside refusing to feel anything.

I always held Addie's hand until that time, but never
since.

I closed my eyes feeling that same horrible way I always
felt when I thought of that weekend. Why hadn't I held her
hand?

I forced myself to remember what happened.

The image of the coffin closing on my dad plagued me –
over and over until I couldn't remember anything about my
dad. The shutting coffin shut everything else out. My life
ended, too. I couldn't stand it. I remembered being so
humiliated as they lowered him into the ground.

Humiliated?

Why had I been so humiliated?

It took me a minute to remember.

I cried. No, I bawled. I even howled a little. When they
closed the coffin for the last time at the funeral, I couldn't
breathe. The preacher had taken my breath with his final

prayer over my dad's soul. I closed my eyes and my dad was gone.

At the grave site, when they lowered him into the earth, I lost it again. Grandma leaned down, her wrinkled chin pressed against my forehead as she slid her mouth to my ear. With an arm around my shoulder as though she comforted me, her voice snapped into my head, "Do the respectable thing and be quiet. At least wait until we're back in the limousine before you sob like a baby—that's what the limousine is for. Really, you are almost fourteen years old, and still such a child. Your mother is so weak. You can no longer be."

When we came to the beach with Mr. Wilson I became a woman. I vowed to be strong. I would take care of Mom and sister. I refused to cry. While becoming a woman I refused Addie, the only thing I had to give. My hand... my comfort. There was no other moment in my life I so thoroughly hated myself for.

But then hadn't Serena taught me? My grandmother was a... was not a nice person? What was so wrong with me crying for my father? Everyone else had hugged me. Other grownups had not only hugged me, many had cried with me as if we were allied in our grief. Why then did I listen to my grandmother's poison? Why didn't I take Addie's hand?

Why did I let the only negative person in my life be my authority?

Regret overwhelmed me.

A wave rushed up the beach, in search of me. I stayed out of reach on the warm dry sand. Perhaps if I bathed in the ocean it would wash away what passed. Perhaps I could go back and hold Addie's hand. Maybe I could even forgive myself for that weekend. The ocean could take the sting of it far away from me.

I wanted the sting taken away. Guilt drenched my soul until no mere human being could bear more. Brought so low, out of humble necessity. What else could I do? I finally let the gentle whispering of the waves in. I'd apologize to Addie, instead of pretending it never happened. I'd apologize, like I had with Tess. Peace settled over me replacing guilt and agony.

My eyes pricked. I did not push the feeling down into my chest like I usually did. Deserved or not, I needed it. I wanted to cry. I needed to feel. I remembered the casket closing, lowering. I remembered the first symbolic shovel of dirt thrown on my father.

Finally, tears trickled down my cheeks beneath my sunglasses. I took the glasses off. I would openly cry for my father. I would cry for his death. Then I would give Addie my hand. I pulled my knees up to my chest and put my hand over my mouth to suppress a moan I could not contain in my chest. The tears came. I'd been saving them up for way too many years.

In that little action, I let go of my thirteen-year-old self's mistake. Relief swept over me. I had only been a child myself. But I wasn't a child anymore. It was time to set my childhood aside. I would make it right with Addie.

Determined, I walked over to my sister. I sat next to Addie's chair in the sand. I took her hand. Addie turned, startled from her repose. She clung to the hand I offered.

"Hey sweet Adeline, can I see what you are looking at?" I asked humbly, not even trying to conceal my red-rimmed eyes. I wouldn't be embarrassed by my tears. They were for my father.

"Oh…um…I was just trying to get a head start on planning the wedding," Addie said. Flustered she fiddled with the magazine on her lap.

"It's the way Charles's mom has just taken over planning the engagement party."

"If you want I'll talk to her for you, tell her to back off," I said squeezing her hand. Addie had told me the whole story on the way up in the car. I simply nodded and returned to obsessing about Ethan. Now, I dismissed my own pain. I engaged in Addie's planning.

"Hey, I know this amazing florist in New York," I said. "She's from generations of florists. She's really artistic. It wouldn't hurt to give her career a boost. I wouldn't chance it, but Addie, she's talented."

"Sure," Addie agreed. A little tentatively she asked, "Can you find me her phone number as soon as we get back so I can get it done?"

"I'll set it up," The new me laughed. A simple phone number would never do. "We'll go together, next week. You can come into the city and we'll have lunch to celebrate your registering for classes as an interior designer. It'll be fun."

Addie laughed a spasm, diving into her bag for the phone Charles gave her as an engagement present, so she could be on a family plan with him.

"Your electronic leash," I said.

"Jealous," she said.

"Oh please! Charles would bribe me with one if I said I'd stop teasing him."

Out of nowhere Addie said:

"Carrie, you know I'm getting married in two months, whether you like it or not, right?"

"I don't agree with it, but I'll respect your decision," I said.

245

"Thanks," she said. "You're my maid of honor, so you have to be on board."

"Ahh, thanks, Addie. I think we may have to say matron of honor, it sounds a little more spinster, doesn't it?

"No, matron means you're married. But then again Ethan's free now, and two months is a long time. You may be a matron by then."

When I made a little noise to show I wasn't amused, Addie laughed.

We sat silent for a while looking out at the lighthouse on the distant peninsula.

"I'm sorry for not holding your hand that weekend. I'm sorry I kinda checked out after Dad died."

"Do you remember those first nights living at Grandma's?" Addie asked.

"I try not to," I admitted.

"I had ... accidents, you know, at night. You cleaned me up, put me in bed with you and quietly told the maid to clean up my bed in the morning. Neither Mom nor Grandma ever knew."

"Oh, well, but I mean that weekend, when I wouldn't –"

"Let it go, Carrie, it was two days. After that, you snuggled with me every night, drowning out the sound of Mom's tears. You took the blame for everything with Grandma. I'd make a mess, or forget to close drawers. Whatever I did and she deemed wrong, you'd take all the blame. She was so mean to you. Every time she called you disorganized, it was for something I did. When I heard you tell Ethan you were disorganized, it broke my heart that you still believed her. It was me."

"No, it was her. She was a ridiculous, malicious woman who never grew up. Please, don't blame yourself."

"Only if you promise not to blame yourself – only if you promise to let go of that time," Addie insisted.

"I'll try," I said.

We sat silently while I remembered all the times I'd stood in front of my sister so my Grandmother couldn't get at her. Maybe I hadn't abandoned her after all. Maybe that's why I still felt an overwhelming need to protect her. As if she could read my mind, Addie said:

"I'm grown woman now. I don't need you to stand in front of me anymore."

"Okay, I'll try," I said watching the ocean roll as if it were the only thing unaffected by time, the only mother that didn't become obsolete to the lives it supported. I was hit with a need to bathe in something so immortal.

"Let's go body surfing," I said.

"The water's too cold," Addie said. Her eyes followed a little girl with swimsuit straps falling off her shoulders carrying a bucket of water for the moat around her sandcastle.

"I think you're scared," I said.

"Whatever," Addie countered, pulling off her ivory straw hat and dumping it in the chair as I stood up. Addie was running toward the surf before I could slide my feet out of my flip flops. I chased Addie onto the firm, wet sand the color of dark brown sugar streaked in places with colors of light brown sugar.

I passed Addie who gradually worked her way into the surf. The ocean sent goose bumps up my legs as I charged into it. Despite my cavalier attitude, I paused at the cold waves lapping over my knees.

"Cold, Carrie?" Addie yelled passing me.

I laughed and ran out into the waves. I dove chest first into the water. The water was so cold it knocked the air out of me. I stood up and spit the taste of brine out of my mouth. Addie, still walking, made it out further than I.

"Are you okay?" she called back to me.

"Of course. I've been doing this since I was a little girl."

We egged each other out until we stood shoulder deep, closer to the sandbar island than the shore. We had to jump so swells of water didn't swamp us.

Suddenly the water curled as if draining. The water leveled for just a moment at my waist, pulling me out to sea. Another wave crashed over my body smashing into the back of my head and pushing me under water. I thrashed in the current, but was unable to swim against its force. After the wave passed, I came up, gasping for air. Panicked, I searched for my little sister.

I found Addie standing ten feet in front of me. Her exhilarated face turned to the setting sun. Addie glowed with pleasure. She twisted to share her exuberance with me but stopped short when she noticed the panic in my eyes.

"Come on, Carrie, you have to jump above it all," she called over the waves. I nodded, remembering, as a wave came down. I jumped and mechanically lifted my feet until my body was riding the top of the water. I started swimming, leaving the current underneath me. I did it perfectly while my amber hair swirled through the water like seaweed. I've always known how to ride waves. It had been so long since I allowed myself to get in the water.

After a few strong waves, I laid next to Addie on the shore laughing while the surf rhythmically came up to tickle our legs.

"You too tired to go again?" Addie called as a little girl ran by, her footprints washing out as soon as she made them. I couldn't answer. The little girl ran to her father, who lifted her up and tossed her into a wave. Oh, how intensely I loved my daddy. I shed another tear for him. I would cry for him whenever I wanted to. It felt better than keeping the pain bottled up, relieving the heavy nothing in my chest.

I jumped up and grabbed Addie's hand. I lifted her up and forward into the water. I yelled with much more gusto than the poet envisioned, "Whatever. I have promises to keep, and miles to go before I sleep."

I'd adjusted to the water; it no longer felt too cold.

CHAPTER THIRTY

Fortunately, Karl kept me busy the next week. Despite having to answer no to the question, "Have you heard from Ethan," time and again, I stayed busy so I couldn't give any extended answer. A new power sustained me. I missed Ethan. I wanted so badly to see him again. I was sad he didn't make an effort to contact me, but I felt supported in my sorrow. It no longer threatened to swamp me. Its rhythm and currents were familiar. The unseen power I gained by forgiving myself buoyed me up. Even in the most vulnerable times when it felt like I lived only for the moment I would see Ethan again, I knew I would make it through the ordeal either way.

With Adam gone, I found work much more satisfying. I wouldn't even mind doing it for a few more years while I earned a teaching certificate.

I finally called Julian back mid-day Monday. I told him I couldn't meet until Thursday morning before the reunion show. I couldn't manage to get time off work before then. To my surprise, Julian agreed.

I refused to reschedule my lunch date with Addie. Wednesday afternoon we waded through Manhattan traffic to a corner flower shop surround by high-rises. Addie behaved agreeably, and the arrangements were beautiful. Addie took home some samples and drawings I did of her ideas made credible by the florist.

Before we parted, Addie gave me an extra invitation to her engagement party on Saturday.

"Just in case there's someone specific at the reunion show you want to invite."

I hesitated, but took the thick envelope from her.

"All's fair in love and war," she said, tilting her head forward at me.

"Um hum," I said, dropping her off at the little BMW convertible Charles bought her. She left it in my parking space because I point blank refused to get into it.

For the reunion show, I took the whole day off work, even though I didn't have to be at the studio until four. I wanted to get my meeting with Julian over in the morning so I could have some time to myself before I performed. Heavy traffic slowed me on my way to the studio. I decided it was time to figure out the subway. I'd been too intimidated to try when I first came to New York.

At the studio, a pretty blonde lady – Julian's secretary – met me in the parking garage. She walked me down long hallways to the innermost belly of the building. She randomly talked to herself, and I quickly figured Julian drove the poor woman mad. As she walked me to the loneliest part of the building, I tried to decide how a therapist would interpret everything she said to her imaginary friends. Then I realized she wore a Bluetooth in her ear under her puffy hair.

As Julian's secretary slowed in front of a door, my stomach knotted.

"Hey, where's Patrick?" I thought to ask, wishing for a friend.

"He's no longer with the company," the woman informed me curtly.

Was that my fault?

I entered Julian's office with a feeling of foreboding. To my surprise a friendly, booming voice greeted me.

251

"Carrie, how are you?" Lance called from the side of Julian's desk.

"Hey Lance, I'm fine, how are you?" I asked as Lance kissed my cheek.

"Exhausted," he replied. "I'll be glad when tonight is over. You're tired out from the week before – all the location filming – and then this last week it's back-to-back publicity. engagements. We interview with the local morning shows all over the country; it's a nightmare how busy they keep us. We interviewed a few extra times trying to make up for Ethan's little blunder."

"What blunder?" I asked. Was this the last week of the show? Hadn't it been a week ago? All this confusion happened inside my head while Julian cut across Lance explaining.

"Carrie, come in. You're late. There's a lot to talk about." Julian put away his phone and came from behind his desk. He held out his hand to me. I allowed him to take mine briefly.

"You've been avoiding me," Julian stated.

"It is possible."

"Ah, that wit gets me every time," Julian said with a spurting, loud chortle.

"What did you need to see me for, Julian?"

"The head of the network wants to meet you. We'll have to talk fast before he gets here," Julian said checking his watch.

I frowned at Lance, who looked just as bewildered.

"Why? Is he single?" I asked, "Because I assure you, I've had quite a few offers lately. Thanks anyway."

"It isn't anything like that... we've found –"

Someone knocked at the door.

"Come in," Julian called trying to keep the annoyance out of his voice. A medium-built man in his mid-thirties with slicked back hair, dressed impeccably, entered. Warily I stepped back. I could tell by the eager look on his face that he wanted something from me.

"This is Richard Blanchard. Well, do you already know him? He is part of your circle in Hartford, I think," Julian observed.

I stretched to remember hearing of Richard Blanchard before *The Whole Package*. Finally, I said, "You'd have to ask Adeline. I've never been a part of all that." Then turning to Richard, I said, "Blanchard. That doesn't sound familiar. But only the old family names ever really do."

I had not meant this as rude. It was simply true. I heard all the old family names since my childhood. I refused to believe myself above or below him. I was just Carrie, and I'd never heard his last name. Despite my intentions, I saw Richard flinch.

"Well, then it's a pleasure to meet you," Richard said. He nodded coolly.

"And you," I nodded back.

"I believe my family's coming to your sister's engagement party Saturday night at the club."

"You'll have to introduce me," I said.

"You're quite the celebrity," Richard said coldly.

"I don't even know what to think about that," I said.

"It's funny what a little breeding and a good sense of humor can do for you."

I nodded again and looked at Lance who had taken a sharp breath in. He looked like he suddenly figured something out.

"Carrie don't –" he started to say.

"Lance, I need something off the printer. Go ask Marge to get it, and then you can go get some sleep before tonight. As you're so exhausted," Julian said.

"I'll come with you," I called feeling vulnerable.

"Carrie – how rude of me – have a seat," Julian said. He followed with his fake chortle and I had to wonder if it hurt his throat.

Lance walked out. I sat down gingerly hoping the chair Julian offered didn't have a pin on it or a broken leg. When nothing poked me, I allowed my entire body weight to sit and then tensely shifted to the back of the chair.

"Aren't Ethan and Veronica just lovely together?" Julian asked. "I always feel so satisfied when I can bring two such charming people together."

I scowled. Julian was playing with me. Richard must have noticed this, too, because he said more politely,

"Can we get you anything?"

"What do you two want?" I asked. Both men started, taken back. They looked at each other confused.

"I know I should sit here politely and wait for it to come out in your own creative way. But I assure you, nothing you can offer is going to tempt me. Please, just spill it."

"You aren't quite the underhanded, charm school graduate, are you?" Richard said.

"Again, you're going to have to talk to my sister, Addie, if you want the charm school act. I've never had a knack for it, though my grandma sure tried to teach me," I said using Julian's fake laugh. Richard cracked a smile at my fairly good imitation.

Julian was going to say something, no doubt to move the conversation back to his level of manipulation. Richard, liking me again for my lack of pretense, said, "We have an opportunity for you."

"What kind?" I asked.

"We've had to cancel a primetime show. We may take *The Whole Package* into the Fall line-up. We'd need a really powerful pull, though. If you were to be the judge, we'd get the ratings to justify giving *The Whole Package* the spot."

"Not a chance," I said without drawing breath.

Richard smiled at me like he expected that answer.

"I figured you pretty much walking off the show was proof enough of you'd not want back on," Richard said. "Julian said he could interest you, though."

I turned to Julian. He didn't look pleased.

"Don't say no just yet," Julian said, "Marge is bringing in a contract for you to look at. You'll like it. It'd mean almost five hundred thousand dollars in revenue for you. Just think what that could do for your sick mom."

I glared at Julian. Richard looked at Julian with a warning in his eyes. Did Richard know about the MS? Had he already told all his Hartford friends about it? I took a deep breath and pushed away the panic this thought brought.

My mother's illness would have to come out eventually. In fact, having a support system might be nice for Mom. Poor Addie couldn't do everything for her now that Mom couldn't drive. I couldn't even remember why we didn't tell people.

After this uncomfortable pause, Marge brought in the contract. She handed it to Julian. In one motion he put it in a manila folder from his desk and then made to hand it to me. I folded my arms and cowered away from the contract.

"We have a quiet room set up for you to review the contract so you can think. I'll come get you before the reunion show. We'll split a cab to the theater. I can answer any questions you have," Julian said.

"You're not even going to pay for the cab?" I teased.

"It's only to the Upper West –"

"You know, Carrie," Richard interrupted. "Right now, you can write your own ticket, if you wanted to host a talk show or… you know with your education and technique, I bet you could do a kid's art show."

"Like Bob Ross?" I asked.

"Educational and fun, but maybe not the afro. You have the training. You'd be great on something like that." Then, amused, he looked at Julian and said, "that is if you've decided not to do *The Whole Package*."

"I have, but I might be open to a kid's art show, if you can afford me." I shrugged at Richard, grinning. I still refused to take the folder Julian held hanging mid-air.

Julian persisted: "*The Whole Package* is only a few months' commitment. It could launch her –"

"Maybe we can talk more Saturday night, Richard. I'm expected at lunch in an hour somewhere else. I only promised Julian a half hour. I've made other arrangements for the rest of my morning. I'll be at the theater by four as I am contractually obligated to be," I said, standing.

I had combed through my contract, calling Charles when I didn't understand something the night before. I resolved never to be so caught off guard by a piece of paper again.

Julian's eyes flashed, perhaps because, for the first time in the history of his contracts, one had been used against him.

"Good luck tonight," Richard said.

"It's been a pleasure. It'll be nice to actually know someone at Addie's party," I said extending my hand out to him.

256

Richard paused and stared at my hand. In an instant, I was transformed back before my father died. I was young and innocent. I could see it in Richard's eyes, what I saw in others eyes so many times in those days. At Grandma's parties, many of the "lowers" or "fillers," as Grandmother called them, expected to be treated inferiorly by me. And I never would answer their expectations.

Now no Grandma cringed at my outstretched hand, often my inducement then. No rewarding smile from my Grandfather. Oh, how I loved my Grandfather, the crinkle at the corners of his eyes when he smiled at me. No dad to see my joke and roll his eyes at me. No sparkling Mom in the background. Mom, now tired and careworn, had once been bright and people craved to be around her. I inherited this quality from Mom. Addie did not shine like I did. Why was that?

When Mom was pure light, I had not given into Grandma's manipulations. Grandma had not a sick mom to hold over my head.

Grandma hadn't forced Gordon on me as a freedom. Let Grandma pick me out a man? Twelve-year-old Carrie would laugh. She would have made fun of the idea until my dad joined in and it was obnoxious to Addie and Mom. With no one left to tell me how to react, or who to be, I chose for myself. I wanted to be a lady – I wanted to be powerful!

Richard released my hand after a rather long and vigorous shake. I was done losing myself. I turned to walk out the door.

"Say, Carrie…" Richard called.

"Yes?"

"Will you dance with me Saturday night?"

I could see Julian grimacing behind Richard. I smiled even more graciously than the situation dictated.

"With pleasure," I agreed.

Then Richard, who must have felt the toxic stance of Julian behind him, said, "Here, let me get the door for you."

We chatted politely all the way to the elevator. My mind was too occupied with the past to hear much of what passed until Richard said, "See you Saturday."

I nodded and climbed into the elevator. Before the door closed I heard him address his mother on his cell phone. He didn't see me put my hand out to stop the doors from closing.

"Mother, you'll never guess who I've engaged to dance with me Saturday night."

"No Caroline Carnegie... she came into the station ...."

I quickly let the doors shut so he didn't notice me still there. I did try not to laugh – I'm not claiming perfection in my transformation. Somewhere beyond my amusement I did wonder if it were people like Richard that had inflated my ego in the first place.

I arranged to tour the art gallery of an old college friend who'd been calling me since I came off the show. I bought a painting for my apartment. For the first time in my adult life, I spent my money how I liked. I relished the experience. A part of James Hall's bonus money went to a painting of the ocean I found intoxicating. My friend offered to sell my art. Painting regularly now, I told her I'd bring a few pieces by in the next week or so.

How many options opened to me when I had enough sense to look for them!

CHAPTER THIRTY-ONE

When I reached the theater, I met Becky pacing back and forth in a makeshift group dressing room. Mirrors on rolling tables lined the middle of the room with folding chairs in front of them. Free standing hanging bars held outfits, turning the room into a maze. Becky sat me in a chair, and instructed the stylist how she wanted my hair done.

"Becky, I saw you're still in the running to win," I said to her.

"I've heard the same of you," she said with a wink that made me smile. She relaxed, and the tension between us from the show disappeared. Until Serena came in and sat next to me that is, then Becky excused herself. She made no effort to hide her escape.

"Carrie, it's so good to see you," Serena said in her most syrupy way.

I looked at her, tired, as if I were about to play a board game with a toddler for the millionth time and I couldn't even stand to look at it. Serena didn't notice. She did notice everything else.

"You shouldn't cross your legs; your make-up is going to be off balance, not to mention your hair," Serena informed. "Have you seen the trend you started? If I were you, I'd never wear that brown dress again, you know, the one with the rose? You can buy it at any department store lately. What's Rebecca Lynn – you know that's what Becky's going by now – putting you in?"

I laughed a little, pointing to a grayish blue dress hanging behind my mirror.

"Erin, you look so cute," I called past Serena, "Didn't you have to grow your hair back out for your dance company? It looks like you cut it shorter!"

Erin came up to me, her hair shorter than it had been before. Totally ignoring her once proclaimed best friend, Serena, she kissed my cheek.

"I'll need the chair," the stylist said to Serena who was already dressed. Serena stood up but didn't leave. Erin sat down.

"I'm choreographing for a different dance company," she said. "I just slick it back for performances."

We spoke for a while about her new opportunities, and I was proud of how well she worked through the ruins of her life after she left the show.

"There's something about how you choose to react," I finally said.

"Yeah," she said glancing at Serena.

"I worried about you after the show. I'm so glad it worked out okay," I said.

"The publicity actually helped me in more ways than one," Erin said.

"How so?" I invited, ignoring Serena clicking her tongue.

"I started dating this guy, he's amazing. He's a sports psychologist; we have so much in common. He watched the show –"

"Um..." I gave her a skeptical look and she defended.

"No, he watched because he was supposed to be Ethan."

"What?" I asked.

"He met with Julian and everything. Six months before the show started, he went in to sign his contract. They dumped him. Said he wasn't right for the show."

"Really," I said.

"Yeah, so he was curious to see who took his place. Then after he saw me, he kept watching," she said with a blush.

"You guys have a lot in common?" I asked.

"Everything," she gushed.

"That's interesting," I said trying to understand what that meant. Erin looked up to see her designer calling her and said, "Oh, gotta go! The benefit of short hair."

I smiled and waved in response, feeling envy at the pull of the curling iron going back in for tighter curls.

A few minutes later Tess came bouncing toward me jubilantly.

"Hey Tess, what's up?" I said.

"Look." Tess shoved a piece of paper in my face.

"It is our pleasure," I read. "Tess, you got accepted to the...Center for Culinary Arts at Lincoln – oh look, that's in Cromwell; that's by Mom's house. Impressive, Tess."

"Yeah, your mom said I could live with her," she said looking tentatively at me.

"It might really help Addie out," I said.

My head yanked back by the curling iron.

"As long as you're okay with it," Tess said.

"It's Mom's house. If she invited you, I think it's a great idea," I said.

She shook her head in the negative to her designer, instead handing her a black halter top meant to cover her whole body. I pointed at an elegant black dress on the rack.

"It's only for a while. I can't mooch off your mom forever. I'll always come for Sunday brunch, though," Tess added. She grinned at me as her designer brought the black silk dress that hung from the shoulders to accentuate Tess's curves in a more mature way.

"It must be nice having a cook for brunch, huh, Carrie? Especially living in Harford, it's near expected to have some kind of hired help," Serena cut in.

Tess and I both looked at Serena, shocked. How did she know I didn't have a cook? This shot was aimed at both Tess and me.

Tess fired back: "Some of us can cook better than hired help."

Serena didn't pretend to look hurt like in the manor house when Tess insulted her.

"At least the world isn't calling me a whore," Serena fired back at Tess. "What you did to poor Carrie – I can't believe you even showed your face here."

I about started in but Tess said, "She's not worth it," and then she shifted her chair so her back was to Serena and said, "Carrie, where's Ethan?"

"I have no clue," I said.

Ethan, Veronica and even Sandra were not in the makeshift dressing room with us. Neither were they funneled into a boxed-off space at the side of the stage, that looked like a corral, where we waited after we were dressed. After a while, we heard the audience shuffle in.

I noticed a trend among all the contestants. We'd all grown up some. With the exception of Serena, who would forever be a reality show star caught up in drama and games. Even one of the drunken sisters confided she attended AA weekly.

The show finally started by giving out the prize to my designer Rebecca Lynn. She won a chance to design a dress for an award show presenter. I liked the picture they used of me the day I left the show. I glowed, almost as if on fire from the inside out.

262

My stomach started to tighten after the drunken sisters went out on stage. Everyone sat with heads cocked upwards watching them interview on a little screen. We all looked like pretty ponies waiting for our turn to canter. I slipped out and went on an expedition.

I stepped into a bustling walkway back stage. I pretended, of course, I should be walking away, and no one stopped me. I made my way through the area where we'd been primped. I had noticed a drinking fountain just outside the stage doors.

I walked in a confident way that, every time I took a step, made my legs spring out from underneath the jagged edges of my dress. My hair sat up on the back of my head in a messy bun. Straying strands of loose curls bounced down my face and back. I looked sheik, and it felt good.

I found the water fountain. I took a refreshing gulp of water and heard someone exclaim my name. With cold water dribbling down my chin, I straightened to see Veronica. I stared at her. What do you say to someone like that?

"Hey, how are you?" I said.

"Stressed kind of, a lot of pressure, you know," she said visibly shaking.

"I'm sure."

I couldn't say anything else. An unpleasant anger bubbled in my chest. I tried to push it back down. I made a silent resolution I wouldn't cry in front of Veronica. I had to leave. How did I leave?

Before either of us could think of something else to say, Julian came out into the hall.

"Oh Veronica, Ethan's getting lonely; he's asking for you," he said as if addressing her, but he watched me. My heart started beating in hurt torrents. I wanted to curl up in a ball and cry. I would not cry for Julian. Oh, where was Ethan? I needed him. I needed to hit him, or kiss him. What I would give just to see him again.

"Sorry... I'm so sorry... I just needed a drink... ur, some air," Veronica said.

"I need you to stay where you're supposed to be, Veronica," Julian continued. "You shouldn't be wandering either, Carrie. We all know how quickly you get lost."

"I'm not lost if I know where I am," I snapped.

"You aren't where you should be," he said, taken back. His conceit overwhelmed me. Just because I didn't stay where he wanted me didn't make me lost. I was where I wanted to be.

"I know Serena was so excited to see you, Carrie," Julian said. His phone started buzzing in his hand. "As for you, Veronica, I'm sure Carrie wants nothing to do with you. Go back to Ethan. Carrie, stay for a minute. I need to talk to you."

Then he turned his back to us sticking a finger in his ear so he could hear his phone call.

My seething anger dispelled. Julian's spell over me broke. I wouldn't see his picture. Veronica didn't look like a tart who, as soon as I left, moved in on the man I loved. She looked like a beaten pony that couldn't even canter properly.

Demoralized with tears welling in her eyes, Veronica turned from me and started walking away. I came to a crossroad. Could I be kind to her? Could I forgive her? I felt lava-like anger for Julian and Adam. I thought that's how I'd feel about Veronica, too. But when it came right down to it, I didn't. Not at all.

Why did Veronica have to be so droopy?

"Hey Ron," I called.

I caught up to Veronica, who'd walked down the hall. I placed a generous hand lightly on her shoulder and whispered in her ear,

"It's almost over. Julian only has as much power over you as you give him. I know it doesn't seem that way, but it is."

I went to let go of Veronica. She threw her arms around my neck and held tightly, crushing my straying curls into my back. Startled, I patted Veronica's back tentatively. I could feel hot tears on my cheek caking both our make-up.

"I didn't mean too ... you lost a bet – you were laughing at me ..." Veronica sobbed. Her whole body shook.

"I never laughed at you. I always thought more highly of you than of myself," I whispered back.

"No, you shouldn't have... I ... I didn't mean to...."

Neither of us meant to become reality TV stars. My eyes began to water. I remembered only too well shoving Tess in public, trying to prove to her Ethan was mine.

Veronica didn't know which way to look or where to set her hands without instruction. Could she seduce Ethan away from me? Was Ethan ever either of ours, or did he belong to Julian?

"Come on, Ron stop that, come on now," I said patting her back.

"I hate myself," she said.

"I remember that night sitting on your bed, lecturing you about love like I had a clue. You were so humble about it. Everything you did was so kind. You are *The Whole Package –* "

"No, I'm not," Veronica insisted.

"You deserved to win –"

"I didn't win anything. I am a poor man's Carrie is all.... I'm sorry I didn't walk out of the house with you."

"No, Veronica, you deserve the money. You always did."

"I don't care about it, it's the pity prize now. I'm so sorry, I'd give back every penny if I could undo –"

"You forgave me. I can do the same for you. I'm sorry too, for, you know, always telling you what to do on the show. I was such a self-righteous jerk," I said. I felt a freedom in my heart from wiping my mistake. And I let it go.

"You're apologizing to me?" Veronica said, flabbergasted, pulling away a little to see if I was serious.

"I'm trying to be *The Whole Package* too," I joked.

At this point, Julian stopped talking on his phone. He pursued us down the hall – annoyed at the picture before him. I could hear someone still talking to him through the phone. I quickly reached into my purse and pulled out the invitation. I turned and handed it to Veronica.

"I want to invite you and Ethan to my sister's engagement party Saturday night."

Then in an act of pure charity, I let go of Ethan. I set all speculation aside. Veronica was my friend again. This was no longer a reality show. Ethan announced they were dating exclusively. In real life, I didn't go after my friend's boyfriend.

"Just to show you there are no hard feelings," I said.

"Really?" Veronica said She looked unsurely at the invitation.

"Sure. Could be stuffy, though," I said, trying to deter Veronica from actually coming. I realized a moment too late it would be uncomfortable watching Veronica with Ethan. I could be Veronica's altruistic friend from afar. A feeling of being inhospitable crept over me, so I finished by saying, "Free food, though, right?"

"Yeah, especially since both Ethan and my contract expire at midnight tomorrow," Veronica said. She smiled coyly at me like she just told a secret. I shrugged. I should feel awful for being such a pushover, but I didn't.

"You're right. I bet Ethan is going to want to see me," Veronica said to Julian, "I'm sure he'll be thrilled. He loves high society parties."

I laughed, remembering Ethan being put off by anything money or status driven. Veronica shrugged. She and I both wore the same unsure, forced smile. Veronica didn't know how Ethan felt any more than I did. But then, how could she? She was engulfed in Julian's world.

Julian had forced us onto opposite teams of dodgeball again. Neither of us wanted to hit the other with a hard ball.

"Carrie, you've got to get back to the staging area. You are going on soon—but we need to talk after the show," Julian snapped. He pushed me off toward my door. I didn't go.

"Veronica, we'll just stick you back with Sandra to get your makeup fixed. Ethan said he needed a break from the ladies anyway."

Veronica paled. Julian turned her and she started walking away.

"Tell her I said hi," I said. Veronica looked at me, but did not look amused. Sandra must not be taking her defeat well. I gave half a wave and walked back where I came from.

"Hey, where've you been?" Tess asked as I entered the corral near the theater stage.

"I needed a drink."

"They just got back from commercial – Erin went on."

"Did I miss anything?"

"Serena got a whole segment to herself. She said how sorry she was that she bashed on you. She said the two of you are best friends. Was that during the week I went home?"

"Okay, something weird is going on," I said.

"Are you all right?" Tess asked, looking perplexed at the smear of mascara on my cheek with no trail to have made it. I didn't have a chance to answer. A woman began frantically touching up my make-up. Then she pushed me out a door to the entryway of the stage.

CHAPTER THIRTY-TWO

Lights shined in my face. People in the room cheered. Their cheers echoed, disorienting me.

"We love you, Carrie," a group of girls yelled.

I smiled and waved. Everything happened so fast. And yet, making nice with Veronica had settled peace in the space around my heart that fear often claimed.

I sat on a love seat next to the hostess, Samantha Prowers. She departed from her suit and wore an orange spaghetti strap dress with a white sash around the middle. Her sleek short hair sat flat to her head as it always did and she looked like a paper doll whose dress was changed.

"Carrie, how did you feel when you heard Ethan declare that if things didn't work out between him and Veronica, he'd be coming after you?" Samantha asked, getting down to business. A calm washed over me. I smiled so well my eyes glittered.

"I don't know. Do you think he meant it in like a psycho-Norman Bates kind of way? Because I didn't actually hear him say it, and when Mom repeated it to me, it kind of sounded that way. I have to wonder how extensive a background check the network does on *The Whole Package* contestants."

Everyone laughed before I finished talking.

"How do you feel about seeing Ethan for the first time since the show?" she asked.

"I don't really know. I guess if I have an epiphany when I see him, I'll let you know," I said.

Samantha laughed. She rehashed a lot of my time on the show, and again brought up my leaving so suddenly. I

269

answered each question with clarity and little emotion. Then she moved onto what I'd been doing since the show ended. I sat poised for her questions.

It was fortunate because Samantha wanted to break me. She leaned in with a glint of determination in her cobalt eyes.

"On a different note, we've heard that your family is in financial ruin?" Samantha asked smugly, her arched eyebrows raised in mock concern. "Will your sister marry quickly enough to save your family home, or will you have to sell?"

"First of all, I'm not sure what that has to do with *The Whole Package*, and secondly who is spewing that garbage?" I asked.

"A very reliable source," Samantha returned, flushing.

"Well Samantha, I've heard a reporter of your caliber should always get at least two sources to confirm their facts."

"Uh, this isn't 60 minutes," she said.

"If it were, you would have done your homework and known Mom's a millionaire many times over. What about you? Do you make a healthy salary?"

"I do all right."

Samantha laughed in a stammer looking at the camera. She cleared her throat.

"How do you feel about your sister being engaged to United State Congress hopeful Parker Goodrich's son? I understand you're not happy about the engagement?"

"Charles is a good man, the kind of person you hope your little sister will marry." As I answered, I surprised myself because I knew it was true.

Samantha looked like she had a lot of other questions but couldn't read me. She didn't want anything else thrown back at her. Giving up, she turned the interview to what she had no difficulty proving – as her source had nothing to do with Julian.

"I heard through the grapevine you'll be meeting our own network head Richard Blanchard at your sister's engagement party. He's very eligible."

"He seems nice," I said.

"He is," Samantha said. She lightly touched her chest with a hint of envy in her voice, "You're a favorite with so many. It's a relief to hear you've moved on from Ethan."

She turned before I could respond to this and said into the camera, "We'll return with Tess after these messages."

"Seriously? Your family isn't in financial trouble?" Samantha snapped as soon as the camera turned off.

"No, we had to sell some stocks last week, but it's not like we didn't have them to sell. Not to brag, but these earrings I'm wearing could buy me a house in Middle America."

Samantha frowned, "Of course, you have assets up this side of the coast and down the other. How did I not catch that?"

"Who told you we're in financial ruin?" I asked.

"Julian's new assistant," Samantha said pointing to the wing.

Adam. Adam stood next to the side entrance of the stadium seating that climbed the back of the theater, wearing Patrick's old headset. Of course. Adam. What had Julian offered him for the intimate details of my life? What's more, what did Adam gain by working with Julian?

"I wonder who will win that pissing war," I said, smiling to myself. How fitting the two men punish each other. Nature's little spankings were on the way. No one can outrun karma.

Samantha looked taken back.

"Excuse me," I shrugged. Samantha Prowers nodded; amused, she warmed up to me. As if I were her equal and no longer a reality TV star, she said: "I don't know about that, but Julian is going to be given a mouthful. I didn't become a nationally recognized reporter to be given false facts about society page gossip. Sorry about that."

"No big deal."

"We need you to make way for Tess," a cameraman informed me.

I made to move, but Samantha said quickly "Is there any truth to Tess living with you?"

"Well, she comes over on the weekends, and she may stay with us when she starts the prestigious cooking school she just enrolled in."

"Good for her," Samantha said bending over her notes and writing quickly.

"In fact, they never showed it, but she cooked for us all the time on the show."

Samantha nodded still focused on her notes, scratching out some and quickly scribbling new ones. Adam smiled and waved at me like we were friends. I nodded in disbelief, then quickly moved to a chair downstage next to Serena. The contestant's chairs made a v shape on the stage. Erin sat across from me. I was stuck looking at Samantha with Adam leering in the background. Serena perched next to me, whispering in my ear. I could paint this.

CHAPTER THIRTY-THREE

Tess's interview stayed positive. Tess represented herself honestly, instead of having to be on the defensive. Samantha openly attributed the improvement to spending time with my family. To my surprise, Tess agreed.

I didn't.

Tess hadn't changed too much. Samantha finally saw beyond her overbearing sexuality. Her funny, amazing personality showed through as a beautiful woman when the whole came together instead of just one blaring piece of her.

Sandra interviewed next. She spoke bitterly about Ethan and Veronica. She complained about the unfair nature of the show, but never illuminated how. Samantha attributed Sandra's attitude entirely to the woman scorned theory. Again, I didn't agree. Being on the show so long, Sandra must have noticed the unethical way Julian ruled his little world. When the commercial finally came, Sandra smoldered, and looked close to tears.

During the commercial Adam started in my direction like he wanted to talk to me. Then he put his hand to his ear like someone pounded on his ear drum. I couldn't see Julian, but the pissing war was a go. Ah, how fortuitous two such people working together are so counterproductive – Adam left me alone, and Julian couldn't reach me.

Veronica came on next. She smiled, but fidgeted like someone shocked her with electricity every few seconds. As she spoke, she sounded rehearsed like she'd been slipped a copy of the questions with a specific answer key. Veronica looked almost like a little kid who had to go to the bathroom–

but she held herself with more composure than in her first days on camera.

Samantha brought me up as competition to Veronica. Thankful for our rendezvous in the hall, I smiled sweetly at Veronica who said, "Norman Bates may be too strong a comparison, Care."

I laughed. Neither Veronica nor I were questioned too enthusiastically about our love triangle. It would come. I tried my best to harden my outside, put up my wall. If a wall, a fake façade, claimed a place in my life, this was that place.

At one point, Samantha asked Veronica what happened when Ethan pushed the camera out of their hotel room after she and Ethan had worked together so well to save that baby boy's life.

"We were exhausted. We played a round of cards and ate all the chocolate dipped strawberries," Veronica said easily. "It was fun."

"Ah, you aren't going to kiss and tell," Samantha said with raised eyebrows.

Veronica just laughed. Fear gripped my heart. Had they... and if they did, what did that mean? Then and there I decided I didn't want a man who didn't equate sex to commitment. But then I'd already given up on Ethan anyway.

During the next commercial break, Julian came out and it appeared that he and Samantha were having it out. Samantha half pointed to me in an angry whisper and Julian snapped back. After Samantha made an angry face they seemed to have come to a compromise.

Then it happened.

Samantha asked the audience to welcome Ethan. All the other women on the stage turned as he came in, but I couldn't. I stayed facing forward. I noticed a young woman in the audience I recognized vaguely but couldn't remember where from. She waved to me. I waved back remembering I'd seen her just after I'd gotten off *The Whole Package*. Samantha gave her tickets to the show. She couldn't be more then fifteen or sixteen, but she felt like a friend when she waved harder with such a nice smile.

I couldn't prolong the inevitable forever. Out of the corner of my eye, I saw his brown leather shoes. He bounced a little. Then I noticed his feet hadn't sat next to Samantha, but on the other side of Veronica.

Was he trying to get as far away from me as possible? Out of pure curiosity, I turned my body to look at him. He looked better than I remembered. His tan brought out his eyes. Overwhelmed, I wondered if I had to talk to him. I caught his eye. A shock of electricity pulsed through me. I quickly looked away to stare at Samantha, unable to breathe correctly.

"Did you know the little boy's condition when you first started to treat him?" Samantha asked.

"I'm sorry. What?" Ethan asked.

Ethan glanced from me to Samantha. It turned out from where Ethan chose to sit, he had a full view of me. He sat next to Veronica, he held her hand, but he stared at me. Was he trying to figure out who he liked better, me or Veronica?

I started. Samantha said something to me:

"Carrie, since Ethan is having such a hard time focusing, any epiphanies you want to share?"

Suddenly my light went on, just like during the filming. I had to show off for Ethan.

"I was reflecting on the theory of relativity and completely forgot about the show. I may have something of interest, but a little off point."

275

Everyone laughed, Ethan a little too loudly.

"Ethan, you've said that you were going after Carrie if it didn't work out with Veronica. Is there anything you'd like to say to her?" Samantha said.

Ethan looked a little embarrassed. I couldn't help it. I smiled at him with a smile that extended to my toes.

"Watch out," Ethan said, smiling back. I laughed and Ethan continued quickly over the screaming audience, "I swear I've never been compared to Norman Bates before – not the most flattering thing ever, Care."

"Really? You want to discuss – not so flattering – with me? Really?" I rebutted.

Ethan nodded. "Fair enough."

I could see Julian. He moved over to stand by Adam. He was smiling. It was at this point Samantha painfully went in for the kill.

"Carrie, when Ethan countered this statement the next day by saying the show brought Veronica into his life and he would never be the same again, did you feel like his backup plan?"

The audience went crazy. They started booing. I wished I hadn't thrown Veronica under the bus. Like the head cheerleader had insisted the whole school hate Veronica. When they quieted to let me answer, I said: "Honestly, I didn't see either comment," trying to fight down the hurt pride swelling in my chest. My wound spoke bitterly, "I'm sure they'll be together for a long time, and like you said, I've moved on. I'm nobody's backup plan."

The audience cheered again. Ethan involuntarily contracted like I'd kicked him in the shins instead of speaking. I shouldn't have said this last part. I could see his hard position. He split himself between two women—

manipulated to do so – now he had to suffer the consequences. But he wasn't the only one with a decision to make. I decided to respect his announcement that he was dating Veronica. Slightly repentant, and, striving for playful, I continued trying to help poor Veronica who shrunk a little each time she was booed:

"Besides, as we're talking about Veronica, who could blame him?" Turning to the audience I said: "I forgave her and moved on. Everyone else should too."

Everyone did a sickening sort of "ah" sound and then Samantha said, almost surprised, "You really are a nice person, Carrie."

"Thanks. I'm really trying to be." I shrugged.

"Veronica, do you feel you betrayed Carrie's friendship by kissing Ethan so soon after she left the show?"

"I wasn't the only one kissing him," Veronica blushed, close to tears.

"Yes, but after all Carrie did for you."

"I know. I'm sorry if I hurt you, Carrie."

"I left. I knew how much you liked him and I left," I said to quiet the audience from booing Veronica. I didn't know how else to help her, but manipulated or not, she made her own choice.

"Ethan, how did you feel when Carrie left?" Samantha asked.

"I…. It hurt, but I understood why she did it," he said.

Again, we had to wait for the audience to calm down, but they cheered Ethan. I wondered why Ethan didn't share Veronica's shame. Ethan kissed me and became the hero of every women's fairytale. He kissed Tess and she'd been the slut. He'd kissed Veronica and she'd betrayed me. Not to mention poor, broken Sandra, sulking on the other side of the stage. Every time, he'd been the one to instigate a physical relationship, manipulated or not. He'd kissed us all. Yet, not once did the audience turn against him. Why was that?

"Well, we're almost to the end of our show. I've heard from a somewhat reliable source," Samantha said somewhat louder than anything else, "That you, Carrie, have been offered a second chance."

"What?" I asked.

Ethan smiled at me expressively. Distracted, I half smiled at Samantha. Did Samantha know how Ethan felt? Instead of some great revelation, Samantha said:

"After we come back from commercial, we'll discuss the spot you've been offered on *The Whole Package* fall lineup, where you will judge ten amazing men who have overcome hardship and made something of themselves. You will be responsible for who is named *The Whole Package.*"

Ethan flinched and his smile faded. Veronica's smile dropped for the first time. Both looked at me in pure horror. Tess laughed out loud, looking to me to share her amusement. Samantha squeamishly added:

"There'll be a twist, though. One of the men that'll automatically make it into the house will be an ex-boyfriend of yours, who worked his way up from nothing. After a word from our sponsors we'll meet him."

The audience screamed their approval. Julian and Adam watched me from off stage. They looked so satisfied like they'd cornered me. This was their plan?

"Carrie, think about what this would do for your mom and sister," Serena leaned over and whispered.

"What's in this for you?" I glared.

278

"This afternoon Lance asked to be one of the men vying for you, and Julian needs all the twists he can get, so I'll be the host," she said smugly.

"Serena, I am so sorry for what happened to you, but putting yourself in bad situations isn't going to make anything better."

"Come on, Care-Bear, you know it'd be the opportunity of a lifetime," Serena said sweetly.

"Not really, not for either of us," I said as I turned my back on Serena, knowing she wasn't likely to be convinced. I looked out at the audience across from me. They were still screaming for me. The young woman in the front row screamed for me. I would hate to disappoint this young woman. A pounding started in my ears. It unnerved me. The pressure of the audience would persuade me. That was Julian's plan. It didn't feel so funny now. This felt very like Adam – take away my choices and put on the pressure, leaving me stranded until I took his solution.

I'd made my decision in Julian's office, but I started weighing it out in my mind. What if, only for a few months, I did play the game. What if I found another Ethan to love? Ethan was with Veronica. I was alone. He moved on. How did I move on? The crowd screeched and cheered for me to let them have a little piece of me. Julian so perfectly matched me before–could he do it again? What would it be like to have men falling all over me for a few months? What could it hurt?

I glanced at Ethan. His face was all sorrow. As I caught his eye, he shook his head at me, only slightly. I couldn't face those eyes. He didn't have any right to tell me what to do. For the last month, he'd been kissing Veronica or Sandra, or whoever stayed still long enough. Some angry part of me felt

279

it would serve him right to have to watch me on television kissing other men.

The young women screamed for me. I saw my grandma telling me the effects MS had on a person's body, and what needed to be done. Gordon proposed – confidently, so sure of himself. He'd known my predicament – he knew I needed him. He knew I would wear his ring.

A woman fixed Adam's hair. He'd taken over the last three years of my life. I'd kick him off first. I'd watch his face as I handed a key to every man but him. A tear started out of my eye. I quickly wiped it. Did I really want to publicly humiliate Adam?

Sitting across from Grandpa once in a run-down Chinese restaurant, he told me to be a lady. He wouldn't tell me what electives to focus my education on. He never once tried to sway me toward his business, his legacy – he was so certain I would make the right choice – I was a lady. He trusted me.

Ethan begged me with his eyes. The young women openly cried. I waved at her stupidly. I put my hand down. People seriously loved me. People I'd never met loved me. I closed my eyes. My father peeked at me out of the corner of his eye after my joke bombed, just to make sure I knew. Then when I caught him, he pretended to laugh so he didn't hurt my feelings. No. Mom held me too tightly, sobbing as the limo pulled away from the cemetery. It scared me. Mom was supposed to be the adult. My grandmother was right. She was weak. I had to be strong. No, I would not be ashamed of anyone's sorrow. How could I ever get into a limo again? A limo took me away from my father. He was gone.

No, he didn't go. He was next to me in the waves showing me how to keep from sinking. He sunk. He was in the coffin sinking into the ground. He was gone. He left me. Then I remembered him telling me after a run-in with my Grandma: "Little one, when it's the hardest to do what's right, that's when it's most important – it doesn't matter what anyone else is doing – you do what's right."

My father hadn't left me. He stood with me when I wouldn't let my grandma torture Addie. He taught me how to joke people out of their bad moods. He was still with me. I needed him. I did not need Julian to match me. I did not need Adam to make money for me. I could never give Julian or Adam control over me again, not ever.

Power emanated from me.

Samantha said, "Welcome back to *The Whole Package* reunion show. We're just going to talk to Carrie about the fall lineup, and meet the lucky man who will have the chance to win one million dollars."

Ethan stared at me. He looked so miserable, poor guy. He wasn't the usual flavor of man candy, hadn't all the make-up artists said so? I had no idea what Julian did to him, but some sort of emotional bullying ran through him and agonized in his eyes. It couldn't have been good. I wished I hadn't been so vindictive towards him. Behind him, I could see Adam preparing to be introduced. Samantha asked:

"Please welcome Adam Pell!"

Adam walked out on stage and sat on a chair that had been placed on the other side of Samantha. He waved to the crowd.

"Carrie, are you surprised to see Adam Pell again?"

"Yes, I'm not really sure what he's doing here. We severed our friendship and I can't work with him again, let alone move into a house with him. Sorry Adam," I said decisively wondering what it would take to get this man out of

281

my life. Adam started to say something, Samantha tried to answer, but I cut both off loudly saying, "Actually Samantha, I'm really confused as to why you're announcing this. I was offered the fall lineup, but I've turned it down—several times."

"Seriously," Samantha asked so forcefully she spit on Adam. She may have apologized, but the audience showed their disappointment in a loud way. Finally, I cut through the noise saying: "I was also offered a chance to create an art show that I'm seriously considering. I was given a lot of fun options. I'm sure I'll be around in the future. Just not on *The Whole Package.*"

Ethan seemed to relax – I wasn't sure. I couldn't look at him. Out of the corner of my eye, I could see Veronica smiling at me. Samantha asked, "Was the show that bad of an experience? You always looked like you were having fun. Why wouldn't you do it again?"

"With something like *The Whole Package,* it's like blowing up your faults and weakness for the whole viewing audience to see. I'm a better person for facing it, I assure you. However, as I learn the lessons I'm taught, I'll not go in for a repeat, thanks."

"Come on, admit it, you're still pining over Ethan. That's why you are not doing it," Samantha lured pleasantly.

"Me and half the women in America," I replied with a playful smile, "Who's not in love with Ethan, really?"

The audience went wild again. I couldn't look directly at Ethan. A sweet, happy feeling surged my heart. This confused me. Then I told myself I would be a good friend to Veronica. The pain of heartbreak surged through me again. Which was right?

Samantha reluctantly turned her toothy grin to the camera. "We're out of time, but we would like to thank all of our contestants and our studio audience."

Everyone clapped while Samantha leaned over to talk to Veronica and Ethan. She turned her back to Adam to let him know he would not be recognized. The show ended abruptly. Julian was on stage ordering everyone around. Serena stood, knocking forcefully into my legs moving toward him. Veronica and Ethan were obligated to stay and sign autographs, and stood looking to Julian for instructions. Julian tried to talk to them and instruct the stage hands to clear the stage so the audience could get on. He snapped at Adam. Adam tried to move toward me, but Julian thwarted him. Adam sneered at Julian but left.

Tess flirted with Lance and he responded nicely. An unseen woman talked into a microphone from somewhere directing the audience into lines. Julian edged his way toward me. I didn't want to talk to him.

I moved over to Sandra, who sat despondently in her chair next to me. She looked up, and seeing Julian right behind me, glared. Julian backed up, apparently not wanting another encounter with her. I sat on the arm of her chair and put my arm around Sandra.

"How you holding up?" I asked.

"I don't know. I just don't know what happened," Sandra said sadly looking at Ethan and Veronica.

"You were manipulated for the sake of ratings on a television show."

Sandra glared with rage across the stage at Julian where he waited for me. He walked further away, snapping at people as he went. Ethan stayed in my vantage point, and I knew he had not lost sight of me, but appeared leery of approaching Sandra.

"Are you going to be all right?" I asked.

"I suppose. I've gotten a few calls from modeling agencies in the last week that may really launch my career," Sandra said, still looking at Ethan. "First, my daddy's sending me on a five-day singles cruise, though."

"That should be fun. You'll have a whole ship full of men following you around after the first few minutes."

Sandra rolled her eyes, but looked more pleased when she said, "Then Ethan will see what he lost."

"Sandra, in my humble opinion you'd do better to focus on your own happiness and let Ethan be. Heaven knows, you'll land on your feet," I answered.

Sandra shrugged, but she was obviously more satisfied, because instead of listening to my little lecture she eyed Lance and Tess flirting. She excused herself to go and have another spar with Tess. I let Sandra go, hoping to slip out before Julian came back. I stepped up to Veronica, who was standing behind Ethan.

"I've got to go," I said.

"Okay, I'll see you," she said, but in an uncertain way.

I nodded and then went in to hug Veronica. Ethan paused talking to Samantha as if just waiting to see if I would find a way to touch him, like I had in the manor house. I didn't, and instead examined Veronica to see if this hurt her feelings. Veronica smiled at me – but it wasn't the happy smile she wore on the television. Her eyes looked ready to cry. I carefully stayed away from Ethan.

Ethan lost his train of thought, trying to excuse himself from Samantha's probelike flirting. I began walking away. I couldn't stop myself. I turned back and called, "Bye, Veronica. Hopefully, I'll see you Saturday."

All pretense thrown aside, Ethan left Samantha mid-sentence and instantly whipped around to look at Veronica with a question in his eyes. Veronica quickly started to explain the invitation. I backed away from them, trying to read Veronica's lips. I saw Ethan's face light up and felt pleased, guilty and confused all at once.

I had to go. Respecting Veronica's attachment to Ethan made my heart break all over again. I caught Ethan's eye. I looked at him for a bit too long wondering if I'd ever see him again. He started toward me, but I turned from him, painfully crushing something deep within me. I slipped back into the corral and retrieved my purse, leaving my microphone with an accommodating stagehand. I was passing the drinking fountain, feeling home free when I heard:

"Carrie."

I turned. My heart dropped in disappointment. Lance jogged across the hallway toward me.

"Hey! where's Tess," I asked.

"Having it out with Sandra. I didn't get to talk to you much. How are you?" he asked focusing on me with an intensity that made me uncomfortable.

"Good, I think," I said, "Can I ask you something?"

"Sure, let's go get a drink," he said.

"Oh, I can't. I have to work tomorrow," I said. I cut in before the convincing started:

"I'm just wondering, was Erin supposed to win, you know, before Adam brought me in?" I asked.

Lance looked at me like I popped a balloon in his face.

"How'd you figure that out?"

"She's dating the perfect guy, and he was supposed to be the judge," I said.

"Yeah, she was supposed to win," he said.

"So then... is he a nice guy? Should I warn her?" I asked.

"He's fine, they're actually very compatible," Lance said.

"Then why don't the couples from this show last? Aren't the guys um...."

"No, no... I mean Ethan was a rock, he was the first judge in the show's history not to sleep with anyone."

"He didn't...um?"

"No, but usually Julian can get the judge to sleep with the final two women if not more."

"Julian manipulates them to sleep with the contestants?"

"Yeah, and it works. Every time!"

"Eww," I said.

"Makes good television. Most of the judges really are decent in normal situations, and wouldn't otherwise sleep with that many different women in such a short amount of time."

"Julian's a real peach," I said.

"That's why Dr. Corbon bailed, so many girls were being... well anyway, no, Erin's fine. He's a nice enough guy, and without the baggage of having slept with half a dozen women at the same time he was sleeping with Erin, they should be fine," Lance said.

"Well that's both a relief and disturbing," I said. A loud commotion broke out. I turned abruptly back in the direction of the theater. Lance cursed and looked up at the ceiling for divine intervention.

"What's that?" I asked.

"I think it's Julian," Lance said turning toward the voices screaming.

"Good luck with that," I said. He grinned, and then waved and went to see what fire he had to put out.

Having no interest in being pulled back into that drama, I left.

CHAPTER THIRTY-FOUR

Karl let me work from my apartment Friday. I received two phone calls of interest. The first came from Tess letting me know Veronica and Ethan planned to come to Addie's engagement party. The second came from Gordon's mom, who called me to decline her invitation to Addie's engagement party. It broke her heart really to be on her Napa Valley vacation, but she couldn't help it. I knew that meant she was in an extremely expensive rehab so I politely told her she'd be missed.

"Carrie," she said in her I'm-about-to-lecture-you voice, "You never actually dated Adam Pell, did you?"

"No, he weaseled his way into my life. How did Gordon know him?" I asked.

"Oh, well Gordon – not our Gordon, but Gordon Senior – my husband's father, tried to help Adam. He always felt so guilty for letting Marcus go," She said.

"What are you talking about?"

"Adam never told you?"

"No," I said.

"Well I suppose, technically speaking, Adam is my nephew," she said.

"What?"

"My husband William's little brother Marcus, in college, fell into some rather questionable business, even dangerous business deals with some underworld types. The family had to legally cut him off after they were sued by multiple people. Marcus disappeared after that. Many years later Adam came along long claiming he was related to us. Gordon Sr. was failing, and asked William to look into it. Marcus didn't marry Adam's mother, but there was some connection there, not to mention Adam looks very much like Marcus and the Shaw side."

"Adam is your nephew?" I asked.

"Yes, but he's not ... it's best to stay away from him. Gordon Sr. tried to help him before he died. William paid for his education, but Adam has a pretty big chip on his shoulder. He thinks he should have everything Gordon had, like it's our fault he wasn't legitimized. Both William and I instructed Gordon to stay away from Adam."

The strangest thought popped into my head.

"Did Gordon ever have political aspirations?" I asked.

"Oh well, William had them. All Gordon ever wanted was to play polo and watch you paint. William was... very insistent Gordon date the right girls so one day he could run for Governor, maybe even President. You were the perfect woman for them both," she said. The tremor in her voice pricked my heart.

"Are you okay?" I asked.

"Yes, Dear, but I've got to go," she said, and I could hear someone talking to her in the background.

"Be safe," I said, disappointed. Gordon's mom could only be counted on for frank information when she was in rehab working with a therapist. She didn't seem to know what transpired between Gordon and Adam anyway, but I couldn't help thinking Gordon must have tried to help Adam. I almost wanted to help for Gordon's sake, until Adam called me leaving a message telling me how I'd humiliated him and had no right to lead him on the way I did. He hated me.

Despite the million questions I had regarding his interactions with Gordon and James Hall, I didn't answer nor call him back. What if he somehow construed any response, as me begging him back into my life? I'd rather be the villain in his mind's melodrama than lose myself to be his heroine. I reconciled myself to the idea that I would probably never know.

And I blocked his number as James had, hoping I cut Adam out of my life forever.

CHAPTER THIRTY-FIVE

On Saturday I woke early, feeling anxious. Trying to force my heart and mind into some kind of liaison, I drove home for Addie's party. Mom and I showed up early to help. I found myself instead the mediator between Addie and her mother-in-law to-be. Marta Goodrich would be an extremely attractive middle-aged woman if she didn't wear her hair so tightly pulled back. It gave her a strange looking facelift.

"Carrie, can you get me that floral arrangement over by the door?" Addie whispered after Marta, as in "my-dearest-Carrie-please-call-me-Marta" moved it.

"Sure." I cautiously jogged the length of the tent. My shoes clicked on the tiles laid out on the grass as a floor. I walked back carefully and handed Addie a vase full of long-stemmed lilies. Her mother-in-law squinted at me but said nothing. She wanted me to like her.

When the violinist to the quartet showed up late, and wearing jeans, Addie almost broke into tears.

"Let me take you back to where you can change. The event begins in half an hour and you're not at all prepared," I said sternly.

Then so proud of myself, I turned and smiled at Addie. Addie, however, did not think this admonishment enough because she started laying into her. I dragged the violinist, clinging to her instrument and costume, away from my sister. The woman explained:

"My daughter started to cough and I had to take her to my mother's – "

"Don't worry about Addie. She's stressed," I said to the overwrought woman. I worked to make sure she smiled before I dropped her off at the dressing room.

When I returned fifteen minutes later, Addie's wary expression nodded in a sad attempt at being pleasant. She stood next to a man whose suit looked like it cost more than it would take to feed a small country. Marta, who already claimed me as family, pulled me over to her and said, "Carrie, oh good. This is my husband, Parker."

Parker Goodrich smiled his perfectly polished smile and took my hand from his wife in both of his.

"We finally meet the famous Carrie Carnegie."

Parker Goodrich's charm gushed forth all over me. Because Mr. Wilson finalized the sale of the stocks two days earlier, I didn't understand Parker Goodrich's strange enthusiasm for me. After his verbally licking my face like an overeager puppy dog, his campaign manager claimed Parker's attention and Marta pulled me away asking: "Are you just heartbroken over the whole Ethan thing?"

"I'm okay," I answered. Addie used this as her opportunity to go find Charles. She left me and Mom to Marta, who obviously did not believe my last statement. I scowled at Addie's retreating head and then put on my brightest smile as I turned to face Marta.

"I actually invited Ethan and Veronica this evening. They didn't RSVP due to time constraint, but sent a message through Tess that they would try to make it," I said.

Marta shrilled something incomprehensible and clapped her perfectly formed hands together. I took an involuntary step back.

"Oh, how great! It'll be like having one of the challenges right here in our midst," Marta said.

I shuddered a little. Then Parker Goodrich turned from the man he had been talking to about points he wanted to hit in his speech. As broad shouldered as his son, his tuxedo cut a little too tight, but for the most part, he looked like a clean-shaven, curly haired politician.

"Charles said he almost has you convinced to campaign for me. I have a debate in a few weeks. I'll be sure to get you tickets," Mr. Goodrich said, turning his full attention on me.

I tried to refuse graciously.

Marta called loudly to me and Mom, "It'll be fun to watch everyone this evening, don't you think, Irene?"

Then she winked at us.

"I'm not sure what you're referring to," Mom said. She carefully patted down her auburn hair.

Parker Goodrich asked me, "What are you doing in September? You would sure be an asset at the call center. Could you imagine people getting a call from Carrie Carnegie? Word would get around and people would wait at home for us to call."

I just nodded because Mrs. Goodrich spoke to Mom: "I'm talking about Matthew Wilson and his daughter, Carly. After all of that guff Lauren said about you when your mom died. You really are the most wholesome little thing alive. Well, she's gotten her comeuppance, hasn't she?"

"What are you talking about?" I asked. Parker Goodrich took this as a need for him to clarify. He began explaining telephone campaigning.

Growing dizzy from trying to keep up with both conversations, I looked back and forth between husband and wife. Couldn't the Goodrich's see they were both talking to me?

As Parker Goodrich explained the importance of personal contact in a political race, Marta said:

"Carrie, of course, you heard, Mr. and Mrs. Matthew Wilson have not lived in the same house for a year. Well, it turns out that Lauren has been having a certain visitor over more often than she should."

"Really," I said. Mom reprimanded me with her eyes. Parker Goodrich said:

"Yes, you'd be surprised how quickly you can change a constituent's mind, by talking to them personally."

Marta said: "Didn't you know? Carly came down for the summer so Lauren would be more prudent. Lauren wouldn't have that. She ran away Tuesday with her thirty-five-year-old friend, a man named Joe."

Parker Goodrich said: "To make personal contact...."

He lost me completely when his wife said:

"Carly told Jane Marks that her mom finally signed the divorce papers she'd been hanging onto for over a year. Lauren has little claim to anything. I wonder if Joe will have to get a job instead of living off her?"

I stared at Marta with my mouth slightly open. I couldn't even pretend to be listening to Mr. Goodrich anymore. It didn't matter he kept on talking about getting to know the people and listening to their concerns.

"I guess we'll judge how the man's doing tonight," said Mrs. Goodrich. "He and Carly are coming, as such old friends of your family, how could he not?" Then in the same breath, she said, "It should be a great night, huh?"

I could not answer. Parker Goodrich was saying, "I've heard you're not going to be recruiting jobs much longer. I'd love for you to join my campaign team."

"Uh...oh," I stammered.

"Mr. Goodrich, something's wrong with the sound equipment," a man from the club said.

"My speech," Mr. Goodrich said, and turning to me, he said, "I'll be back."

Both Mr. and Mrs. Goodrich, apparently knowing more about sound equipment than the man hired to take care of it, left. I let out an exasperated sigh in Mom's direction.

"Consider dearest. They raised Charles and he's a very good man. They must also be very good people," Mom said.

I nodded, not caring one way or the other about the Goodrich's with so much pressing information just drooled forth.

"Did you know that?" I whispered.

Feigning innocence, Mom refused to understand what I was talking about.

"About the Wilsons," I said.

"Matthew has been our friend: we need not repeat his heartache," Mom answered.

"Of course not, Mom, but...." Here I stopped. I wasn't sure what to say. I was scared. I had to know, "Are you pleased that he's getting a divorce?"

"Carrie, he's been humiliated in an extremely public way. Now he'll have to cut off ties he thought would last his whole life. That's a painful and awful ordeal. Who would be pleased?" Mom reproved.

"I didn't mean that," I stammered, "Of course, not the pain of it, but that he'll be free. Are you pleased that he'll be free?"

"Carrie!" Mom said blushing. She prudently walked away. My stomach tightened. Mom wanted to be loved.

After a half hour, people chatted and ate hors d'oeuvres all around me. Neither Veronica nor Ethan arrived. Everyone tried to get my attention, to please me, to impress me. I will own, I have always liked attention. Yet having it so abundantly grew overwhelming. These weren't star-struck teenagers anymore. These were members of my community, and I couldn't even go to the bathroom without being followed.

To add to the awkward situation, Tess brought Lance with her. He tried to talk to me through people. Distracted to the point of chaos, I couldn't respond. I did find a way to watch the entrance expectantly, though. I wouldn't admit why, when Tess and Andrea teased me. My eyes, without my permission, glanced toward the entryway of the tent at every chance. I became so conscious of time passing that when Mr. Wilson and his daughter, Carly, come in, I noticed they were forty-three minutes late.

They were slighted to one side by head nods and "excuse-me-won't-you". It was almost like they had the plague, and no one wanted to catch it. Somehow people thought the rumors circulating about them would rub off. Addie nodded to me from across a crowd and we both headed straight toward them, once we were free.

"Hello Wilsons. Thank you so much for coming," Addie said, opening her arms as we walked up to the pair. I pushed my way up behind her.

"Thank you for having us," Carly said. She stood with relief almost to tears and hugged Addie.

"Mom would be here, but she's indisposed this evening."

"Of course," Addie answered. "Carly, I haven't seen you all summer. How are you?"

"Fine, thank you," Carly said, "Is that Tess, and the host from *The Whole Package,* Carrie?"

"Yes," I said glancing at the door for the rest of the cast to show up. Still no Ethan – I couldn't even pretend it was Veronica I wanted to see.

Carly looked interested so Addie said loudly, interrupting my absent-minded stare at the door, "Come meet them. I don't really know Lance, but Tess's great. The show just made her appear horrid."

Addie put her arm around Carly whispering as they moved away. I moved to follow them but noticed Mr. Wilson hadn't budged.

"Won't you come and join our group, Mr. Wilson?" I asked.

"I'm sure I'm not wanted over there," Mr. Wilson said. His jaw remained clenched and he tapped his foot. Mr. Wilson eyed Mom.

"Why would you think that?" I asked sitting down next to him.

Mr. Wilson appraised me. I'd been peevish toward him in the last couple days. His increasing phone calls to my mother with every tiny detail he could share about the sale of the stocks seemed unnecessary.

"You know, as you are an adult now, you could call me Matthew," he said.

"Oh yeah, I guess," I said fidgeting uncomfortably. "Just come over to our table."

"I'm the social outcast," he said, letting out a little laugh, "I'm sure by now you've heard my wife left me."

"I'm really sorry," I said, caught off guard. I didn't think he would so openly admit this after Carly so openly denied it. "How would that affect you coming over to our group? You're pretty much family and family sticks together through the cruddy times."

297

"Why didn't your mom come and say hello to me, then?" Mr. Wilson said, glancing at her.

"You make her nervous for some reason," I teased very gently.

"Nervous?" Mr. Wilson asked, confused.

"In a good way." I forced a laugh. Would I really do this? Would I pave the way for another man in my mother's life?

Mr. Wilson looked as if he didn't believe me. He watched Mom in the little circle Carly joined. She stood aloof, silently worrying.

I wanted Mom to sparkle again.

"She's worried about you," I said, swallowing down the bile that came up my throat.

"Oh, she is kind," he said, and yes, even Mr. Wilson blushes. I wondered if Mr. Wilson's long marriage to a woman, who could rival my grandmother, made him ripe to appreciate, nay, perhaps near worship, my mother and her gentle spirit.

Charles whispered something to Mom and she glanced over at us before walking away with him.

"I suppose Addie will marry Charles," Mr. Wilson said.

"Yes," I said.

"He's a good man. Despite our asking Addie not to say anything, he knew about the stocks before they sold.

"That Addie!" I said, shaking my head, exasperated and looking away. She ditched me with her mother-in-law-to-be: fair is fair.

"Well, he let the stocks sell. He didn't interfere. I spoke to some of Charles' business partners right after they found out about the stocks being sold back to the Ellis family. They respect him for choosing Addie over the stocks. They're more willing to work with him than they've ever been."

"Good. I know he wants to make a name for himself," I said. Charles walked back toward Addie like he needed to be near her. Mr. Wilson said:

"...Everyone thinks you were behind the selling of the stocks so it didn't cause contention with Addie and Charles. Nobody even suspects you were struggling. You sustained your family so this could happen."

"I guess," I said.

"You have every right to be proud of yourself. You took good care of your mom and sister. Now Charles will be Addie's family and I'll take care of your mom ... ur, I mean, I'll watch her financially and make sure –"

"My dad loved you like a brother," I interrupted. "I think he'd be okay with you taking care of Mom."

"Perhaps I should go make sure she's doing all right," Mr. Wilson said, stepping away from his seat when my mother reappeared.

"Oh, look there's your Uncle Brock," Mr. Wilson said turning back to me.

My dad's brother looked like he may ignore Mr. Wilson's contagion to come over. He didn't care for Mr. Wilson paying attention to Addie and me in public. He felt it his job to dote on the children of his famous dead brother when in public, despite his having cut us off. The Goodrich's were still held at bay by Mr. Wilson's cooties. The man was running for public office, after all.

Mr. Wilson seemed to relax and began reminiscing.

"When we were seventeen, your dad and I went to Brock's engagement party," he said. "We...um never mind."

"What?" I asked.

299

"I miss your dad," he said.

My eyes glistened as I said, with an undefined irritation, "I wish he hadn't worked himself to death. If he could've stayed with me for a little longer, until I was more grown up, I'd have –"

"Carrie," Mr. Wilson snapped, "He died of cancer."

"We could've caught some of the warning signs. We could have treated it if he hadn't always been exhausted from working," I said.

Mr. Wilson put an arm around my shoulder, thinking about how to word what he was going to say to defend his best friend. If another man had to love Mom it should be someone who would defend my dad – every time:

"Little one, your dad valued hard work. There's nothing wrong with that. Plus, you can't say 'what if' we caught it sooner. The fact is the cancer was so far along when they did discover it, he didn't have a chance."

I didn't answer.

"You know what he said about getting cancer don't you?" Mr. Wilson said trying to pull my solemn expression from looking at the door. I gave Mr. Wilson my attention and caught hold of everyone else's as I laughed my pretty laugh.

"It was because of the Hartford Inbreeding program, better known as high society dating. He said maybe if his parents hadn't been second cousins, he'd have had a chance."

We laughed. I remembered my dad being so accepting and funny about his illness.

"A person can't deny you inherited his sense of humor," he said.

"I guess that's something."

The music stopped playing. The club manager announced dinner. The attendant moved to close the French doors of the tent. As he pulled the first door shut my heart dropped. The attendant pulled at the second door, but paused for just a moment. Two people slipped past him into the tent. Then he let the door fall shut.

Ethan and Veronica arrived.

CHAPTER THIRTY-SIX

Veronica and Ethan clustered by the door. Tess, as instructed by Addie, would show them where to sit. She and Lance went to greet them. Head down, charging like a bull, Marta pushed her way toward them. Veronica, over the course of many interviews, learned to greet everyone, even Marta, with a smile. I could see something like panic in her eyes, and a little shake in her, but the smile never left Veronica's face.

Only one group didn't drift toward *The Whole Package* reunion at the doors of the tent. Mom, Andrea, Phil, Addie, Charles, Carly and Richard Blanchard, waited for me. The latter because he felt sure I would have to rejoin my family eventually.

"Come on. It looks like your sister's trying to get your attention," Mr. Wilson said, taking pity on me.

Dinner was announced again; due to the disturbance by the door, nobody found their seats. We started walking again. I eyed Ethan, lost in the admiration of the women present. I grimaced when Marta hugged him.

"I believe you're at my table for dinner, Mr. Wilson," I said, distracted, finally looking at the floor.

"Carrie," Uncle Brock said, ushering me toward him. He pulled out my chair for me, his trim body, facial features and grey hair cropped to his head so like my father's, only his blue eyes held a dull lackluster quality in them that made him entirely different in a way that was frustrating, like he wasted his potential as a human being. I nodded my thanks. Mr. Wilson grinned and sat next to me in my uncle's seat.

My uncle assessed the situation. He glanced at me and I willed myself to look innocent. Forced to sit in Mr. Wilson's seat, my uncle walked to the other side of the table with my aunt who dreaded making any kind of a scene. Carly ended up in my aunt's seat after looking terribly confused. Others filled in between us. Mr. Wilson was now acknowledged by everyone.

Dinner dragged out forever. Ethan wouldn't even look at me. I kept reminding myself he was dating Veronica, but my eyes didn't get the memo; they were drawn to him. During dessert Mr. Goodrich spoke for only a minute. His microphone inexplicably shorted out again. I saw one of Charles' cousins wink at him after it happen and I couldn't help grinning.

A man in a white tux with tails held his trumpet and claimed his band didn't need amplification. They replaced the string quartet with dancing music. Charles and Addie started the couples by dancing in the center of the room while everyone applauded.

I had a mouthful of chocolate torte when Richard Blanchard came shortly after to claim his dance. He stuck his hand out to me in a showy, expressive way that annoyed me. I glanced at Ethan and he looked livid about something. Confused, I nodded and placed my white linen napkin over the back of my chair. As I walked, I tried to swallow the rich chocolate that coated my mouth.

People slyly glanced at me. I couldn't nonchalantly look at Ethan. Every time I tried, I caught eyes smiling at me. I smiled back until aware chocolate coated my teeth. Then I nodded somberly when I couldn't avoid someone's glance. I didn't really know what to do. People seemed so fond of me.

"Did you see the whole mess I'm cleaning up with Julian?" Richard asked, pulling me toward him and from my thoughts.

"No. What happened?" I asked.

"He tried to strong-arm Samantha Prowers, my Number One morning personality. I guess he fed her a bunch of false information, and Samantha got pretty angry. She said either Julian went or she did. Like we'd let her go – she pulls in more revenue than Julian ever could."

"Yeah, she seemed mad when I corrected her," I said.

"I have to cancel *The Whole Package* now," Richard said.

"Really?" I asked. Something that was clenched inside of me relaxed.

"We started to get reports that Julian was involved in bad business practices. You were one of his favorites, so I'm sure he never did it to you, but turns out some of the participants, especially Sandra, felt he was a bit of a bully. Sandra's father is outraged Ethan didn't choose her after some of the stuff Julian told her."

"Oh, I don't doubt it," I said.

"Anyway, I apologize to you for his behavior. I don't know why he announced you were doing the fall lineup. He didn't have permission to do that. I haven't had half as much trouble from all my other reality show producers put together," Richard said.

I nodded. I looked over to Lance for answers. Ethan stared at me with sad eyes. When he noticed me looking at him he tried to smile, but he looked annoyed.

I didn't hear anything Richard said from that point on. I covertly watched Ethan. He was not talking to anyone and if someone did talk to him he had very little to say to them. Then I remembered how down on society Ethan had always been. After the dance ended, Richard took me back to my table. It looked as though he was going to stay, and I started to think of how to get rid of him. But something changed. I lost all awareness of Richard Blanchard. The air around me filled with an electric charge bringing me back to life. I knew he was in my face before he reached out and touched my arm. Every one of my nerve endings moved to the place where his fingers brushed my skin to get my attention. I turned.

"Carrie, will you dance with me?"

Ethan stood inches from my face. I stammered, unable to answer with his breath warm on my ear. He stood right in front of me. My hand reached for him to see if he was real. I stopped mid-reach and put my hand on my stomach. Ethan, more of a dream than reality, finally stood before me.

"Oh ... a, yeah. Of course," I said. I wanted him to throw his arms around me and make everything better. I managed a nonchalant, "Sure, why not."

The whole room saw Ethan walk to me because everyone stared at us, not in a polite glancing way, but openly gaping. The room went strangely silent as the band flipped through their music to start in on the next song. Some old friends of my parents, most of whom had placed employment candidates for me, were happily talking to Mr. Wilson and Mom. They glanced up to see if I needed anything, just as they had been doing since my dad died. I smiled at them, but lifted my hand and placed it in Ethan's.

His touch coursed through my hand and torched my entire body. I couldn't help feeling the intense physical connection between us as powerful as ever. I tried to reprimand it down, but every nerve in my body focused on the place where Ethan held limply to my hand. He did nothing to pull me to him once on the dance floor. He put a loose hand on my waist and danced like we were in junior high being chaperoned.

His removed demeanor doused me in cold water. The festering hope, one that burned deep down inside me where I couldn't seem to extinguish it, fizzled out under his withdrawn behavior.

"How's work?" he asked, looking around the room.

"Fine," I whispered. He didn't say anything to me after that. No smiles. Not even a grip on my hand. We danced. He had been forced to play a part, after all. He'd never cared about me. I wished the last glance I gave him after the reunion show was my final memory of Ethan.

Anything would be better than him showing up late, and then dancing with me coldly. Was he proving he didn't love me? Did he feel he owed me that, after I'd desperately sent him an invitation to a party he would hate?

He chose Veronica. He probably felt annoyed with her for making him come into the very core of high society. Of course, Veronica would bring him. Of course, she would give me my chance. She was my friend.

After the song ended, I wanted to run away from the horribly polite and reserved Ethan. How did I get out the closed doors? His grasp that once held me so desperately now felt like a cooled noodle against me. I could not bear it.

Ethan did not let go of me, nor indicate we should walk back to my table where I noticed Richard Blanchard hovered. The music began again. Ethan wouldn't look at me, but he started swaying to the music again. Then I noticed he did not look impassive. He looked mad. This confused me.

Wait a minute. I got to be mad – not him!

"What's the matter with you?" I snapped.

"Did you invite me here to throw your new relationship with Richard Blanchard in my face?"

"What?" I asked confused.

"You said you didn't even know him," Ethan snapped trying to keep his voice under control.

"I don't," I said confused trying to get my bearings.

"He and your ex-boyfriend Adam are fighting over you? I thought Adam was just your work associate. Turns out let's-make-a-bet-Adam is your ex?"

"Wow, none of that is accurate. Adam is crazy, I never dated him. I don't even work with him anymore. And Richard Blanchard asked me to dance when I met him, for the first time, on Thursday. You think I lied to you on the show when I told you that I don't know him?"

"We said a lot of things on the show," Ethan said, looking away, and upset.

"Really, you get to question my loyalty – really?" I stammered.

Ethan kissed all the other women on the show. I got to be mad, not him.

"Julian said you were getting cozy with Mr. Blanchard because he's a part of this world where you belong," Ethan accused.

"I don't know him! Julian's a manipulative jerk and his show's being canceled. How do you, of all people, not see that?"

Ethan closed his eyes a little and took a breath like it was the first one in some time. Then to my great surprise he pulled me toward him, tightening his grip on me.

"You don't really know him?" he asked.

"Not at all," I answered.

After everything we'd been through, this was the conversation I was having with Ethan?

"Why did run away Thursday night," he asked.

"Oh, Julian was trying to strong arm me into doing the show in the fall. I had to leave."

"Oh, I thought … Care," Ethan said. His face held so close to mine. Agony brimmed in his eyes. This broke my reserve and I said anxiously, "What? What's the matter?"

"I'm sorry…" Ethan said. Here Ethan paused. He couldn't put a finger on all he was sorry for. So he said again miserably, "I am so sorry."

"I know…" I said rubbing his arm, trying to get the awful look from his face, "I know. Julian's a jerk. We were in a bad situation. I'm sorry you got sucked into going on *The Whole Package* in the first place."

Ethan shook his head in the negative, and I said, "What?"

"I can't be sorry for going on the show," Ethan said looking embarrassed. Ethan nervously reached out to play with a piece of my hair bouncing down my back. I closed my eyes at his touch. I couldn't help it. He continued:

"I'd never have met you if I hadn't gone on the show. I know I hurt you. I'm a total idiot. It's so selfish, but I'll always be glad I went on the show – and you went on the show. Can we start over? I swear I will sweep you off your feet. Please?"

"What about Veronica? Aren't you dating her … you love her …?" I stammered trying to focus – Ethan held me tightly now. His eyes were begging me.

"Carrie, Julian's a manipulative jerk, remember? We've only been away long enough for me to realize just what I lost. How could I already be in love with Veronica?" Ethan asked. I could see he tried to understand where I was even coming from, despite his many televised make-out sessions.

"Does Veronica know that?" I asked trying to fight the relief and pure joy purging my overwrought mind to feel bad for my friend.

"We could talk about the contestants that left the show. All we ever talk about is you, Care. She knows."

I looked over my shoulder. We were surprisingly close to Ethan's table. Veronica sat a few feet away and watched us with a sad smile. She'd mucked up the water. Ethan kissed her so much. How could she have known?

I gave her a pleading look, begging her with my eyes to understand. Veronica kissed her hand to me in a submissive, understanding way. Just by the way Ethan held to the back of my dress like he couldn't get me close enough, Veronica knew.

"Thank-you," I mouthed to her and I could feel tears of pure gratitude forming as Veronica's sad eyes relinquished Ethan. I loved her for this. I would be her friend forever; she was *The Whole Package*.

"Will you give me another chance? I will never give you another reason to…. You'll never have to wonder. Just give me another chance," Ethan pleaded.

I didn't trust my voice, tears welled fat in my eyes, so I nodded.

"Hi, I'm Ethan, I'm a pediatrician – oh right – twenty-nine years old –"

"Knock it off," I said, laughing, but losing the tear. Ethan reached up and wiped it with his thumb. With the tear, he also took away all the miserable rejection I'd felt while I ran frantically down a rocky beach, swearing I'd never try again.

I saw no one beyond Ethan – which was good because everyone saw us. The song ended as it begun, in silence. It was too perfect a moment to talk through. Ethan creased the back of my dress pulling on it to bring me closer.

Richard Blanchard came toward us like he would try to cut in. Ethan pulled me into him further with his greedy grasp and started to sway to the music again. He glared and Richard sulked away.

I started humming along to the song in Ethan's ear. Ethan couldn't resist being so close to me. He rounded his face to mine and kissed me like we never parted.

A light flashed. A woman in a black gown with a professional camera began pushing her way out of the vinyl tent. She looked frantically over her shoulder. She obviously thought someone would try to stop her. After shaking the stability of the structure, the club manager escorted her out.

"Carrie, seriously – propriety," Addie whispered, sidling up behind me.

"Addie, they've seen it before, it's just like seeing the conclusion, only live," I said.

"Should we do it again? We don't want to leave anyone unsatisfied," Ethan chimed in.

"Especially not you," I said.

"At least you could go to the tennis courts like the self-respecting teenagers," Charles countered.

Addie rolled her eyes. "Please, Carrie," she implored.

"Okay," I said trying to look at Ethan like I meant it because he had a mischievous gleam in his eye.

We swayed to the center of the dance floor while Ethan tried to get me to tell him where the tennis courts were. I wanted him to kiss me again. I longed for his arms to be around me all the time. Then, I didn't care what anyone thought. No, I remembered Veronica. Oh, poor Veronica. I quickly looked over to Veronica, but I couldn't focus enough to see if she was okay.

Ethan moved a little closer to me. Then I forgot everything except I had to avert Ethan's attention from my mouth. Poor Veronica. I laid my forehead against his cheek.

Ethan gently pulled away so he could see my blushing face. He stared at me transfixed. His eyes became watery. He started to move his lips toward mine. I watched him do it with a mixture of excitement, layered with prudence.

This was Addie's night – was I really as bad as Mr. Goodrich – just forgetting that? I tried to muster the strength to ask Ethan not to kiss me. I couldn't even look away from Ethan to see where Addie was. Ethan turned at the last moment just enough to brush my face with his and he nuzzled into my ear.

"I love you. I always have, and I always will," he whispered.

I laughed, a little dismayed, and punched him on the shoulder joint.

"Come on, Care, you know you love me," Ethan said grinning.

"I must, to put up with that," I said.

Ethan kissed my cheek and smirked at Richard Blanchard. Then he put his forehead on mine so I couldn't see anyone but him.

"Please," I pleaded, "I can't resist you and this has to be Addie's night."

"I can live with that," he grinned, showing he did, in fact, possess restraint.

Ethan and I talked and danced until the musicians gave up and packed up their instruments. Pulling all the satisfaction life has to offer, I held his hand while he impressed my friends, or leaned in close as we danced. I couldn't see how the musicians could be tired; it was barely three in the morning – maybe four at the most.

Then our first big dilemma arrived. As Ethan had been a ward of the studios up until the previous evening, he'd not thought about his lodging. I started considering. Veronica left at midnight from sheer exhaustion. Mom kindly offered her the last maintained guest room at the estate.

I suggested that Ethan could sleep on the couch in the recreation room if he didn't mind.

Ethan wasn't concerned. He didn't mind the couch. He said he could get a room at a hotel if that would be weird for my family. Charles offered Ethan a place to stay so he didn't have to get a hotel room, considering everything nearby would be closed.

Charles was sure that there would be room in his pool house for him. I volunteered to drive him the thirty minutes to Charles' house. What other option was there?

Veronica drove Mom home in her car. Charles had to get Addie safely home, so he couldn't ride with them. Of course, Ethan could just take my car. Maybe we could meet up with Charles and Addie at the house and talk about it in the kitchen over the other half of Tess's chocolate cake. We couldn't help but feel unwelcome in the tent, now being cleared in a hurried manner that implied the caterer and waiters wanted to get home.

After the bustle over such a taxing dilemma, the problem resolved itself. Drawn to the cool air, we stepped outside the oversized, stuffy tent. I moved over onto the path heading toward the tennis courts with my shoes in my hand. Ethan found he couldn't resist a walk around the impeccably kept grounds. Addie, near collapsing, leaned against Charles. He wrapped his arms around her waist and pulled her to his car. He waved goodbye to Ethan and me.

Neither Ethan nor I noticed; we were immersed in conversation, which lasted until the morning light peeked over the clubhouse. Mostly, neither of us could talk fast enough to satisfy all there was to say.

www.ingramcontent.com/pod-product-compliance
Lightning Source LLC
Chambersburg PA
CBHW031548240626
47153CB00002B/424